LEOPOLD
BLUE

LEOPOLD BLUE

ROSIE ROWELL

HOT
KEY
BOOKS

First published in Great Britain in 2014 by Hot Key Books
Northburgh House, 10 Northburgh Street, London EC1V 0AT

A CIP catalogue record for this book is available from the British Library.

ISBN: 978-1-4714-0125-1

1

This book is typeset in 10.5 Berling LT Std using Atomik ePublisher

Printed and bound by Clays Ltd, St Ives Plc

FSC

Hot Key Books supports the Forest Stewardship Council (FSC),
the leading international forest certification organisation, and is
committed to printing only on Greenpeace-approved FSC-certified paper.

www.hotkeybooks.com

Hot Key Books is part of the Bonnier Publishing Group
www.bonnierpublishing.com

For Johnny

CHAPTER ONE

I lay across the middle of the Main Street. The sky above was a relentless blue. 'Leopold blue' was what Mum would have said were she not off making a nuisance of herself, but she was wrong. *Leopold* blue was the deep, fiery summer sky. This was a thin-lipped, wintery version, still waiting to be pumped with the warmth of spring. I rolled my head to the side. My sister Beth sat on the edge of the pavement, her head resting on her arms. Her long brown hair curtained over her legs, the curls limp with dust. Behind her and the row of rooftops, Bosmansberg loomed, a rolling wave caught in stone.

In the last two hours there had been no evidence of life – not a human being, not a car, not even a drifting dog. Across the road Pep Stores advertised its Birthday Bonanza savings in yellow and blue. Yesterday, the last Saturday of July, the store had been bursting with farm workers on their monthly trip to town. The manager stood on the pavement with a loudspeaker and a boombox, inviting people in and laughing at his own jokes. Now the double doors were padlocked shut, an iron bar across the front. A Shoprite plastic bag humped off the pavement in a brief gust of air before settling back down.

This morning I had opened my eyes to the same noises as yesterday, in the room I had slept in all my fifteeen and a quarter years, but today my bed – with its half scratched-off My Little Pony stickers – felt too small. The purple patchwork print curtains that hung limply in my window ridiculed me.

Now, a sob slipped out, like trapped air needing to escape.

Beth lifted her head. 'What?'

She didn't feel the choking toxicity of the air here; she didn't see that behind Bosmansberg, the rest of the world crackled and buzzed, while we remained caught in an endless empty afternoon.

'Nothing.' I stood up. 'I'm going home.'

'But nothing's happened!'

'You can't play chicken when there aren't any cars, Beth. It's pathetic.' An empty Fanta Grape can lay in front of me. I kicked it, ferociously. It *clitter-clattered* on the cement, unnaturally loud in the canyon of the Main Street.

'Fine. I'm staying.' Beth lay down in my abandoned spot with the air of a South African Joan of Arc – only there was nothing at stake. Dying of boredom, perhaps.

After a few paces Beth popped up in front of me, hands curled under her armpits, flapping her arms. '*Pu-u-u-u-k-puk-puk*!' She danced about, mimicking the throaty next-door rooster.

Despite myself, I laughed.

When she had finished, overplaying the joke as usual, we started together up the middle of the road, the last two people left in the world. A banner along the white-washed wall of the old Dutch Reformed church read 'Leopold Flower Show 1993'. It actually read 'Leopold Flower Show 1985'; a white

8

page with the numbers 93 had been sticky-taped over the 85.

Next to the church was the mechanics shop with its life-size cut-out of Naas Botha kicking his rugby ball into the window; and the library where tannie* Hester kept a stock of English romances for Mum, although she couldn't bear them; and the pebble-dashed Volkskas bank.

Beth stopped and sniffed the air. 'Can you smell candyfloss?'

'No,' I replied. The town smelled musty, like a left-behind suitcase. It smelled of Sunday.

'Let's make milkshakes when we get home,' she said.

Even the Royal Hotel and its adjoining off-licence were deserted today. When we reached the Anglican church, I looked towards the sprinkling of gravestones in the churchyard. In the far right-hand corner, under a jacaranda tree, were four little crosses in a row. Between 1899 and 1902 a mother had lost four children in successive years. It was the saddest corner in the world. But that was Leopold.

Beyond the church was the magistrate's office and the bronze statue of the founder of our town, Johannes Basson Leopold, standing proud and tall. Prouder and taller, apparently, than in reality, but Dad said one couldn't have one's town founded by a little runt of a man. It wasn't good for morale. The statue was a constant source of irritation to Mum, because the San bushmen were here a long time before Leopold and his ox wagons arrived, so the statue should be of a bushman. Of course bushmen weren't particularly tall either.

We passed the police station. The evil Rottweiler police dog, <u>Kaptein, thump</u>ed his tail from his outstretched position on

* An auntie or an old lady

the front steps, but didn't bother lifting his head.

'Do you think Mum and Dad will be home when we get back?'

'I don't know, Beth.'

'Do you think she is going to do this every weekend?'

'How should I know?' I snapped.

'I hate Sundays without her and Dad. And Ronel's mum says she is stirring up trouble.'

'What?'

'She says all this talk about a deadly disease is upsetting the volk* and making the farmers angry with Mum.'

I felt a familiar thud in my stomach. 'So tell her.'

Beth shot me a look. We both knew it would only invite a long lecture about social responsibility and righting the wrongs and AIDS is a reality and education is the only way. We'd heard it too many times.

Dad blamed Mum's social conscience on her bleeding-heart, lentil-eating leftie friends in England. But I thought she was being selfish – what was the point of spending your weekends travelling the countryside, visiting desperately poor people, only to tell them about a disease that was probably going to kill them and their children? How did that improve their quality of life? It was typical of Mum; no doubt she secretly likened herself to Princess Diana, when she was simply making everyone miserable.

At the top of the Main Street we stopped and looked back down the length of the town. Nothing in this snapshot bedded us in the present. On an afternoon like this, Leopold's dead seemed more alive than the living. If, with a blink, you could

* Farm labourers

shift your focus, or change the lens, what ghosts would we see crossing the street? What would they stop and say to each other?

'I've got to do a tourist brochure for English,' Beth said. She was dyslexic and not much taken with school. When she was six, Dad had asked her what she wanted to be when she grew up. She'd looked at him blankly and said, 'Me.' Beth didn't need to be anything to complete her.

'For where?' I asked.

'For Leopold, dummy.'

'Jeez.'

Only two events might entice a stranger to Leopold: the wild flower show in August, or the annual agricultural show in April. Other than that you would have to be very lost to wind up here. The town wasn't signposted – local opinion was that if you didn't know where you were you had no business being here. Mrs Franklin, the girls' school headmistress, had suggested linking the town with a Dutch equivalent, so that we could have a board that said 'Leopold – twinned with Schoonvergeet, Holland'. This, she said, would set us apart from the handful of other hopelessly small towns of the surrounding valleys. But the locals, most of whom preferred not to leave the region, had no intention of being linked to a town full of foreigners.

'Write about the tea,' I said, 'or the veldskoen* factory that makes David Kramer's red shoes.'

'Nah.' Beth wrinkled up her nose.

'Or the bushmen paintings. Or the mountain hikes.'

Beth shook her head.

'You have to write about something.'

---

* Traditional leather shoes, originally homemade, worn in the bush

11

Beth scuffed her takkie* back and forth on the road. 'I'm going to write about Dad and Mum and Simon and Marta. And you. All the people I love in this town.'

I looked at her and shook my head. I worried about Beth. She was content living here. She was happy.

Out of a rattle and a roar and a cloud of dust emerged a battered Toyota Cressida, electric blue apart from the front passenger door, which was yellow. It stopped abruptly a few metres off. Marta emerged from the canary-coloured door, in the blue and purple Mothers' Union uniform she wore to church every Sunday. She leaned back through the open passenger window and said something to the driver, who reversed and clattered away in the direction of the Camp, Leopold's name for the overcrowded streets where the coloured community lived.

'God have mercy, children! What business do you have here?' she scolded as she walked towards us, her small body favouring her right side more than usual after a day on her feet praising the Lord.

'We were –'

I stood on Beth's foot and said, 'We were taking a walk.'

'Don't you "taking a walk" me!' she said. Father Basil must have produced a particularly fiery sermon because Marta's crinkled black eyes looked fearsome. 'Look at the sight of you, sulke skollie** children wandering the streets on a Sunday afternoon. *Wragtie!**** The shame of it. Take my hat, child,' she

---

* Trainer
** Such hooligan
*** Truly!

said, shedding her burdens, 'and my coat.'

'We're going to make milkshakes,' said Beth as we turned in the direction of home.

'You are not!'

'But Mum's doing her thing again. And Dad has to go with her in case she gets a puncture. So we're in charge.'

I glanced at Marta. Her lips were drawn in a disapproving line. 'How did you know where we were?' I asked her.

She clicked her tongue. 'My Father in heaven tells me everything. There are no secrets between us.'

We turned the corner and saw our house. It was a squat square with white-washed walls. Its heavy thatched roof gave the impression that it was sinking back into the ground rather than rising out of it. It was built around the remains of Leopold's original homestead and was therefore the oldest house in town. This had not impressed my English grandmother, whose house in Salisbury was only a little younger but still standing very nicely. But the most unfortunate thing about the house, according to Salisbury standards, was that it sat directly on the street. 'Not that it's not much of a street,' she'd added, looking around.

With no sign of our maroon station wagon, Beth turned to Marta and squeezed her arm. 'I love you, Marta!' she said, 'And so does Meg. You'll never leave us, will you?'

'What?' said Marta. 'I'm waiting for my Romeo and then I'm off!'

'Where will you go?' asked Beth.

Marta turned and looked up at Bosmansberg. We were surrounded by hills. Our valley was wedged between a series

13

of foothills that rose gradually into the actual mountains a slow hour's drive away. 'Saldahna,' she answered, referring to the fishing town she grew up in. 'I'll end my days sitting in a chair, watching the boats and getting fat on calamari and chips.'

I smiled and felt worse than before. When I was little I had liked to think of myself as a Georgiana (Meg was not a heroine's name), a mix of Anne of Green Gables, Nancy Drew and Queen Isabella of Spain, the protagonist of countless adventures; beautiful, steadfast and astonishingly brave. But no adventure or tragedy had come my way, nor ever would, not in Leopold – even though Leopold was a pretty tragic town. Despair hovered in doorways and oozed down telephone receivers. It formed a film over the eyes of those who had lived here forever, who would and could never leave. It was contagious. And I was Meg, not Georgiana, with my straight, muddy-brown hair and rooinek* complexion, and time was running out. Without some miraculous intervention, I was in danger of getting stuck here, being me for the rest of my life.

* Englishman

14

CHAPTER TWO

Marta had two children: Angelika, whom everyone called Angel, and Simon. Angel had been Marta's favourite until she fell pregnant by a 'good-for-nothing-rubbish' at the age of thirteen, the same age that Marta had given birth to her. Angel now lived two hours away in Portaville with the child and we didn't talk about her anymore.

Since Angel's 'fall', Simon had become the focus of Marta's life. She took to bringing him to work every day rather than leave him with her sister. Simon became a sort of big brother, four years faster, taller and brighter than me. However I wasn't allowed to yell at or tell tales on him as one would one's own brother because he had so little. It wasn't unusual to grow up with your maid's children. The difference was that in our house Mum used it as a way of 'fighting the system'. Mum was devoted to fighting the system, hence her current campaign of scaring the farm workers with her AIDS education. Dad didn't find the system as intolerable as Mum, but he liked having Simon around because he doubled the number of boys in our house. The arrangement didn't win us any friends amongst the townsfolk. Here in Leopold, it made us downright odd.

When Simon was twelve, his teacher declared him too clever for the tiny coloured school up the road. Marta was distraught. Everyone knew that bright kids were the first to get into trouble. Dad secured him a scholarship to a private school in Cape Town. Simon was the first coloured boy to be educated outside of Leopold; he would be the first person in his family to finish school.

'He carries a heavy burden, that boy,' Mum said the first time he'd left.

'What burden?' I'd asked, feeling the first twist of my stomach that would return each time his name was mentioned.

'The hopes of a community.' She looked wistfully after the retreating car.

I had burdens too, but Mum wasn't interested in mine. For five long years we were fed one Simon story after another, until I'd automatically stop listening at the mention of his name. There was a photo of him stuck on our fridge, taken on his last day of school, wearing an academic gown. His short, curly black hair was hidden under a square cap with a tassel hanging down. His eyes were crinkled almost shut. His normally wide smile was pulled tight with embarrassment and impatience. He was trying to look ironic. His skin was brown ochre. We knew this because one day we had found an old paint sample colour wheel and decided to code ourselves. Beth's hair was chestnut brown; my eyes were dolphin blue. Beth claimed they were pigeon blue but she was jealous because her eyes were definitely rusty. Mum said my eyes were the colour of the sea in winter.

Simon's glorious 'A' won him a place on an international

exchange programme. He left as soon as he'd finished school and had spent six months travelling around Europe. At first Marta couldn't wait to show off the postcards he sent home. Every sentence she spoke started with 'Simon says'. But now that Simon was due back in a couple of months, Marta hadn't mentioned him recently. I tried not to think about his return. My life was bad enough without him prancing around with his academic genius and overseas adventure.

Marta stayed to cook us a Sunday roast. She insisted that we bring our unfinished homework to the kitchen table.

'Start that again,' she said, leaning over Beth's exercise book.

'Why?' asked Beth.

'Because neatliness is next to Godliness.'

'It's good enough for me,' said Beth.

Marta leaned close to Beth and said, 'Well, it's not good enough for me,' and straightened up with a menacing look.

Beth laughed. 'Why do you have to go back to church, Marta? You spent all morning there.'

'Don't whine,' I said. 'You sound like a baby.'

'Until the peoples of this country put down their guns and pick up their bibles, we should all be down on our knees.'

'That too,' I said. Beth pulled a face at me and turned back to Marta.

'Will there be koeksisters* and cakes and samoosas** and doughnuts at the end?' Beth had never forgotten the one post-service tea Marta had taken us to.

* Deep-fried syrup-coated doughnut in a braided shape
** Fried pastry with a spicy, savoury filling

17

'Of course!' Marta sniffed. 'Father Basil's services feed the soul; it is up to the Mothers' Union to feed the body.'

By the time my parents returned Beth and I were at the bottom of the garden, spread out under the pecanut tree. The last of the winter sun was making a slow retreat across the lawn. Beth flipped through a pile of Archie comics. On my lap lay *The Grapes of Wrath*, but I was thinking about Sinead O'Connor. She sang into my Walkman; her voice filled my head. The tape was stretched and the batteries were running low, but when I played it at full volume, all her anger and longing were trapped inside me and I felt better.

'I fee-eel soooo different,' I sang with my heart full and my eyes closed.

Beth pinched my arm.

I opened my eyes. 'What?'

'You *are* different,' she said, and sat up. Mum was approaching across the lawn. I picked up my book. She was alone; Dad had no doubt taken refuge in his study after a long day with Florence Nightingale. Watching her from behind the pages, I despaired. Her thick, rusty-brown hair was long – too long and heavy for her lean frame. It hung around her face like an old velvet curtain. When I was little I'd loved to weave my fingers between the thick strands, but long hair did nothing for middle-aged women. And it was unhygienic. Strands of it clogged up the bathroom plugholes and clung to the sofa and cushions, as though she was everywhere.

She hesitated halfway across the garden, her tall figure uncomfortably straight, and looked around, as if from behind an invisible screen. The longer she lived here, the more English she became. Whereas local women softened and spread, she was becoming stiff and knobbly. Each year her voice sounded harsher. It rang out on the Main Street, distinguishable above all the other noise.

She tucked her mane behind her ears and launched questions as she strode closer: 'Take those things off your ears so that I can talk to you. What are you doing out here? Have you finished your homework? What did you have for lunch? It's getting late – are your uniforms ready?' Her words flew at us, *rat-a-tat-a-tat-a-tat*, splintering our peaceful afternoon. I flicked over the tape in my Walkman and lay down.

'Why was Marta here? Did you call her?'

'No,' said Beth.

'Marta loves us,' I said pointedly.

'What did the two of you get up to today?' Mum asked in her most tolerant voice.

'Nothing,' I sat up quickly, before Beth could reply, 'Nothing of interest.'

Mum's eyes finally flashed as she looked at me. 'If you want to be part of this conversation, take those silly headphones off.'

'What? I can't hear you,' I said loudly, pointing to my ears.

'It's time to come inside,' she said, shaking her head, then turned back to the house. I winked at Beth. But Beth was watching Mum. After a moment she ran to join her.

I followed them in. The sun had slipped behind the house, a blanket of cold air settling over the garden. A dikkop* broke into song – its ghostly, mournful whistles confirmed the coming

* Cape dikkop: spotted 'thick-knee' bird

19

night. I paused on the stoep* and looked out across the lawn. From inside it would already look dark. But in the last light I could make out the pecanut tree, its spindly, bare branches reaching up into the night. The watchman. It marked the unofficial end of the garden, even though, like the other two houses in our road, our land stretched five acres down to the river. Dad had strung up a chicken-wire fence behind it when we were little in a fit of parental diligence, to keep us from wandering off and getting into trouble. Then it had seemed like a dare: to climb over, to go beyond. These days it represented a battered frontier line, a weak attempt at keeping the advancing wilderness at bay. The magistrate's property next door was by contrast the essence of order and control. Past the rolled lawn and neat flowerbeds lay a large vegetable garden and beyond that pastureland, where up until two years ago the magistrate's wife had kept a cow. This wasn't legal, but as the cow had kept the houses along our road in milk and butter, and as the magistrate's wife was a sensitive woman and uncommonly attached to her cow, it had been overlooked. But when her beloved Bessie was bitten by a cobra and had to be shot, she let it be known that she blamed our 'English wilderness' next door. She and Mum had not since exchanged a word. But the name had stuck – Dad was very much taken with the idea of the 'English wilderness'. He used it regularly to refer to the general chaos of our house.

The air in the kitchen was heavy with roast chicken and onions and sweet potatoes. Dad and Beth were already seated

* Veranda

at the table. Mum carved the chicken at the counter next to the stove. I ruffled Dad's hair as I passed. It was thick and dark and somehow always carried the sharp, lemony smell of boegoe* leaves. He winked in reply. Dad was a man of the earth. His natural habitat was out in the mountains, studying his precious rock formations. There his conversation leaped about, trying to keep up as his mind raced on ahead. Inside he preferred to keep his thoughts to himself.

The kitchen table was the centre of our family. The history of our lives was etched into it with our crayons and scissors and pens. We had chiselled out crevices on the side deep enough to stash forbidden bubble gum or a Brussels sprout.

In the corner of the kitchen, on the old black and white TV, a newsreader announced another weekend of violence and death.

'Where were the police in all of this?' Mum demanded of the newsreader. 'The so-called peace-keepers!' She kept talking, as did he, neither of them interested in the other's reply.

I looked at Dad. He raised his bushy eyebrows in a way that made me giggle.

'This is *exactly*,' Mum waved the carving fork at the TV, 'the kind of reporting that incites violence. And hatred.' She jabbed again at the unfortunate TV reader. This time she was going for his heart.

'Turn off the TV before your mother sends her fork through it,' Dad said to Beth.

'It's downright irresponsible,' said Mum to the suddenly quiet room, as she delivered the butchered chicken and vegetables

* Indigenous South African plant with a strong odour, used in traditional medicines

21

to the table.

'Yes, Vivvy.' Dad looked tired.

'It is,' she insisted as she sat down.

As we began to eat, she sat up and glanced at the yellow clock above the door. She pushed her chair away from the table and looked at Dad. 'It was exactly a week ago.'

'I know,' he replied. He put down his knife and fork and closed his eyes.

'What?' I asked into the silence. When no one replied, I repeated: '*What?*'

Mum turned to me. 'Don't be obtuse, Margaret. The St James Church killings. When those men burst in on the evening service, spraying bullets across the church, killing eleven people. Did any of this tragedy register with you?'

'Yes, *Mother*, it did,' I said. Of course I knew about it, it was a shocking thing to have happened. It was terrible. But what iota of difference could Mum make to the future of this country? In what way would her being angry at the government, or the newsreader, change anything?

We all sat and thought about the killings and the families of the dead people until Mum decided that it was OK to start eating. As though waiting until our food was thoroughly cold was our small way of honouring those who had lost their lives.

'Yummy!' I said after a silence. 'This is delicious. Well done, Marta!'

Dad shook his head at me.

'Does no one have anything cheerful to talk about?' I asked.

'The under-12s netball team is being announced on Monday,'

22

said Beth, 'and Juffrou* Kat said I'll be in it. Well, she said maybe, but she winked, so I'm pretty sure.'

'Good girl!' said Dad.

'And,' Beth continued, 'and, for camp, next year, guess where we're going? Guess!'

'Sun City,' I replied.

'Don't be a spaz,' said Beth.

'Where then?'

'Strandfontein! We're going to the beach!'

'Rubbish. They'll never take you there. They'll take you to Juffrou du Plessis' farm, because that's where the standard fives** always go.'

'This time it's different. Juffrou said it's because we're the best year. All the teachers think so.'

'Sorry to crash the party, but I have even better news,' said Dad.

He waited, enjoying a rare moment of our full attention. 'My book is finally due to be out next year.'

'Fantastic!' said Mum.

'What are you going to call it, Dad?' asked Beth.

'*Hot Rocks and Flirty Fossils*.'

'Timothy!' Mum groaned.

'That's more likely to sell than "A Palaeontological History of the Cederberg Region".' He turned to me. 'How about you, princess? Any good news to share?'

'Nothing,' I said. 'But don't let that dampen the mood.'

'Oh, darling! The sweet agony of being fifteen!' said Mum.

---

* Miss or lady teacher
** Year Sevens

I rolled my eyes.

'All those hormones, all those *feelings*,' said Beth, shaking her head.

'Hello! You're eleven years old. What do you know?'

Dad put down his fork and cleared his throat. 'Beth, under no circumstances are you to enter adolescence until Meg is safely out the other side. This household will not survive both of you wandering the valley of despair at the same time.'

'So hurry up!' said Beth, leaning forward over the table.

'Actually, I have some good news,' said Mum.

'You're pregnant!' said Beth.

I snorted.

'Pregnant?' Mum looked confused. 'No! Thank God,' she added, which caused Dad to sink. 'My friend Bibi wants to write a feature for an English newspaper on the AIDS education I'm doing. Isn't that great?' She put a forkful into her mouth and chewed on it for a moment. 'Who knows, maybe we'll even get some funding out of it.'

'I thought you said you had good news,' I said. It slipped out too quickly. I glanced at Mum to see her reaction. She made a show of breathing in slowly.

'When are you going to stop this?' Beth asked.

Mum looked at Beth. 'Sweetheart, if by "this" you mean telling very poor, uneducated people how they can avoid getting a disease that will kill them and their children, the answer is I'm not. It's important.'

'No, it's not,' replied Beth, unusually stubborn.

'Yes, it is,' Mum laughed, her eyes darting to Dad for support.

'You're not listening!' I said.

24

'How about for once in your life –' Mum started, her voice rising.

'Ronel's mum says you're upsetting the volk and making the famers cross,' Beth spoke over her. Her face was red. 'And everyone wants you to stop.'

'*Every*one,' I nodded.

Mum stared at Beth a moment, then scraped her chair back against the linoleum floor and left.

I looked at Dad, but he held up his hand and finished his supper in silence.

I couldn't remember when my allergic reaction to Mum began. Everything she did annoyed me; everything I said to her sounded childish or whiny. I loved her of course; but recently I'd found it difficult to be in the same room. I lay on my bed, staring up at the poster of Kirk Cameron that was stuck to my ceiling. A nagging guilt wormed its way into my thoughts. 'I'm not going to apologise,' I said aloud to the grinning Kirk. 'Somebody has to stand up to her!' Dad was incapable of doing it. Nevertheless the look on Mum's face at supper made me feel mean. Many things made Mum angry, but she rarely got upset.

'Oh, all right,' I muttered, getting up with heavy feet. I would apologise for being rude. Then I would tell her about the way people looked at us, the parties I wasn't invited to, the raised eyebrows when her back was turned. Surely her family was more important to her than the farm workers?

I walked across the courtyard around which our square house was built and into the family room. There was no reason for it to be called that – it had no purpose other than to link the courtyard to the stoep and garden. The far wall was a graveyard of discarded passions – our baby books, Dad's record collection, the upright piano and Mum's knitting machine. Ahead of me was the sitting room. I paused. Although I couldn't see them, I knew my parents were spread out on the old brown corduroy sofa. While everyone else in South Africa sat on a couch in their lounge, we had a sofa in our sitting room. 'Airports have lounges,' was one of Mum's mantras, 'people have sitting rooms.'

'But Timothy,' came her voice through the open door, 'AIDS is not a construct of my imagination! It's an epidemic, not a scare story. All the evidence you need is there.' Her tone was softer alone with Dad. 'It will be on the new government's agenda – there's a committee drawing up a national response.'

'A committee, hey? This *is* serious,' Dad teased. The sofa creaked. He sipped loudly a couple of times. I couldn't bear the way Dad slurped – it was the only thing about him that I didn't like.

'Life is short and hard, Vivvy, for the people you're trying to help. You're not bringing them good news. And you're asking them to talk about the only thing in their lives that is private.'

'I don't understand you!' Mum sounded tired. 'You're talking about a community where alcoholism and domestic abuse are diseases themselves. Surely this is a perfect opportunity to change some of that?'

'The things people are most ashamed about are the things they are least likely to talk about. It will take time. You're not going to change ideas overnight because of some numbers on a piece of paper.'

'But there isn't time, Timothy! That's why Bibi's article is so important.'

'That woman has too much time on her hands,' replied Dad, 'She needs to settle down.' Then he added. 'You know what she needs, Vivvy…'

Mum laughed. 'I don't think it's a man she's after,' she said.

'Huh! That's only because she hasn't met a real man yet. A South African man would sort that problem out. What about Hannes?' Their laughter was warm and private. I didn't want to be near them. I felt left out; my awkwardness would make me rude. As I turned away, Mum spoke again.

'I don't know how to deal with that child, Tim.'

I stopped.

'She's fine,' came Dad's reply.

'She's a pain in the bloody arse.'

My heart constricted at Mum's words; I knew I shouldn't be listening. But I couldn't move.

She sighed. 'I don't blame her.'

Outside the crickets seemed unbearably loud.

Mum continued: 'I'm worried about her. She has no friends.'

I bit my bottom lip and squeezed my eyes shut.

Dad clicked his tongue. 'Come now.'

'It's true,' replied Mum, 'We should be hanging up on boyfriends and barring her from using the phone, we should be finding cigarettes in her bag and gating her for months on end.'

I wanted to burst in on them and scream, 'It's not my fault I'm a social retard! It's yours! It's this town!' I wanted to shake her and yell: 'Don't you see, you stupid woman, don't you get it? I would do anything to have a friend, let alone a *boyfriend*, anything!'

27

But I could not bear to face their pity. What was there to say? Nothing they could say would make it any better.

The door leading out onto the stoep was slightly open. I pushed it further and stepped out. The moon had risen late. It was full and heavy and as it climbed silver light bathed the garden. Despite the cold air I sat down on the bench by the door until my breathing returned to normal and the tears dried up. Up in the Camp, Marta would be making her way back from her prayer service, along the narrow streets where even at this time there would be kids playing out on the road, light spilling out from open doors, radios playing and bursts of laughter or shouting. Here the *creek-creek* of the crickets and the distant frogs were the only things that kept us from being swallowed up in the silence altogether.

CHAPTER THREE

Juffrou du Plessis, the grande dame of Leopold, sat at the front of the classroom, the regulation school chair hidden underneath her. I held my breath as I skirted around her large table – it was a reflex action, a poor substitute for being able to make myself disappear altogether. Being invisible to Juffrou du Plessis had been my priority ever since she had been appointed my homeroom teacher two years ago. It was a priority for anyone with any sense. At first glance my Afrikaans teacher looked uncannily like the granny on the Ouma rusks box. She had an unchanging rotation of floral or polka-dot dresses in the summer or pleated skirts in winter, from which the hemline of her apricot petticoat often protruded. Her dark brown hair, which she wore pinned back in a severe roll, was streaked with a top layer of white, like a Top Deck chocolate. Juffrou herself was an unpalatable mixture of disappointment and meanness. Her tongue's lashings hurt more than a sjambok*.

She was marking books, something she did infrequently. Her red pen flew disdainfully through the pages, scattering a spray of little red arrows that would leave an imprint several

* Cowhide whip

pages deep. Every so often another book landed on the growing pile on the floor beside her. We took our seats – fifteen girls in total, seven pairs of two, and me – and still she continued. The silence slid into lesson time, long enough for a shiver of anticipation to pass around the room. Finally, without slowing the speed of the marking, she said: 'The good Lord created the world in six days. On the seventh day,' she paused to draw breath, 'what did He do on the seventh day, Isabel?'

Isabel looked flummoxed. This was supposed to be Afrikaans grammar.

'Isabel?' Juffrou's red pen hovered in the air.

'Rested?' Isabel offered, screwing up her face with the effort.

'Exactly!' agreed Juffrou du Plessis, with a final slash into the page before she plonked the book on the pile. We watched as she opened the next. She shook her head and sighed, then picked up her ruler. She drew a red line diagonally across the double page and continued: 'and He calls upon His children to do the same.' *Smack* went the ruler on her table as she lifted her head to look directly at me.

'Sunday is a day of rest, to be spent in fellowship at church and at home, not careering around the countryside, upsetting hard-working people.'

I lowered my eyes, and sank into the wooden seat. Juffrou pushed her chair back and stood up. In the social hierarchy of Leopold, Juffrou du Plessis was second only to Mevrou* Dominee, the Dutch Reformed church minister's wife. The du Plessis family had been farming in the area for almost 200

* 'Dominee' is the church minister, and the minister's wife is referred to as 'Mevrou Dominee'

years. Juffrou ran the Kinderkrans* group, and presided over the flower show committee and the Leopold Women's Circle. She could smell out mischief before it had been committed. She was the public opinion. On matters of interest that arose outside town, her friend Santie de Vries, who worked the telephone exchange, fed her daily updates. Now it appeared that Mum was beginning to annoy her.

'Trappe van vergelyken**.' She picked up her ruler and pointed to the blackboard, across which three examples were written. She started down a row. The ruler was poised, ready to smash onto a desk as she passed.

'Right,' she barked at Martie.

'More right, the most right,' replied Martie quickly.

'No, Martie, if you are right, you are right. End of story,' said Juffrou, looking in my direction. She stopped at the back of the classroom and leaned briefly against the display board. It was dedicated to her 'Home-Grown Heroes'. The opera singer Mimi Coertse had been there so long that she was beginning to fade. Next to her were Chris Barnard, Bles Bridges, and Gary Player. In the centre of the display were her two favourites – Naas Botha and Steve Hofmeyr. 'Proper young men, those two. Decent boys,' she'd say, nodding at the *Huis Genoot**** pull-outs.

'Foolish.' She was off again, this time pouncing on Sunette. I twisted the skirt of my dress as she made her way towards me. Dad had laughed when I told him I was terrified of Juffrou. 'Sonja du Plessis?' he'd said. 'It's all bark. She's a big softie

* Children's bible school
** Degrees of comparison
*** Local Afrikaans magazine

really.' By now the Big Softie had reached the top of my row and I was finding it difficult to breathe. As she started towards me, something caught her eye and she turned to the door. Through the centre pane of glass we saw tannie Hanneke, the school secretary, beckoning her.

Juffrou called out an exercise before hurrying away.

I breathed out slowly.

'You're in trouble!' Esna swivelled around in her desk and picked up my pen. Esna had completely bypassed adolescence – she'd left for the holidays at the end of last year with a bit too much puppy fat and returned in January a tannie.

'No I'm not,' I said, taking the pen out of her sticky fingers.

'No man, not her, her mother!' said Elmarie next to her. Elmarie Goosen was the only person who ever offered to be my best friend. We were eight years old. I'd been to stay with her a few times. She lived on a large family farm in the mountains. Our weekends were spent jumping down into the silos filled with acorns for the pigs and making tea parties for her dolls and running away from her demonic younger brother Flip. At mealtimes Elmarie's mother practised her English words on me. 'Chutney' was her favourite – it made Elmarie and Flip laugh. On Sunday we gathered in her grandfather's lounge for a hymn and prayers while P.W. Botha smiled benignly down at us from his gold-framed photograph on the wall, in a manner not unlike the Pope. Then on Monday morning, while it was still dark, we drank sweet moer koffie* and ate beskuit** under

* Stove-top brewed, sweet coffee
** Rusk

crocheted blankets in the back of the bakkie* and drove to town in time for school. I loved it.

Our friendship lasted until the day I let slip that my second-best friend was Simon. This put Elmarie in an impossible position. My admission made me a rooinek kaffir-dogtertjie** and no friendship could survive that. I ran home in tears and found my parents sitting at the kitchen table, about to have lunch. Dad gave me a squeeze and told me that it wasn't Elmarie's fault; she was operating from a very limited gene pool. Mum gathered me on to her lap, and for a moment looked ready to cry. Then she stood up, deposited me on a chair and announced she was taking this matter to the headmistress. Dad disagreed. Under the circumstances it would only damage 'relations'. Mum put her finger on her lips and they moved off to continue their discussion behind a closed door. I was left on the kitchen chair, clutching my damp tissue. It was only then that I noticed Marta, who must have been there all along. She placed my favourite peanut butter and cheese sandwich and a glass of Oros on the table. She turned my chair to face her and knelt down, leaning in so that her browny-black eyes were inches from mine.

'You listen to me,' she said, her knobbly finger poking my shoulder, 'Never again do you let that Elmarie Goosen make you cry, do you understand?' I nodded, fighting back another bout of tears, 'You are Margaret Bergman, you do not cry for no one.'

---

* Pick-up truck
** Extremely negative term for a white person ('dogtertjie' meaning 'little girl') who sympathised with the cause of the black community

'OK,' I'd promised and started on my sandwich in case I started all over again. I never did cry after that day, but neither did I mention Simon again.

Elmarie and Esna had been best friends ever since, and to prove it they spent lunch breaks doing French plaits in each other's hair.

'It's your mother,' Elmarie smirked now. 'She's causing trouble. My dad says so, he says she's making mischief.'

I rolled my eyes. Everything Elmarie said was qualified by 'my dad says'.

But she was not finished. 'He says she's upsetting the volk on all the farms with stories about some disease and saying they must go the clinic for check-ups.'

Esna looked alarmed.

'My dad says it's giving the farmers a big bladdy headache. And for what? What business is it of hers?'

They looked at me, as if I knew the answer. I looked down. One of Mum's strands of hair had snaked itself around the sleeve of my school jersey. I picked it off and flicked it away. How dare she do this to me? I wouldn't defend her, I couldn't. Instead I looked out the window. 'Ooh, look over there! It's Jaco Visagie! What's he doing here?'

'Where?' Esna jumped out of her desk, sending the wooden seat clattering back and knocking her books to the floor. She had been devoted to Jaco, the local hunk from the agricultural college, for over a year. She hadn't said a word to him, but according to her he was spoken for.

'*Vark!*' she sneered at me, resembling a pig herself.

'I wonder if Jaco will be asked to the matric dance?' I

continued. Elmarie hid a smile. Dates for the school leavers'
dance were hard to find in Leopold. The agricultural college
was the only source of boys in town. Unless you knew someone
who was willing to drive three hours to drink Coke and Fanta
and dance to the local squashbox band, you were stuck with
one of them.

Juffrou reappeared. Her face was red and in a burst of energy
unlike her, she started calling out commands before she'd sat
down: 'Come, come! Top of page 152.' She pulled out her
hankie from inside the top of her dress and dabbed away a
few crumbs from her top lip. '*Ag genade**, Isabel, why are you
not ready?'

Juffrou glowered from her table, her ruler and pencil poised
like a knife and fork. Once and then again she glanced at the
closed classroom door.

'Begin, child, begin,' she said as Isabel haltingly started to
read.

A few moments later came the *clack, clack, clack* of the
headmistress Mrs Franklin's stilettos down the corridor.

A rap on the door, followed without pause by her entry, had
us all clambering to our feet. Mrs Franklin was small and fierce.
Even in the sweltering heat she remained crisp and efficient.
We rattled off our greeting as Juffrou tugged her hemline back
over her petticoat.

'Juffrou du Plessis.' Mrs Franklin smiled broadly.

'Headmistress.' Juffrou beamed back, her hands folded one
on top of the other. Their perfect manners highlighted their
mutual dislike.

---

* Oh mercy

Mrs Franklin turned to us. 'We have a newcomer today.' She looked back over her shoulder towards the classroom door with an impatient frown, before the bright smile returned. 'I'm sure you will all make her feel welcome, just as I am assured she will make every effort,' here she paused, 'to make the best of her time here.'

It was the same each time a new girl arrived. In the moments before she stepped into the classroom I would clutch at a wild hope that at last I might have a friend. And then she would step in and have long blonde hair caught back in a scrunchie and her ankle socks would be rolled right down over her carefully tanned legs and I knew that to her, I was one of the dim locals. Nothing would make her want to speak to me.

'Her name is Xanthe, and she will join your class as soon as she can find her way back from the school boarding house. Ah! There you are!' She beckoned at the doorway and into the classroom stepped a tall, pale girl with very black hair. Mrs Franklin pointed to the empty space next to me. 'Margaret, we will assign Xanthe to your capable care.'

I looked at my fingers to hide my blush.

'That's all.' With a last nod at Juffrou, Mrs Franklin left. For a few moments the only sound was the echo of her shoes disappearing down the corridor.

CHAPTER FOUR

Xanthe stood at the front of the classroom, satchel hanging off her left hand. In those first moments it wasn't her pale, long, skinny legs that caught my attention, or the way the blue school shift hung from her like a tent, as though her body had rejected it as it would an invasion of foreign cells. It wasn't her sharp pixie hairstyle, or its aggressively black colour that struck me, or even her arctic-blue eyes – what impressed me about this girl, standing alone at the front of the class, was her lack of interest in her surroundings. She stared ahead; her eyes were fixed on the wall behind Juffrou.

'Bye, then, darling, bye!' called a motherly voice from the corridor. It sounded twinkly and bright, like a mum in a washing powder advert. The girl turned briefly but made no reply. Juffrou eyed her for a moment, not bothering to disguise her thoughts, then clapped her hands, shooing her towards the desk.

Elmarie swung around, delighted that I had been dumped with this odd-looking girl. I flicked the top of my third finger against my thumb at her. I didn't want her ruining what had turned into an interesting afternoon. As the girl sat down, I shifted away, to give her space. When she didn't say anything, or even return my smile, I had a horrible feeling that I had moved too far. I had been rude. I moved back, but now I was almost on top of her. Red-faced and hot, I sat in the middle of my seat, determined not to move for the rest of the lesson.

Juffrou du Plessis made her bark of a cough to bring the class back to order then fixed her eyes on the new girl: 'Well, now, Santie, welcome to our class. Let's add you to our register,' she said opening the wide book; 'So that's s - a - n?' she raised an eyebrow.

'X.'

'I beg your pardon?'

'X - a - n - t - h - e.' The girl spelled her name with an admirable slowness. It stopped a shadow short of being rude. Her accent sounded virtually foreign. That would make her from Cape Town. They often did that.

Juffrou frowned in confusion. 'Really?' Her heavy Afrikaans accent lingered on the vowel sounds.

'Yes.'

Juffrou did not approve of outlandish names. A few years back there had been a Hermione. Juffrou had called her Hester. She raised her eyebrows as she entered the name on the register. 'I've never heard of that name myself. But then one learns something new every day, don't you think, Sonia?' The last sentence was delivered in a loud voice and accompanied by a small piece of chalk that landed inches from Sonia's left hand. Juffrou waited for silence. 'Of course the local indigenous people, the Xhosa,' she rested on the 'osa' and took a breath, 'use all their "x"s to make a click sound, so why not use an "s" for a "z" sound instead,' she said with a little laugh.

38

We stared back.

Another cough. 'Exercise five. Sonia, seeing you have so much to say today, why don't you proceed.'

Xanthe unzipped her Tipp-Ex-graphitised pencil case. Her fingernails were filed into a square shape. A couple of pencils spilled out of the case. She reached in and pulled out a thick silver fountain pen. It looked old and heavy. The lid was bordered at the top and bottom with a gold rim. Midway up the brushed silver base was an inscription. She stared at it for a moment and then put it back in the pencil case and took out a black ballpoint pen.

What was a smart pen doing in a scruffy pencil case? It was the most beautiful pen I'd ever seen. It was the first time I'd considered that a pen could be beautiful.

A few minutes before the end of the lesson Juffrou left again. As the door shut Elmarie and Esna swung around. Elmarie frowned at Xanthe before saying in Afrikaans: 'What happened to your hair?'

Esna clapped her hands to her mouth and giggled.

Xanthe lifted her gaze to Elmarie, then closed her eyes.

I smiled. Elmarie had no choice but to swivel back in her seat.

'Did you see her eyes?' Elmarie said loudly in Afrikaans. 'Like a witch.'

'Don't witches have yellow eyes? Like werewolves? Her eyes were icy blue,' replied Esna.

Elmarie clicked her tongue. 'It was her expression, then. But there was definitely something witch-like about her.'

'I thought she looked more like a cat,' replied Esna.

'Why are you two being so rude?' I said, purposefully in English, sounding too much like Mum. 'She's not stupid, you know. She understands everything you're saying.'

Dad called the local white community's attitude 'frontier philosophy'. 'When you're the obvious minority,' he'd explained to Mum many times, 'your existence is constantly under threat. There is no room for diversity.'

'Actually, I try not to understand anything in that language,' said Xanthe, the first words she'd spoken.

They swivelled back. 'You will have a very bad time in Leopold, then,' said Esna in her severe English.

'Not long before it's bye-bye Santie,' added Elmarie.

'Let's hope so,' said Xanthe. 'And don't ever call me Santie again – it's a *zuh* sound – as in xenophobia.'

I laughed at the blank expression on their faces. '*Zuh* as in zulu.'

'OK, Santie,' Esna said, getting up as the bell rang.

We were the last two left in the classroom. After my bizarre behaviour ealier, I wanted to start again. Xanthe stuffed her notepad and pencil case into her satchel and picked up a printed map of the school. She looked up at me and smiled. Or maybe she didn't, and I assumed she had, and I rushed in with, 'Hi! I'm Margaret!'

At the same time she said: 'Uh – where is the secretaries' office?'

I smiled, too brightly. 'Straight down the passage.'

'Thanks,' she said, walking out the classroom.

'Hang on, I'll show you!' I called, grabbing my bag.

But she was gone.

40

I slumped into the desk. I had not met many people before – everyone I knew had been here forever, occupying their place on the canvas of our town, moving in and out of focus as they became more or less relevant to me. Sometimes, out of boredom, Simon and I used to assign each other characters for the day, but that wasn't the same. Simon could never be anyone but himself. The first time Mum saw Dad she had apparently walked up to him and started talking, as if they had been in the middle of a conversation five minutes previously. Mum said she was so nervous that she had to pretend they were already friends. Dad said he felt hypnotised, like a helpless chicken, and by the time he came to, a strange woman had taken control of his life.

What did this girl Xanthe think of me? What would I think of me on first meeting? A freckly girl with honey-brown (not 'mousy', as Beth claimed) hair; tall but podgy ('puppy fat,' Mum insisted) with a permanent frown. I kicked the seat in front of me so that it clattered down on its hinges. At the front of the room, Juffrou's handwriting, warm, warmer, die warmste, looped its way across the blackboard. *Boring, more boring, the most boring*, said a voice in my head. Even Esna left an impression. Xanthe had forgotten me before she'd even left the classroom. Worse than that, it was if she hadn't registered me at all.

The voice in my head spoke again, with such cold, clear force that I gripped the edge of the desk: maybe it wasn't this town that was the problem. Maybe it was me.

I left the classroom, dragging my despondency behind me. At the front of the building I paused. All that was waiting for me at home was my black mood, skulking about my bedroom. I could afford to take my time.

From the steps you could see the whole valley. Today Bosmansberg looked like a cardboard cut-out against the sharp sky. A few waterfalls remained from the recent rains. They leaked down the creases of the rocky hillside like silver tendrils.

At the foot of Bosmansberg was the clump of factory-like buildings of the agricultural college and its surrounding fields, separated from the town by the river. Its fat green banks snaked up the valley floor like a lazy boomslang*, all the way to the pine and cedar forests in the distance.

Leopold's three longest roads, Main Street, De Wet Street and Voortrekker Street, ran parallel to the river. Nobody knew who De Wet was or why he had a street named after him. A fire in the town hall in the early 1900s had destroyed all the original town records.

The streets, like stripes across the town, made me think of my English grandmother who'd told me, on her only visit to South Africa, that one should never wear horizontal stripes as they made one look fat.

This had made Mum very angry. 'Why do you say these things?'

'*Somebody* needs to,' my grandmother replied, fixing her eyes on Mum. 'These are things your children need to know.'

'No they don't! Outside your tiny world, Mother, is another one where people are not judged solely by their appearance.'

'Tosh!' had been my grandmother's response. I'd never decided whether she was dismissing Mum or the idea.

* A long, greenish venomous tree snake

Leopold's horizontal roads didn't make the town look fatter; from my position above they seemed to squash the town into the narrow valley bed.

Inside the school a door slammed shut. A few moments later came the sound of Buddy, the school janitor, whistling and jangling his keys. As I turned around Juffrou du Plessis emered from the gloom. I sank to my haunches and rummaged around in my satchel, pretending to have lost something.

Juffrou stopped next to me and looked out over the valley. 'Pragtig*,' she murmured, admiring the view. '"I will lift up mine eyes unto the hills, from whence cometh my help."'

I stood up and stared across at Bosmansberg, silently begging any form of help to make her leave. Eventually she turned to me, opened her mouth to say something, but decided against it. As she started down the stairs, she muttered, 'Poor child.'

Juffrou took a while to shrink. I watched her lumber down the hill. In a bigger world my problems would be far smaller – Juffrou would be nothing more than a grumpy teacher; Mum an average freak. When Xanthe walked into the classroom, she'd stepped out of a world that was everything I had been longing for. I wanted to be part of that world so much that it ached.

---

* Beautiful

CHAPTER FIVE

The steeples of Leopold's churches formed a triangle above the tree line. The largest was the face brick clock tower of the new Dutch Reformed church. At the bottom end of the Main Street was the gothic-shaped steeple of the old Dutch Reformed church, at the top end the sandstone Anglican church.

The new Dutch Reformed church, set in the heart of the well-to-do properties with their arched gables and front rose gardens, was designed to be the single most important building in town. The clock tower steeple could be seen from any position. Its 1950s face brick design was windowless apart from a row of square panes along the top. Mum called it 'the bunker'.

The Anglican church had been built by the English missionaries. As Mum was the only white member of the congregation, Father Basil held services in the community hall in the Camp. The church was unused except for weddings and funerals.

I cut through its churchyard on my way down to the Main Street. In the far corner of the graveyeard, near the cluster of children's gravestones, was the bent figure of Witbooi, the self-appointed verger. He had always looked 150 years old. Even in the hottest weather he wore the same brown nylon trouser suit over a threadbare blue V-neck jersey. Dad called him 'Meneer* Professor' despite the fact that Witbooi was illiterate. He claimed that Witbooi carried in his head an uninterrupted history of the region for the last hundred years. More than that, Dad said he was a 'seer'. I tried to avoid the tiny, age-stiff man with his toothless smile and creased face, in case he might see too far into me.

He straightened up as I passed and beckoned me over. On the ground in front of him was a bird's nest with three tiny Francolin chicks inside. The mauled mother lay to the side of the tree. I pulled the sleeve of my jersey over my hand and covered my nose.

'Devil dog,' he breathed and inclined his head towards the police station. His voice was whispery, like tissue paper. 'Take them.' He picked up the nest and put it inside an old cardboard Castle beer crate.

'What? No.' I looked around. 'I don't think they will survive, Witbooi. They're tiny.'

'Take them to Marta,' he insisted.

The balls of brown fluff looked blindly upwards, mewling for their mother. They would continue to do that until they were too weak to hold their necks up any longer. Beth and I had rescued enough baby birds to know that these ones had very little chance. But Beth had a rule that if you didn't try and save something you were complicit with its death.

'Alright, then,' I said and took the cardboard box.

* Mr

45

At home I went in search of Marta. 'A present from Witbooi,' I said, placing the box on the kitchen counter.

'Silly old fool.' She peered at the nest and shook her head. 'They won't survive the night. No doubt full of fleas.'

'You know the rules, Marta,' said Beth, who had come to have a look at the chicks. 'Are you happy to have their blood on your hands?'

'That's not rules, that's nonsense!' said Marta but she abandoned the ironing, set about mixing up a bowl of milky Pronutro and found me a syringe.

That evening I stood next to Dad and peered down at the birds, a sense of responsibility tugging at me. Marta had transferred them to a Wilson's tennis shoebox padded with an old towel and shredded newspaper. The box, under the desk lamp in Dad's study, was a makeshift incubator.

'Poor little buggers, not likely to survive the night,' said Dad.

'They enjoyed the Pronutro,' I said.

Dad shook his head. 'Why do people think birds like Pronutro?'

'What else would you feed them?'

He frowned at me. 'Regurgitated worms.'

'Be my guest!' I lingered over the box. Dad's study always made me feel better. It felt safe to be surrounded by stacks of his notebooks full of his neat spidery cursive. His handwriting was contained and measured. Mum's handwriting was so erratic that sometimes even she couldn't read it.

'There was a new girl at school today,' I said, thinking back to Xanthe's pencil case and the beautiful pen.

'Nice?'

I wrinkled up my nose. 'Can weird be nice?'

He looked up. 'You're nice.'

I smacked his arm. 'Maybe not weird, exactly. Different, I suppose.'

'Well now, different is always nice, especially around these parts.'

'*Ja*, right,' I said, thinking of Esna and Elmarie and Juffrou's reaction to my very different mother. 'Dad, you have to talk to Mum.'

'Do you think so? I said hello to her just last week.'

'You're not funny,' I scolded. 'Juffrou had a go at me at school today. She says Mum's a troublemaker and . . . she could get arrested,' I finished weakly.

Dad frowned. 'She's educating people about a disease. She's saving the farmers a lot of time and money.'

'But standing in front of the clinic with a bucket of condoms?'

He chuckled.

I stamped my foot. 'You need to stop her, Dad.'

'Shhh, you're upsetting the chicks. They're fighting for their lives, they don't care about condoms.'

I left him at his desk. He was no help. He didn't have to put up with Juffrou and Elmarie and Esna. At any sign of trouble he disappeared behind his books and his rocks like a dassie* darting out of sight.

I woke the next morning thinking of the chicks. As I reached over the box and picked up the nearest one, I held my breath.

* Rock rabbit

Its tiny claws tickled my palm. Its racing heartbeat pulsed into my carefully closed hand and up my arm.

'Well, I never,' said Dad, peering over my shoulder.

'Isn't it amazing,' I whispered.

'Not sure I'm *amazed*,' replied Dad.

I was in awe. They had survived! It was a sign – from God – that life had taken a dramatic turn for the better. Perhaps they would grow up and live in the courtyard and every time I passed they would fly down and perch on my shoulder. At the very least, it meant that Xanthe would be my friend.

'They're still more likely to die than not,' added Dad.

I couldn't wait to get to school. It was as though a suffocating cloak had been lifted from my shoulders.

'What's the matter with you?' asked Elmarie halfway through Afrikaans.

'What do you mean?'

'You're different today.'

'This is the way I always am!' I said, laughing loudly. I stole a glance at Xanthe, but she hadn't been listening. It didn't matter. I didn't mind when later in the day she chose to sit at another pair of empty desks rather than next to me. Everything would work out – it was all a matter of time.

At home, Marta had made banana bread. Banana bread was delicious at any time of year. In winter it was comforting and wholesome. In summer, when Marta kept it in the fridge and served it with a thick smear of butter, it was cool and moist. Today, when spring sunshine mingled with the sweet oozing fruit and hovered in the kitchen, it was sublime.

Mum and Beth were at the table. I sat down and cut a large slice.

Beth was talking at Mum with her mouth full. 'It was so unfair on the Romanovs, don't you think?'

The loaf was still warm from the oven. It fell apart exquisitely in my mouth.

'Don't you think, Mum?' repeated Beth.

'Hmm?' said Mum without looking up. It was her standard 'Shhh! I'm busy,' reply. She sat at the far end of the table, letters and newspapers spread out around her, her reading glasses balanced at a ridiculous angle on her nose. Behind her Marta leaned against the sink, examining a piece of paper in her hands.

'You're a mother,' continued Beth. 'Imagine what the poor Tsarina felt, seeing her children herded off to that grotty holding house, when they'd never before left a palace in their lives. And the boys were haemophiliacs, you know. And then,' Beth looked around the table, 'they shot them!'

Marta clicked her tongue. 'The acts of evil men.' She shared Beth's love of a good drama.

Mum took off her glasses and looked up. 'It wasn't that simple.'

'Complicated murder is OK,' I said, cutting another slice of bread.

'No,' said Mum, drawing out the 'o' sound. Her tone suggested she was talking to a very stupid and potentially dangerous person. 'There is no excuse for killing, but you must understand it in the context of revolution and war. Change is painful,' she added, looking meaningfully at me.

'What?' I said. 'Do you think I don't like change?'

The smallest inclination of her head. A raised eyebrow.

'Are you joking?' I said. 'I'm dying for a bit of change around here.'

'Ha, ha,' said Mum severely.

'Those men were evil!' said Beth loudly, annoyed by the deviation. 'That poor Romanov family. Did you know, Marta, that they sewed their rubies and diamonds and tiaras into their coats? I wonder whether the Tsarina knew they were going to die, but made them do it to keep the childrens' hopes up.' Beth fell into a reflective silence, before saying, 'Thank goodness Anastasia survived!'

'Praise God!' said Marta.

'What?' said Mum.

'She got away! She ran away from the men with guns!' Beth paused for a sip of water. 'Do you know that after all she went through some people doubted that she was in fact Anastasia. But it was obvious – she had absolutely no idea what money was!' Beth shook her head in wonderment. 'I'm going to call my daughter Anastasia.'

I turned to Mum. Four years ago I had brought home the same story. She threatened to call the Cape Provincial Education Department. When I begged her not to, she'd shouted: 'But it's not true! How can they teach you things that aren't true?'

But she appeared to be softening with age. Or perhaps it was Beth. She leaned towards Beth. 'Do you remember old Mrs Schultz?' she said in a low voice. 'She was a Russian émigré. She arrived here in 1920 without any money. Perhaps Anastasia ended up *here*.'

Beth narrowed her eyes at Mum, then returned to her banana bread. 'Don't be pathetic.'

Marta had been fiddling with the letter all through Beth's anti-Bolshevik rant. Twice she had been about to say something, but each time turned back to the sink. It must be important.

I kicked Mum's foot under the table and motioned towards Marta.

Mum looked up. 'Marta?'

'Miss Viv?'

Mum looked back at me.

I mouthed, 'The letter!'

She shot me an exasperated look and then said, 'What's in the letter, Marta?'

Marta picked up a washed pot, and put it back down. 'It's Simon,' she said. She turned and studied Simon's photo on the fridge.

'Anything the matter?' Mum's voice was unnaturally bright. Beth forgot about her dead Russians. I felt my wonderful day begin to lose definition and dissolve, like heat rising off tarmac.

'He will be back in a few weeks. He's coming home,' said Marta quietly.

'But he was supposed to be away the whole year. It's only August!' I burst out. I felt Mum's eyes on me.

'It will be September by the time he's back,' said Marta. 'Anyway, it's time he came home and made himself useful. All this nonsense travelling the world, and with Mister Tim paying so much money . . . The child needs to get a job.'

'Nonsense,' said Mum. 'He's a star and we are so proud of him.'

51

Blood thumped against my skull. Of course you are, Mother! I thought. You can't wait to have him back, never mind your own children!

Then I looked up to see the smile that Marta couldn't hide and felt bad. I knew Marta missed her son, but I didn't want him home. It was easy for Beth, with her dyslexia. All she had to do was bring home a pass and be showered with a gruff 'That's my girl!' from Dad and a wobbly smile from Mum. Yet my 'B' aggregates infuriated Mum. Her mouth would set, even if I was one of the top five girls in the class. 'You're not up against your *class*, Margaret,' she'd say in an intense whisper that was supposed to inspire, 'you're up against yourself.' As far as she was concerned, not 'reaching your potential' was worse than lazy. It was unethical. But if you already knew you could do something, what was the point? What sense of personal achievement was there to be gained from that?

That night I couldn't sleep. I checked on the chicks, I sang them a song. I lay on my side, I flopped over onto my tummy. I curled myself into a small ball, I spread myself out like a starfish. I focused on a pure green light between my eyes. It was hopeless. The only sound was the intermittent chime of the grandfather clock in the hall, wheezing its way through the night: 11.30, 12 o'clock. 12.30. My back hurt, my eyes ached. My skin itched as though insects were crawling all over me. I searched my sheets. I changed my nightie. Nothing. Nothing but this endless night.

It was Simon, of course. It was the news that Simon was coming home.

52

Once upon a time I'd thought Simon the smartest person in the world. After Dad. And MacGyver. But that was when he had grasshopper legs and his ears stood out at forty-five degrees and it looked as though he had slipped on an extra-large pair of hands over his own.

'*Karraboosh*,' I said to the dark night.

Karraboosh was Simon's word. In a house that buzzed with what Dad called the 'unfathomable female disposition', Simon commanded attention by being silent. Hours passed without him saying a word. Then he'd tell a screamingly naughty joke or he'd start talking, very quickly, about a jumble of topics: a story he'd heard at school or the names and order of the planets or the gestational period of an elephant cow. Often he'd simply say '*karraboosh*.'

It made Marta furious. 'For God's sake, Simon, stop that nonsense!' she'd scold. 'It's not even a word!'

He'd raise his eyebrow in disagreement. '*Karraboosh*,' he'd whisper, loud enough to set Beth and I off.

Karraboosh lasted many years. Beth and I still used it sometimes as a private deal-sealer.

The trouble with Simon was that he had everything I wanted and it wasn't fair. My parents had used *our* money to pay for him to go away. When I'd asked to go to boarding school they'd refused. 'Why would you want to leave me, princess?' Dad had looked horrified. 'You've got the rest of your life to discover that Leopold is the best place on earth.'

While I resented the way Mum heralded Simon's every success, I hated it when Dad took him fishing. One day I found Simon and Dad packing the car. It was not long after Elmarie had informed me that P.W. Botha would be very upset that I'd called Simon my second-best friend. I was sick of watching the two of them drive off together. I bet P.W. Botha wouldn't be pleased about that either.

'Why should Dad take Simon fishing again?' I shouted, stamping my foot.

Another closed door, more fierce whispering lest Simon's feelings be hurt. Simon didn't have a dad.

'So he gets to take mine? That's not fair!' I kept shouting.

'No, so you get to share. You're very lucky to be in a position to share,' replied Mum, looking pained by my insolence.

I wasn't lucky, I was left out.

As the clock chimed a lonely stroke, I sat up and switched on the light. I had a bad feeling about Simon's return. Why did his letter have to arrive today? It felt like a challenge. He'd had enough good fortune in the past few years. It was my turn now, and I wouldn't let anything ruin that.

By the time I arrived home from school the next day the chicks had died. We buried them in the Wilson's tennis shoebox at the bottom of the garden, next to a cluster of other rescued birds, a hamster and three goldfish that the cat had eaten before it had been bitten by a snake. Beth sang the whole of 'All things bright and beautiful', although one verse would have done, and planted another handmade cross.

'I don't know what you're so cheerful about,' I said as we walked back across the lawn. She had no idea what these deaths signified. Although I knew it was ridiculous, I blamed Simon's letter.

'I was thinking of all the things we can do when Simon's back,' Beth said. 'We should go down to the river and rebuild our swimming pool!' She grabbed my wrist. 'We can go camping!'

'Don't be silly,' I said, shaking my arm free.

'Why is that silly?'

'Simon is nineteen,' I said, 'Why would he want to hang out with a snotty little eleven-year-old?'

'Because he's Simon,' she said simply.

I shook my head.

'He's your friend, Meg,' said Beth. 'Don't be weird.'

'He's not my friend, stop saying that!' I snapped.

Beth stepped back at my tone. Then she broke into a run and cartwheeled across the rest of the lawn.

Inside I found Marta bent over a newspaper on the dining-room table. 'What are you reading?' I asked, walking towards her.

'Nothing.' She straightened up and picked up the dishcloth on the table. It was one of Mum's English newspapers. The headline read: NO REFUGE FROM THE SOUTH AFRICAN VIOLENCE. It was about the St James massacre.

'Oh,' I said, 'more of that.'

'*Genade*, child, watch yourself! It's terrible that the European people read these things about us.'

'England.'

She frowned at me.

'The newspaper is from England, not Europe.'

'Don't be cute, or I'll wash your mouth out.'

I laughed. 'I'll show you.' I fetched Mum's world atlas from the bookshelf. 'See,' I said, pointing out the ink smudge of an island next to the larger Europe, 'England – Europe.'

I was about to show her all the countries that Simon had visited, but the look on her face stopped me. She stared at the page for a long time. Then she smacked the dishcloth over her shoulder and turned away.

I watched her disappear into the kitchen. I thought I had been kind. Marta was so proud that she would hate to make such an obvious error. Mum stepped up next to me and squeezed my shoulder. I hadn't seen her behind us. 'Marta's waiting for Simon to return from a continent and countries that are nothing more than words to her. He might as well have been in space.'

I shook off Mum's hand and stepped out onto the stoep, into the last of the afternoon sunshine. Simon had been through a stage of wanting to be an astronaut.

'Don't be ridiculous,' I'd scoffed, 'you're Simon from Leopold, you'll never get to the moon.'

'I will too,' he'd replied, 'and I'll leave you behind if you're going to be like that.'

On Friday morning Juffrou stood next to her desk. Her eyes scanned the class like a jackal buzzard flying low. They came to rest on Xanthe and me.

'So,' she said, 'this morning Mrs Franklin asked me how the new girl was settling in, whether our two English speakers had struck up a friendship. And I had to say, "No, Headmistress, they've not exchanged a word."'

I prickled with shame.

'I suppose we should be grateful,' Juffrou continued. 'The last thing we need is for our two English troublemakers to be

56

in cahoots.'

Next to me Xanthe stirred, like a dozing cat who senses a bird and opens one eye.

At lunchtime I sat on the steps outside the biology lab, peeling soggy tomato off my brown-bread sandwich. I spent most of my lunch breaks here. Beth and her friends never came to this part of the school.

Xanthe had been here a week. It was obvious that she wasn't interested in being friends with me. In every other class but Afrikaans she had chosen to sit alone rather than next to me. The birds were dead; my 'lucky break' had turned out to be a mean joke. Fat tears plopped onto the concrete step in front of me. They dissolved into the stone, leaving no trace. I didn't want to be me anymore. It was too difficult. I wanted to be the kind of person Xanthe would like. I dug my hands into my eyes and sniffed loudly.

A yellow tissue appeared in front of me. A moment later it jiggled. I looked up. Xanthe was sitting next to me, tactfully avoiding eye contact.

'Thank you,' I muttered, blowing my nose.

When she didn't reply, I picked up my sandwich and flicked away the last piece of tomato.

'Yuck.' Her voice startled me.

'I know.' I gave up and returned the remains of the sandwich to the Tupperware sandwich box and shut the lid. 'My mother's idea of a nutritious lunch.'

'Have some of these. Much healthier.' She reached into her school bag and pulled out a bag of Big Korn Bites.

57

As I dug my hand into the packet, she said: 'How long have you been here, Madge?'

'You make it sound like a prison.' I laughed but stopped when I realised that for her it was. I followed her gaze across the gravel-dusty quad at the thirsty clump of tall, tatty orange cannas in the central rockery. They stood like a group of convicts chained together. On the far side of the quad a mess of pink bougainvillea flowers lay trampled into the ground by a thousand feet.

'Forever,' I replied eventually. 'I was born here.'

She whistled. 'Je-sus, Madge, that's bad luck.'

'Margaret,' I corrected her. 'Or Meg.'

She looked at me, head cocked to one side, her cat's eyes narrow. 'Nah, it's definitely Madge,' she said, the corners of her mouth twitching.

CHAPTER SIX

My new name stayed with me all weekend. 'Madge,' I practised when no one was around. 'My name is Madge.' It made me stand differently; it changed the angle of my head. It was a second chance. I could step out of everything I didn't like about Meg and fill Madge with all the things I wanted to be. Meg was a hen's name – it rhymed with peg and beg and dreg. Madge was too gritty to rhyme with much at all.

I made a list of Madge things to do. I managed 'hang out with best friend; have a boyfriend; go for milkshakes' before I realised that was what the characters did on *Beverly Hills 90210*. More than that, the last two items on my list were currently impossible in Leopold.

I studied myself in the mirror, searching for signs of Madge. I needed a look. Xanthe had one without even trying. Her mouth was subversive. Her eyes were steely. They made me think she enjoyed having secrets. Most of all she looked experienced. You couldn't fake that. At this my Madge mood started to slip.

Mum found Beth and me on the stoep, locked in a hyperventilating competition.

'Dad says there's a new girl in your class.'

59

I grunted without looking up from the stopwatch.

'Why don't you invite her for lunch?'

'No thanks,' I said.

'They're not actually friends,' panted Beth, forfeiting her time.

'Yes, we are!'

'So then,' said Beth, still red in the face. 'Invite her for lunch.'

Later that week I stood over the kitchen sink, staring at a mug in my hand. I had left the washing-up long enough for Mum to be fuming but not yet thundering through to my room. The mug was brown with a pattern of square orange flowers embossed on it. It was the last remaining of a set of four.

Xanthe would hate this mug. It was old and chipped. The handle had been glued back on several times. I dumped it on the drying rack. What would she think about the old yellow clock on the wall and the kitchen table and the net curtains? Mum insisted on the curtains; she said they were ironic. They were tatty and beige with age. Two weeks ago the kitchen had been fine. Now I knew it was awful. It hadn't occurred to me before then that the dishtowel lying on the counter was a puke shade of yellow, it had simply been a dishcloth. I leaned over and chucked it away in disgust, but that didn't feel like enough. I picked up the brown mug and smashed it onto the floor.

My parents appeared.

'I'm sorry,' I said quickly. 'It slipped out of my hand.'

'It was my favourite,' said Mum quietly as she bent down to pick up the pieces.

'I know,' I said. I stared at the chunks of thick brown porcelain on the floor. 'Why did you call me Margaret?'

Mum peered up at me. 'What?'

'Margaret, of all names?'

'It's a very pretty name,' she said.

'It's not! It's clumpy and stuffy and so 1970s,' I said.

'But darling, you were born in the 1970s.' Her confusion made me want to scream.

'Margaret wasn't my choice,' said Dad, as he picked the dishtowel up off the floor.

'A-ha!' I said to Mum.

'I wanted to call you Petronella, after my grandmother,' he said. He folded the dishcloth over the oven rail. Mum giggled and left the kitchen.

'What do you think about that dishcloth?' I turned on Dad.

He glanced after Mum, then turned back to me, his head on one side.

'The cloth,' I said, 'the colour, what do you think?'

He looked down at his hands and back at me. 'It's . . . nice? Different? Nicely weird and a little bit different?'

But I didn't want to be teased. I wanted to tell him that at last I thought I had found a friend who was fun and even made me feel fun. She embodied everything I wanted to be, but as a result everything else seemed insufferable. I had a 'Xanthe' voice in my head and it was loud and funny and brighter than me. It was also meaner than me. But that sounded ridiculous. The best I could manage was: 'Do you ever hear voices in your head?'

'Sure,' he shrugged. 'All the time.' He picked up a jug of custard and scooped a large dollop into his mouth. 'Take this custard, for instance. I don't want it. It's the voices! They're screaming out for it, they won't give me any rest.'

I was beginning to suspect that his simple-mindedness was cultivated. 'Dad, I hate to say it, but you're a bit of a moron.'

'Funny,' he replied as he left the kitchen, 'The voices were saying the same thing about you.'

Xanthe had been in Leopold for three weeks. Sometimes she appeared at lunchtime on the steps of the biology lab, but not every day. I was always there, although never again with my soggy sandwich. I ate that quickly standing behind my open locker door.

Some days she was relaxed and chatty. But that could change without warning and she'd be monosyllabic and constantly looking over her shoulder. Then I had nothing to say.

Xanthe arrived near the end of lunch break. She never mentioned where she'd been and I wasn't brave enough to ask. She had taken to bringing me packets of Big Korn Bites. I found it unnerving – it was such a motherly thing to do. I felt I should give her something in return, but there was nothing she'd want from me.

'What's next?' she asked as the bell rang.

'Swimming,' I muttered.

'Swimming?' she shouted. 'With that woman – Juffrou Kat? Fuck that. There's no way I'm getting undressed in front of her.'

I laughed. 'Why not?'

'She's a complete lessie.'

'A what?'

'Les-bi-an.'

'Seriously?'

Xanthe didn't bother responding. She stalked off, in the opposite direction to the pool.

'Where are you going?' I called, and bit my lip at the sound of my voice.

Girls streamed past, criss-crossing the space between us on their way to class. Xanthe stopped and looked back. 'Come on,' she said eventually.

I swallowed and looked around. Juffrou Kat emerged from the building, a bundle of hula hoops over one shoulder and a sack of netball balls over the other. Juffrou Kat was taller than anyone else in the school. Her year-round uniform was a tennis skirt and a white polo shirt that stretched tight across her shelf-like breasts. Her thighs were thicker than Dad's. She blasted the whistle that hung around her neck with a strength that made you pee in your pants. I turned towards the swimming pool. But a moment later, Xanthe's hand on my arm stopped me.

'Why aren't you two up at the pool getting changed?' Juffrou Kat demanded.

I looked down to avoid Xanthe's smile.

'Juffrou, we were on our way to find you,' Xanthe replied, her voice like the distant hum of bees. 'How are you?'

Juffrou frowned at Xanthe.

'Great,' said Xanthe, with another quick smile. 'Juffrou, the thing is, I'm far behind in maths, and Margaret has offered to help me catch up. If I don't, my father –' She broke off, and looked over her shoulder, as Juffrou Kat and I watched. 'There will be trouble at home if I don't improve my marks,' Xanthe said softly. 'Would you mind if we used this one hour to work in the library? It would make such a difference.' Xanthe smiled at the teacher, who astonishingly smiled back, if only for a second. Then Juffrou Kat turned to me.

'Maths,' I said, nodding.

Juffrou Kat's eyes drilled holes straight into my lying soul. She sniffed once and said, 'Just this once.'

'Absolutely,' said Xanthe, nodding. 'Come on, Margaret, let's get going.'

I followed Xanthe around the building. 'This isn't the way –' I started, but Xanthe carried on walking. 'Are we not going to do maths?' I asked.

She laughed. Excitement and fear collided in my veins.

We were outside the side door of the new hall, the door that led to the stage. Xanthe looked around, her face suddenly so serious that I wanted to laugh. She opened the door and slipped inside.

I followed her in and up the steps to the stage. The new hall was in fact the school's only hall. It was not that new either, but it had stage lights and a sound system and was a source of great pride. She walked past the three rows of chairs where the staff sat during our daily assembly, and then waited for me, holding back the long black curtain that separated the front of the stage from the back. Her normally mirror-like eyes danced. Her grin was wide. Wolfish, I thought, and then disregarded it. How could a girl be wolfish?

At the back of the stage, behind two rows of wooden chairs and benches and next to a collection of stacked sets was a stepladder attached to the wall. The ladder led up to a metal walkway that framed the stage from above. At the front left corner of the stage was another ladder, even narrower than the last. This led up into the ceiling. Oh dear God! I thought. Oh, please no!

Xanthe started climbing. My hands were wet and tingling. She looked back at me from the top of the first ladder. 'Say something!' I instructed myself. 'Tell her you don't like heights. She'll understand. Don't be such a scaredy-cat!' But the look on her face quickly shattered that hope. She didn't move until I started up after her.

By the time I had climbed five rungs, I thought I was going to throw up. Xanthe had reached the suspended metal walkway. It swayed as she walked.

'Where are you going?' I asked.

She looked around, expecting me to be behind her, and frowned to find me still only a few rungs above the floor.

'We're going up there.' She pointed to the ceiling midway along the hall where a row of spotlights was fixed, like the bottom row of teeth in an open mouth. 'We're going to the gods!' She laughed. 'Or are you too scared?'

I had lied to a teacher. I was supposed to be in the swimming pool, attempting an underwater backwards somersault in time to 'The Final Countdown'. Instead, I was following Xanthe up a set of ladders that were strictly off limits to all girls. This was so obviously bad it was comical. What if I got stuck and needed rescuing, or fell? Or Juffrou Kat went to the library to check up on us? Why would I risk all this on a ladder I didn't want to climb?

At the same time I knew that if I turned around now, Xanthe

would never speak to me again. 'What is your *problem*?' shouted the voice in my head. 'Move!'

Nauseous and sweating horribly, I made it onto the steel walkway. The side door opened below us. Heavy footsteps approached. I froze. The footsteps climbed the stage steps; they were almost below us. I was far too scared to cry. My hands were so wet that they slipped back and forth over the metal railings. One step, I kept thinking, one wrong step and you're dead. No – maimed. Ahead of me, Xanthe leaned far over the side railing to see who it was. She let out a long, low whistle. A few more footsteps and Buddy came into view.

'*Howzit*, my man?' Xanthe called softly.

He chuckled, shaking his head. 'It's the cat lady.' He waved his hand in farewell and disappeared.

'The cat lady?' I asked, but Xanthe was already at the top of the second ladder. The next moment she disappeared into the ceiling.

At last I crawled next to her, behind the spotlights, grubby from sweat and dust.

'Cool, huh,' she said.

I nodded, feeling dizzy. It was as though we were perched high in a tree. All I had to do was stretch out my arms and take off. I laughed.

'What?'

I shook my head. The giggles bubbled up, unstoppable.

She started laughing at me. 'Shh!' she said.

'Sorry.' I pressed my lips together to try and stop. 'Sorry,' I said again. I held my nose, and snorted like a pig, which made her laugh a generous, full-throttle laugh that transformed her face. It made it look kind.

I followed her back with barely a downwards glance. This was a Madge thing to have done. I bet Simon had never done this type of thing. He would have been too busy coming top of the class.

'My mum thought you might want to come for lunch,' I said, trying to sound off-hand. 'The boarding house must be pretty dull on a Sunday.'

'Sure,' replied Xanthe after the slightest pause. 'Why not.'

'What does your dad do?' I asked as we started down the bottom ladder. I made my voice light, as though the question had only then occurred to me, not one of a stack of things I was dying to know.

She stopped. 'I'm not really sure.'

My heart lurched. 'I'm sorry. Your parents are divorced?'

'No.'

No wonder she was so odd! 'Did he die?' I asked quietly.

She threw her head back and laughed.

I clutched the railing.

'My dad is very much alive,' she said, 'He's a businessman. He spends a lot of time in Russia. Mostly to get away from Shirley, I suspect.'

'Shirley?'

'My mum.'

'Nice name,' I said, grasping at something to say. I tried to imagine a life where my father travelled to Russia and my mother was called Shirley. Xanthe stopped to deliver a particularly withering look.

The end-of-day bell rang as we emerged from the hall. The

afternoon burst into slamming doors and shouts and running feet. At the entrance of the main building, where I would turn down towards home, and she towards the boarding house, she paused. 'You're alright, Madgie,' she said. Then she grinned.

I looked down to hide the blush that spread through my cheeks. 'You're OK too,' I said, but she had vanished into the bustle of girls without a backwards glance.

CHAPTER SEVEN

My stomach woke me early on Sunday morning. It squeezed and pinched like a coiled-up dishcloth. I stared at the purple curtains above my bed. They made me sick. Six months ago, flicking through one of Mum's *Fair Lady* magazines, I had seen the curtains that would change my life. The fabric was a pattern of spring blossom in dusty pink and yellow and green against a cream background. They were airy and sophisticated and if only I were only lying in bed looking at them, I'd have had nothing to worry about.

I groaned and turned my back on them, to face an aged and curling poster of Munch's 'The Scream'.

The night before, in a fit of nerves, I had torn down the 'Too cute to care' kittens poster that had been on my wall so long that large greasy spots marked each corner. The Garfield poster followed that and the breaching Bottlenose dolphins. All that remained was Kirk Cameron smiling down at me from the ceiling. He had to stay – he knew too many secrets to be thrown away.

Beth had appeared as I stared at the grubby, flecked walls. 'Do you want to borrow my Bon Jovi posters?' she'd asked.

It was a big offer. 'But if she likes them you have to say they are mine.' she added.

I couldn't imagine what music Xanthe listened to but I had a feeling it wasn't Bon Jovi. In the end I had settled on 'The Scream' from a box of posters in the attic. Last night it seemed edgy and cool. Today it looked ridiculous alone on the dirty white wall. What was I going to do with Xanthe all day? How would I ever manage to be cool when I didn't know what cool was?

Outisde on the stoep I cradled a mug of tea in the milky morning. Mum was bent over her sweet peas in a nearby flowerbed. She muttered as she worked – curses and promises of imminent death. Each spring she waged war against the fat green caterpillars that ravaged her flowers. In sheer persistence, they were perfectly matched.

Her head appeared, red and blotchy from bending over. Her eyes gleamed from a morning's killing. She was wearing one of Dad's blue overalls and had tried unsuccessfully to tie back her hair in what we called her Corgi scarf. She looked around and blinked a few times. 'Morning, sweetheart!'

I turned away, because if you have nothing nice to say, it's better to say nothing at all. Dad was at the bottom of the garden, brandishing the weed-eater. He cut the power when he saw me and performed a little turn to show off his khaki safari suit. 'All in honour of our lunch guest!' he shouted.

I felt like throwing up. The potential for any one of my family to embarrass me today was overwhelming.

Our family did not keep the Sabbath in the way that the Leopold townsfolk thought correct. Occasionally Mum attended Father Basil's church in the Camp, to prove a point. Dad said he took his religion him everywhere; he did not need to put it on every Sunday morning. Nonetheless we had our rituals, when Mum wasn't tearing around the countryside spreading the bad news.

One such ritual was the Sunday Lunch Braai*. When it came to braaing, Dad was a fundamentalist. A real braai was an upturned half oil drum. It was made with wood, not charcoal. The occasion demanded beer and decently marinated meat. It required family assistance but never intervention. Dad lit the fire at noon. At that point Mum's duties lay in the kitchen. Beth and I were the messengers, and the replenishers of empty beer bottles.

'Beth, tell your mum I'm ready for the meat.'

'Beth, go and check that the mielies** are on.'

'Meg, tell Vivienne we're fifteen minutes away. And another beer, princess.'

As the meat neared perfection, he'd bypass the reluctant handmaidens. 'Vivienne, are the potatoes done? Let's eat!'

At this point, Mum had to appear with salads, potatoes, bread rolls, beetroot, pickles and more beer. When all that remained was chicken-sticky fingers and a purple, green and red-stained plate, Dad would lean back in his chair, close his eyes and pass the afternoon in deep meditation.

I opened the front door to find Xanthe looking cross. She wore a white polo T-shirt and a pretty floral skirt and sandals.

* Barbecue
** Corn on the cob

71

A canvas bag was slung over her shoulder.

'So, like, firstly they forced me go to church, bunch of religious freaks, and then the matron, what's her name, the one with the enormous bum, wouldn't let me leave the boarding house without wearing this, this . . .' She yanked at her skirt in disgust as she stepped inside. As her eyes accustomed to the gloom, she stopped. 'You live in a museum!' She looked around. 'This is like of those funny little houses in Stellenbosch we visited on school outings. You know, the ones with the loo in the kitchen.'

I smiled and felt disappointed. I led her past Dad's study into the courtyard.

The rows of overhead vines that ran across the courtyard had trapped in the early morning freshness. The air smelled of old stone and thatch and damp earth. The courtyard was a refuge for Mum's delicate English plants that would never survive Leopold's summer. Pots of roses and fuchsias and lavender lined the walls. Honeysuckle covered the family room wall, jasmine competed opposite it. A water feature tucked into the far corner burbled and gurgled all day long. It was supposed to instill a sense of well-being. Outside the kitchen door Mum tended her rosemary and mint and lemon basil. As with everything she did, it was too much. Springtime in the courtyard was an assault on the senses.

Through the kitchen swing-door came the low murmur of male voices. Every now and then Mum's voice interrupted them with 'Not true!' or 'Rubbish!' and 'Oh, for pity's sake!'

Xanthe stepped forward.

'Uh – that's my mother. It's her politics programme. We're

72

better off in the garden.'

'Really?" Xanthe looked disappointed.

'Oh yes,' I said and led her through the family room and on to the stoep. The day had ripened into a busy spring blue, the breeze retreated to the shadows and crevices.

'Hello.' Beth appeared.

'Where's Dad?' I asked.

Beth pointed towards the garden without taking her eyes off Xanthe. 'He's lost the matches again. Do you want to help us find the matches?' she asked Xanthe.

'No,' I said quickly and made a swift u-turn. The only place left was my bedroom.

Xanthe flopped down on the bed and looked around. 'I saw the original of that, in the Louvre,' she said finally, jutting her chin towards the Munch poster. 'It's much smaller than you'd expect.'

With Xanthe stretched out on my bed, I opted for the floor. Since that first day at school I was wary of being too close to her.

'Kirk Cameron, hey?' she said, looking up at my ceiling.

Away from school and Juffrou and Elmarie and Esna, I couldn't think of anything to say. The day stretched ahead, huge and silent. As I thought it couldn't get any worse, Beth appeared again.

'Have you ever been overseas, Xanthe?'

'Of course,' said Xanthe, without looking at Beth. As she picked up an out-of-date copy of *Fair Lady* magazine, I mouthed 'Go away!' at Beth and pulled my finger across my neck.

'How many times?' Beth persisted.

73

Xanthe looked up from her magazine. 'Twice. To England and Italy and France, before you ask.'

'Wow!' Beth's three favourite things in the world were all from 'overseas': Princess Di, A-Ha, and anything from the Body Shop. 'We've never been,' she added.

'I have,' I said quickly.

'No, you haven't.'

'I have too, before you were born.'

'But you were a baby – that doesn't count.'

'The stamp's in my passport,' I said.

Xanthe laughed.

Somehow Beth had sidled into my room and was sitting at the bottom of my bed. I shot her a death glare, but it bounced off.

Xanthe reached into her bag and pulled out a magazine.

'*Just Seventeen*!' Beth stroked the glossy cover. 'Look at the price tag – it was bought in England! *And* it's last month's issue!'

I watched the two of them and bit the inside of my cheek. Xanthe wasn't supposed to be laughing at Beth, she was supposed to be laughing at me. Instead, Beth was making her lovely brown eyes grow bigger with excitement, laughing in her stupid half-laugh-half-snort way. Beth in a good mood was like someone switching on the light in a room at dusk.

Xanthe waited until she had Beth's full attention before she produced a small bottle of nail polish, the colour of congealed blood with a purple glint.

Beth dropped the magazine in order to examine the bottle.

'This is the sold-out new colour. My mother says in England it's the only colour anyone wants to wear,' said Xanthe.

Beth wrinkled her nose. 'It's not very pretty.'

'It's not supposed to be pretty. It's called –' Xanthe leaned forward and lowered her voice '– Vixen.'

Beth glanced at me, a moment's hesitation. She took the bottle from Xanthe, and turning it around in her hand, whispered, 'Vixen.'

My parents had pulled themselves together by lunchtime; Mum had even changed into a dress and brushed her hair. Dad cast an eye over us all, seated at the table on the stoep. He picked up the roasting pan of meat.

'Don't be shy, Xanthe. There's one hang of a lot of meat here.'

'I'm vegetarian,' she said.

'Hey?' Dad looked at her, putting the roasting dish down. 'That's not healthy, my girl. Our bodies need meat. We're hunters, after all. Ask the doctor,' he said, motioning to Mum. 'She'll tell you.'

Instead Mum passed Xanthe the salad. 'Tell us about your family,' she said.

'My father is a businessman and my mother is a busybody.'

'Busybody!' Beth snorted.

'I'm sure she has a lot on,' said Mum.

'Not really, if you discount bridge and tennis,' replied Xanthe. 'Do you work?' Xanthe couldn't have chosen a worse subject. The topic of Mum's career was avoided in our house.

'No, I don't,' Mum said in her sarcastic, *'here's-an-amusing-little-story-that's-not'* tone. 'After my fifth application to the hospital, the superintendent took pity on me and explained that not even a black man would consider it proper to be treated by a woman.' Mum laughed. 'So.'

The only way the townsfolk understood Mum was to treat her as a 'character', like Witbooi. Mum was the token English person: predictably outspoken and unfathomably odd. She didn't seem to mind it, but I did. I wanted her to be normal. I wanted to be proud of her.

I glanced at Dad. What Mum never noticed was that every time she told that story Dad looked as though she were blaming him, not the town.

'It's not all bad though,' I said brightly. 'It's freed up your time to harass the workers about your killer disease and hand out condoms at the clinic.'

Mum was ready with a reply but thought better of it.

'Such a lovely name, Xanthe,' she said as she passed Xanthe the mealies. 'Very unusual for this country. Of course, in Greek it means –'

'Golden,' said Xanthe.

'Yes.' Mum's surprise made her voice high.

'My mother chose it because of my blonde hair.' Xanthe replied nonchalantly. She leaned across the table and helped herself to the salt and pepper.

'When did it turn so dark?' I asked.

'Every two weeks, when I colour it,' replied Xanthe, now buttering the bread roll on her side plate.

'Why would you do that?' exclaimed Beth. She ached to have Barbie-blonde hair.

'To piss my mother off,' said Xanthe with a grin, looking directly at Mum.

My hand froze with my fork halfway to my mouth. Beth and

76

I exchanged glances. Mum didn't tolerate swearing. It showed 'a lack of imagination'. But Mum laughed and shook her head,

'Honestly, Xanthe, you're a dreadful child. Margaret comes from Greek too,' she continued, looking at me. Her face was softer than I'd seen for a long time. 'It means pearl.'

After lunch we moved to the lawn. Beth and I sat in our rust-rickety garden chairs; faces tilted up and awkwardly back, carefully positioned to allow our lemon-drenched hair as much sun as possible. Peach yoghurt formed a thin crust on our faces. You were supposed to use unflavoured, but nobody in our house ate plain yoghurt. Covering each eyelid was a damp teabag. We were following *Just Seventeen's* 'Beverly Hills Blitz'; we were metamorphosising into Babes. Xanthe took shelter under the pecanut tree. The sharp, chemical smell of her Vixen nail polish hovered over us, unable to soften into the honeysuckle sky. As she waited for each coat to dry, Xanthe read us articles from the magazine.

A thwack of a page. 'Listen up, Beth!' Xanthe cleared her throat: '*Jason Priestley in steamy 90210 love triangle.*'

A sigh slipped out of Beth. 'Jason Priestley is divine, don't you think, Xanthe? Don't you want to die when you see a picture of him?'

Xanthe laughed.

'Who is Jason Priestley?' Mum's voice broke our spell. I bristled. Despite the fact that I'd have seen her approach if I hadn't had teabags covering my eyes, I felt as though she'd snuck up on us.

'He's like, he's like so . . .' Beth gave up. 'You wouldn't understand, Ma.'

'Careful with that lemon juice, Meg. Too much and your hair will go green.'

Beth and I laughed.

'You think you invented hair bleaching?' she said.

A short humph and a creak of her knee as she sat down. 'There is nothing in this world more lovely than Leopold in spring,' she said. 'It teases and beguiles you with its colours and warmth. But it never lasts.'

Shut up! I shouted at her in my head. Beth was bad enough. I imagined Mum sitting on the rug next to Xanthe – surely it was too small for both of them? The teabags were making me panicky. It was as though I wasn't there.

'Which poor woodland animal's blood are you smearing over your toes, Xanthe?' she continued.

'It's called "Vixen",' I said in a strangled voice.

'It's the only colour to be wearing right now,' Beth added.

My mother laughed. 'Says who?'

Beth snorted. 'Everybody.'

'I don't know,' replied Mum. 'Walk around this town wearing that colour and you'll have the Dominee* knocking on the door.'

'This town is intolerable,' I said. Even as the words came out, I cringed at the sound of my tone. It was the teabags still covering my eyes that was intolerable, but I couldn't take them off. Not before Beth had.

Mum spoke again, in what Dad called her 'Oxbridge' voice, with her vowels round and long, as though she were reading a BBC audiotape. She put on this voice whenever she quoted 'great literature', as though the literature would cease to be

* The Dutch Reformed Church minister

impressive in a normal voice.

'"The town was a little one, worse than a village, and it was inhabited by scarcely any but old people who died with an infrequency that was really annoying."'

'Stop!' I pleaded.

'She likes to quote Shakespeare from time to time,' Beth said, addressing Xanthe. 'It's an English thing.'

'It's Chekhov,' said Xanthe. 'It's a Russian thing.'

The teabags plopped down into my lap as I sat up. Mum claimed you hadn't read literature until you'd read the Russians. It had made me determined to avoid them.

'Yes, it is,' Mum admitted with a little laugh.

'I like Chekhov,' Xanthe said. She stretched out her legs in front of her and examined her finished toes.

I sat back in the chair and looked up at the sky. It was late afternoon, the birds were beginning to chatter. I was filled with an unusual feeling – a mixture of laziness and contentment. I smiled as I realised what it was. Perhaps this was how it felt to be normal.

Only one thing ruined the day and it wasn't Xanthe's fault, I decided later, it was Beth's. She never knew when to stop. The afternoon heat had leaked away and we returned to my room. Beth hung in the doorway, midway through a story about netball trials.

'Beth,' said Xanthe.

'Ja?'

'Scram. Go play with your Barbies.'

I looked up. Xanthe had returned to the *Fair Lady* magazine.

If it weren't for the look on Beth's face, I would have been sure I had dreamt up her words, her cutting tone.

'I'm standing on my side of the doorway,' Beth replied, pointing to her feet. 'I can stay here all day if I want.'

Xanthe rolled her eyes and flicked over the page.

I looked at Beth beseechingly, but there was no hope. Beth was the baby, she was used to being adored. A horrible silence followed, in which I should have come to Beth's defence, or said something funny. But I didn't.

'If I give you this, will you go?' Xanthe reached for her bag and pulled out a Bar One.

Beth looked at me.

'Go on,' I said.

She took the chocolate bar and slammed the door.

Mum was right about the lemon juice. The strands of hair I'd so carefully smothered in lemon juice had turned snot-green.

'Look!' I wailed, running into the kitchen, where Beth and my parents were eating supper.

'The lady of the lake,' said Dad.

Mum smacked his hand. 'Luckily, I know a trick.'

She returned from the pantry cupboard with a bottle of violently red tomato sauce. 'Wash your hair with this,' she said.

'I will not!'

'Fine. Don't,' she said, sitting back down, as if it didn't matter whether I had green hair or not.

When I returned, Mum was in the study, phoning her friend Bibi in England. It was her once-a-month Sunday night call.

'You smell like a hotdog,' said Beth. She had not forgiven

me for Xanthe's behaviour. Then, with a mouth full of toast, she said, 'Dad, did Meg tell you that Xanthe was expelled?'

I froze. 'That's a big fat lie, Beth,' I said, looking from her to Dad. He raised one eyebrow.

'No it's not,' she said happily. After another bite of toast, she added: 'Not just once, either!'

'Liar!'

'Am not. Ronel's mother works in the office. She's seen her school record.'

Dad digested the news. 'Meg?'

'I'm sure it's not true,' I said.

Beth sat back in her chair, grinning.

Of course it made sense. It was the reason Xanthe had arrived mid-term, it was apparent in the way the teachers treated her. I turned to Dad: 'Even if it is, you've often said that everyone deserves a second chance.'

'Or third,' Beth butted in.

'Shut *up*!'

'Enough, both of you! You know better than to tell tales, Beth.'

I glared at Beth but she made a face and left the table. We used to be a team. Before Xanthe arrived she'd never have done that. She could only be jealous.

Before bed I stood in front of my mirror, repeating Xanthe's words and mannerisms that had seemed to charm Mum rather than infuriate her. But my cheeky grin looked like a disfigured sneer and my nonchalant face sulky. I lifted my hair up and back to see what it would look like short and chopped off. I

81

looked like an overfed baby. Suddenly I caught sight of Mum in the reflection of the mirror. My arms dropped down to my sides. Dad would have told her about Xanthe's school record. I braced myself for an inquisition.

Instead, she stepped up behind me and wrapped her arms around my waist. 'I like your friend. She has . . . character.' She kissed my hair, and rested her chin on my shoulder. I tried to lean back into her as I knew she wanted me to, but my joints felt locked. She smiled at me in the mirror and after a moment whispered, 'You're far more beautiful than Xanthe, you know.'

CHAPTER EIGHT

Sometimes I wondered what Mum had been thinking when she married Dad. She had left England, her home and friends and career to live in a small community where she would never belong. She had gambled her whole life on him. Much as I loved him, it seemed like an awfully big risk.

Mum hadn't made any farm visits since Xanthe had arrived. She had stopped standing in front of the clinic, harassing lactating mothers. She seemed more relaxed. She had even tried being funny.

A week and a half after Xanthe came to lunch, Mum arrived at the supper table holding a sheet of folded newsprint. Beth was fretting about finishing supper in time to see *Beverly Hills 90210*. The radio was set up next to the TV so that we could listen to the simulcast original English dialogue, rather than endure SABC's Afrikaans translation. Last week Shannen Doherty had found a lump in her breast. The episode before that she'd had a pregnancy scare.

'Ridiculous!' Mum would mutter, but that didn't stop her watching. I only stayed for Luke Perry.

After a few mouthfuls of spaghetti Mum put down her

fork. She glanced at Dad and then turned to me. 'Have a read about your famous mum! Bibi wrote a feature for *The Herald* about the HIV/AIDS awareness workshops I've been doing.'

'What? Why?' I asked, taking the newspaper from her.

In the depths of the Karoo region of South Africa a small Afrikaans farming community run huge tracks of land with the help of a large quasi-feudal labour system. In stark contrast to their white Afrikaner bosses, these labourers own nothing, not their house, their own futures, barely even the clothes on their backs. Education is scant, illiteracy is common. Many farms still practise the 'dop' system: they pay their labourers in alcohol.

'This is rubbish,' I said. 'We don't live in the Karoo.'
Mum rolled her eyes.

Malnutrition is high, pneumonia and tuberculosis everyday diseases. Add to this the bleak reality of the HIV/AIDS virus and the terrible result is a potentially dreadful loss of human life.

One woman is trying to make a difference, despite the enormous pressure of the white Afrikaans community. Dr Vivienne Bergman, a Cambridge graduate originally from Salisbury, has been living in the region for almost twenty years. She has taken it upon herself to roll out a series of workshops to educate and inform these abject communities about the spread and terrible consequences of HIV, much to the chagrin of the Boer community.

I looked at Dad. This was appalling. If anyone ever saw this, Mum would be ostracised forever. We would all be. The throbbing in my head made it impossible to clutch at the right words.

'I wouldn't worry too much about it, Meg. Your grandmother once told me that only black lesbians read *The Herald*,' he said.

'Well, it's nice that the black lesbians of England know that I'm trying to make a difference!' Mum laughed. 'I'm sorry you can't see the good in it, Meg. Not to say a little disappointed. The thing is,' she paused and looked at Dad, '*The Sunday Times Magazine* is going to publish the article this weekend.'

'I beg your pardon?' I said. 'You said no, right?'

Her laughter rattled around the room, searching for somewhere to settle. 'Why would I refuse? This disease is about to become a national crisis. This article could save peoples' lives.' She looked back at Dad. 'It really could.' Her voice was firm.

He was silent. His elbows dug down into the tablecloth; his left hand covered his right fist. He knocked his hands back and forth against his chin.

'You didn't even ask Dad!' I said.

Mum turned to me. 'This is not the nineteenth century. I do not have to ask your father's permission. The appropriate response is, "Well done, Mum, that's great news!"'

'Fuck that,' I muttered.

'I beg your pardon?'

'How can you put a bunch of farm workers ahead of your family? You know exactly how people are going to react here.'

'It's a piece of journalism, Meg. No one here reads *The Sunday Times*.'

'Are you insane? Everyone from here to bloody Bloemfontein will know about this before lunchtime on Sunday!'

'That's enough,' said Dad, the warning shot.

'Well done, Mum, that's great news!' I said in my sweetest voice. 'As if you don't make life difficult enough already.' I pushed back my chair and stood up.

'Sit. Down.' Mum's voice wobbled with barely controlled anger. 'Sit *down*, bloody child, and finish your supper. I am sick to death of your tantrums. As long as you're under this roof you will behave like a civilised person.'

'Or what?' I said. Through tunnels of rushing blood I heard Beth's intake of breath.

'Or I'll ground you for the rest of the year.'

'Don't be ridiculous! That's more than two months, you fat witch!' I felt like shouting. But I knew she'd do it, on principle if nothing else. I sat down noisily and stared down at my untouched plate. Knives and forks clattered through the silence. The hall clock struck a single chime. Out of the corner of my eye, I saw Beth reach across and squeeze Mum's hand. She responded with a watery smile. How dare she? She was the one causing all the trouble! I bit my tongue until the pain took my mind off the desire to burst into tears.

Dad was the first to finish. He folded his napkin next to his plate and left the room. In an amplified silence we listened to his study door shut.

Later that evening he appeared at my bedroom. He leaned wearily against the doorframe, as though it were propping him up.

'Meg, your behaviour –'

'You know what damage this article will do, Dad. The people she's writing about are your friends.'

'I know.'

'So how can you stand by and let it get printed?'

He screwed his eyes shut, and rubbed his forehead a few times. 'Your rudeness was unacceptable, Meg.'

'Come on, Dad!'

He sighed. 'Soon after your mother and I met, I travelled with her to England. She needed to complete her internship and I thought, Why not – how bad could it be?' He smiled. 'I tried living there.' He shook his head. 'In the end I realised I am not made to survive outside my natural territory – I was like a plant dug up and replanted in alien soil.

'Your grandmother found me a job in a life insurance company. I sorted files all day on the top floor of a huge, ugly building, surrounded by mountains of boxed paper. There was one window, right up at the top of the vast room, and I'd climb up a stack of boxes and spend hours looking out through the filthy glass at the green hills in the distance.' He rubbed his chin. 'By coming to live here, your mother has done something for me that I wouldn't ever have been able to do for her.'

'So you're going to feel guilty for the rest of your life?'

'One day you'll understand.' He smiled. 'Sleep tight, princess.' He blew me a kiss that did not make it across the room.

CHAPTER NINE

I paused at the stop sign and waited for Xanthe to catch up.

'It's rather hot for a mystery bike ride,' she called. She was wobbling slightly on her bicycle. I remembered too late that the saddle on that one was loose.

'This is not hot, Xanthe,' I muttered to myself.

'Do you know,' she said as she stopped next to me, 'where I come from, they've invented things called gears for bicycles.'

'My mother brought them with her from England.'

'Go figure,' Xanthe muttered.

I pushed off and turned towards Bosmansberg.

'We're leaving town?' Xanthe asked behind me.

'We're leaving town!' I shouted as I pedalled away. After the bridge I turned onto the road that led past the agricultural college.

'Are we going to meet some boys?' called Xanthe, speeding up momentarily.

'Not exactly,' I replied, struggling to contain the dread. I'd shown Xanthe the library. We'd tried the double-size flake 99 soft-serve ice creams at Ricci's café. The park, she said, resembled a parking lot gone to seed. The flower show had been 'Nice, if you're into flowers'. If I took her to the river Beth would follow us. Leopold's grave was the only place left to go.

I knew she'd rather have stayed at home. 'I like it at your house,' she said after Sunday lunch. 'Your family is so, I don't know how to describe it . . .'

'Weird,' I'd suggested.

'Obviously, but in an unusual way.'

But I couldn't be at home today. I couldn't bear to watch Xanthe charm Mum and I didn't trust Beth not to make a scene.

Long-armed sprinklers stretched across the college rugby fields, mechanical albatrosses lining up to take off. The grounds were deserted. Past the red-brick buildings, the land was neatly divided, a life-size 'let's play farm' board game. To our left were green mielie fields, and beyond those, as far as the surrounding hills would allow, citrus orchards. The fields on our right stretched down to the river. This was where the boys practised ploughing, spraying, harvesting and crop rotation and where the school's small herds of cattle and sheep grazed.

A bend in the road acted as the boundary. Bosmansberg rose up too steeply to allow any form of cultivation, and rocky scrub took over. It was also where the tar stopped. Within minutes the itch in my arms from riding over gravel was unbearable. Behind me Xanthe cursed.

On our right the river dipped away. We were surrounded by veld and sky. Leopold's grave was around the corner, a few minutes' walk from the road. It was in the middle of a clearing, on the site of an ancient San stopover point. With a little digging you could still find their sharp-edged stones and pounded-out rocks. Mum claimed it was deeply insulting to

89

the San to have Leopold buried there. It was 'blanket bullying' and 'a prime example of the rampant cultural insensitivity of the minority rule'. It was one of the few subjects on which my parents did not agree.

'Why would Leopold have asked to be buried all the way out here rather than in the church graveyard?' I'd asked the last time we'd visited it.

'Because he had a soul,' Dad had replied.

Mum snorted.

'Are you denying a man a soul because he is born Dutch and not a San huntsman?' Dad knew how to make a point.

I gripped the handlebars at the thought of Mum. Far worse than her annoyance with me was the politeness that had wedged itself between her and Dad. Each day passed more slowly than the last. The second hand of the hall clock kept time to our waiting. On it ticked towards tomorrow and the publication of the article, like the timer attached to a bomb.

A large gum tree marked the entrance to the grave. 'Here we are.' I looked back.

Xanthe's pale skin was blotchy, her glacial eyes had retreated from view. A greasy chain print patterned her ankle. She absorbed the vast expanse of nothingness with a raised eyebrow.

I slung the satchel around my shoulder and let my bicycle fall at the side of the road.

'Aren't you worried someone will take it?'

'Like who?'

'I don't know.'

'Like a baboon?' I teased.

Instead of the expected laugh, Xanthe hesitated. 'Baboons

are dangerous.'

'They can be.'

'They jump on your car and steal your food.'

For the first time I understood the look Dad often gave me. 'We're OK, then.'

'Seriously, Madge, what we're doing here?'

I started up the path, pushing aside spear-tipped grass reeds and overgrown fynbos* as we walked. I thought about mentioning the possibility of snakes, but after her reaction to baboons, decided against it. 'We're going to Leopold's grave. It's nothing special. I used to come here with Simon.' I stopped.

'Who's Simon?'

I looked up at the empty sky. 'Marta's boy.'

'Chilling out in a graveyard. That's pretty dark for you, Madge.'

'You've seen the alternatives,' I replied, ignoring the smile twitching about on Xanthe's lips.

The silence in the clearing was older than the world. The air had not let go of the recent rain. I dropped the bag under the sprawling wild olive tree and wandered towards the cave. It was shallow, as though a hand had reached in and scooped out the front section. As well as their discarded tools, the San had left behind the story of an elephant hunt on the back wall. Simon and I believed there was something magical about this cave. The sun reached a point mid-afternoon where its rays fell directly on to the smooth rockface. As it did so, the yellow-brown stone turned an orangey-red; the ochre San huntsmen golden. We had a game: if we sat very still, held our

* Natural shrubland vegetation of the Western Cape

91

breath and half-closed our eyes, we were sure we could see them move. I'd never tell Xanthe about that.

Leopold's grave was in the middle of the clearing. The raised cement casing was enclosed in a rusted iron fence. The original gravestone had been replaced a few years ago with a grand grey slab. Xanthe leaned over and read the carved words: "'Yeah though I walk through the valley of the shadow of death, I will fear no ill."' She humphed. 'But you didn't, did you?'

'Hey?'

'This Leopold guy.' She turned and jabbed her finger at the gravestone. 'You, Johannes Basson Leopold, you didn't keep walking, And now Madge has to live in the valley of death. You should be ashamed of yourself.'

My first instinct was to snap: 'Come on, Xanthe, it's not that bad,' but I caught myself and said, 'They say he's a restless soul.'

'You don't scare me, Madgie.'

She sat down next to me on a rock. I pulled out two oranges from my bag and handed one to her.

'What exactly did you two do here?' she asked, peeling her orange. She stood up, letting her peel fall to the ground, and walked into the cave. It took her a few moments to find the paintings. She ate her orange in silence, standing in front of the copper hunstmen pursuing their elephant.

I picked up her peel and put it in the backpack.

'Is this yours?'

I looked up. She walked towards me, holding a stick. Quivering on the end of it was something limp and rubbery. Bits of dirt and leaf stuck to it. I stood up to see what it was. She waved the stick, dangling the thing at me.

'Yuck!' I laughed and jumped out of her way. Then I saw the white and blue plastic wrapper on the ground. It came from Mum's bucket.

'You and your friend?' Xanthe asked.

'Xanthe!'

She held out the stick between us, a drawn sword. 'Have you kissed him?'

'Don't be weird.'

The stick hovered a moment longer, then she chucked it into the nearby bushes.

'Just kidding. Have you kissed anyone?'

I looked down. 'So this is all there is to see. A grave in a cave.'

'Aha! I knew it,' she said, and we both knew what she was referring to.

I walked back to the satchel on the rock. I needed to say something funny, but I was so humiliated that I didn't trust myself not to cry. With my back still turned, I fished out the bottle of water and took a sip.

'Madge, come on, I was teasing.' Xanthe's voice was much closer than I expected. 'Hey, listen, it's not your fault, it's this town. The real worry would be if you *had* kissed someone here!' She laughed.

I smiled into the plastic bottle and sipped again.

'But tell me, Margaret Bergman, are you really planning on saving yourself until you're married?' she asked, in Juffrou du Plessis' heavily accented English.

I choked on the water. Half of it went up my nose, which hurt so much that my eyes stung. The rest landed up on the ground.

'You have to think about these things, Madge. What if you don't get married?'

'I don't know.' I wiped my nose on the back of my arm. 'Maybe if I'm like sixty and haven't gotten married I'll have sex, to know what it's like.'

Xanthe snorted.

'Or fifty,' I said. 'You're probably too old to have sex at sixty.'

'Sex is the biggest lie.'

'What?'

'All that shit they tell you, that you have to really love someone before you "give yourself to them". It's a means of control.'

'Really?'

'Totally. Sex is basic animal mating, Madge. Sometimes it's nice, other times not. The rest is all crap.'

What did she mean 'sometimes it's nice'? I retreated to the cave and sat down on a rock. In the corner lay the charcoaled remains of a recent fire and a couple of empty beer bottles.

'Having said that,' Xanthe continued. 'It's all guys think about. It's all they want. As soon as you give in, they lose interest.'

'Well,' I said, releasing a sigh. 'Good to know.'

She sat down next to me and leaned back against the wall. The sun broke through the canopy of leaves and shone directly on to the back wall, on to our faces. I closed my eyes, to find Simon staring at me from the inside cave of my eyelids.

'Do you miss home?' I asked, blinking rapidly.

'Nope,' she said. 'Don't get me wrong, I can't believe my father sent me to this shithole and I miss going out and that, but not home.'

Silence curled around the branches of the wild olive tree. 'But what about your friends?' I said.

'Ja, I mean –' She paused. 'I've never been a big friends person. It just seems a bit . . . silly.'

'What?'

'Take my mother. Her whole life is about her tennis and bridge friends and someone said this and now they haven't been invited there. She's a grown woman, for God's sake!'

'It's all I ever wanted.'

She turned to me. 'That's exactly your problem.'

I smiled. There it was, spilled out on the dirt in front of us. My very big problem.

The sun had slipped off the back wall. I knew we should be getting home, but I couldn't yet move.

She stood up and turned to face me.

For a moment I thought she might apologise, then I realised she was bored. 'Time to go,' I mumbled.

'So where is he?' she asked when we reached the bicycles.

'Who?'

'Marta's boy. Simon.'

'Overseas. Travelling.' Due home soon, I thought, deciding not to mention that.

Once we reached the tar Xanthe speeded up and rode alongside me. 'If it makes you feel better, I will be your friend, Madge. But for the record, historically I'm not very good at it and I'm not making any promises.'

'Lucky me,' I said, biting the inside of my cheek to hide my smile.

CHAPTER TEN

The day after the article appeared – spread across a double page and impossible to miss – I arrived at school early. Juffrou du Plessis would be waiting, with all the righteous wrath of the Afrikaner nation. I'd rather she unleashed it without an audience. I was not that lucky. I had to sit in my desk and endure the stares and remarks of the rest of the class as they trickled in. While *The Sunday Times* would have done well to sell ten copies in Leopold, there was no doubt that everyone would have heard about it.

Elmarie marched up to me. 'My dad says, he says –'

'I don't care what your father says,' I cut her off. 'Leave me alone.'

Xanthe was nowhere to be seen.

Juffrou arrived, and made a point of ignoring me as she distributed a pile of excercise books. My palms were sweaty. There was a ringing in my ears. Juffrou was now at the top of our row. Elmarie and Esna turned around in anticipation. As Juffrou reached my desk, Xanthe appeared and sank down next to me, out of breath.

'Jammer*, Juffrou.' Xanthe attempted an apology in stuttering Afrikaans. But Juffrou only had eyes for me.

'The English Doctor has been busy.' Juffrou's voice slithered like a furious cobra.

Xanthe looked from Juffrou to me.

'Perhaps in England children are not taught the simple rules of community. Perhaps they do not feel pride in their town.' She tossed my book down onto my desk. 'Perhaps the English Doctor has forgotten what she owes to the people who took her in so many years ago.'

As Juffrou marched on Xanthe started laughing. 'What was that?'

I shot Xanthe a warning glare, but she wouldn't let it go. Adopting a heavy Afrikaans accent, she continued, 'The English Doctor would do well to remember that Big Sister is watching.'

Juffrou swung back around.

'For the love of God, Xanthe, shut up!' I snapped.

After school I went in search of support. Marta and Beth were in the garden.

'Did you see the article, Marta?'

'Juffrou Engelbrecht was almost in tears,' said Beth. 'She wanted to know who was this Bibi person who had written such lies about Leopold. She said Leopold would be tainted forever.'

Marta sighed. 'It was a shameful day.'

'I know. How could Mum do it?' I said.

Marta stiffened. 'It was shameful because it is all true.'

* Sorry

97

Everyone knew about the article. The Dominee went on regional radio to denounce the article as hysterical propaganda by an uninformed and dimwitted foreign journalist. But we all knew he was talking about Mum.

Our house felt battered, as if somebody had died.

'Hendrik wouldn't serve me in the post office this morning,' said Mum on Tuesday. 'Sonia du Plessis crossed the road when she saw me coming.'

'It will blow over. These things always do.' But Dad didn't look at her as he spoke.

'I don't think it will,' replied Mum. 'They've always hated me. At last they have a reason.'

'I thought you were going to change the names,' he said quietly.

'That's not journalism,' Mum replied, watching Dad. She watched him for the rest of the week. It was a side of Dad I'd never before seen. His skin seemed to hang off him, as if all his essence had been sucked out of him. This was what I'd been wanting him to do, to stand up to her. But instead of feeling triumphant, I felt worried.

Mum didn't work without Dad. I found her staring out of the window in the sitting room.

'I can't remember the name of the fabric your grandmother covered the sitting-room chairs with,' she said, looking out at Bosmansberg. 'Morris-something. I can't even picture the room anymore.'

Dad clattered into the sitting room on Friday afternoon. His footsteps kicked back the silence that had blanketed us all week. Beth and I were spread out on the sofa, watching an old copy of *The Bodyguard*. Mum was in the armchair next to us, pretending to read a science journal.

'Look who I found lolling around in town!' he said. Dad loved Fridays. It was market day in Leopold, when the farmers and their wives came to town. The wagon-wide Main Street became a slow-moving procession of 'King Cab' bakkies and 1970s Mercedes sedans. While the wives went to the bank and the post office and caught up on a week's gossip, the men congregated up the hill at the Co Op. They stood about in solid khaki clusters, swapping news, as they collected feed or a new supply of cattle dip or tractor parts. Dad could spend all day up there.

'Who did you find lolling around?' I asked, because he appeared to be alone.

Dad looked back, took a few steps towards the door then called out, 'Hannes!'

Beth and I swivelled back to Mum, in time to see the horror cross her face. All Mum's speechifying about 'fighting inbred prejudice' and all people being created equal came to nothing in the way she reacted to Hannes. Hannes was Dad's oldest friend, Dad's favourite person in the world after us. He made Mum knuckle-crunchingly uncomfortable. Not that she saw him often: sightings of Hannes beyond the boundaries of his farm were rare. Other than Christmas and Easter, his visits to town were made only under duress.

Hannes appeared, stooping as he negotiated the doorframe. With each passing year Hannes seemed to blend more with the land he farmed. His skin, like dried-out clay, told of hot, long summers; his restless eyes of the worry of coaxing another harvest out of the tired ground. He was dressed, as always, in his khaki short-sleeved shirt, shorts and veldskoen. Instead of a watch he wore two copper bracelets on his left wrist. The skin around it was stained green.

He stood next to Dad and blinked a few times in the shuttered light, fiddling with the hat in his hands.

'Hello, Hannes!' we chanted dutifully. He swallowed and nodded at us.

When he turned to Mum, he blushed deeply and muttered, 'Mevrou,' into the carpet.

'What a lovely surprise!' said Mum, her voice too loud. I looked at Beth and bit my lip. On the TV, the music stopped. There was a single drumbeat, as Whitney Houston's lower jaw dropped for her to deliver her final, heart-stopping chorus of 'And I will always love you!'

Hannes' eyes widened in alarm.

Dad stepped in to rescue his friend. 'If you'll excuse us, Hannes and I have an important business meeting on the stoep.'

As soon as they were out of hearing, Mum said in a loud whisper: 'That was odd, don't you think?'

'No,' said Beth.

'But he's so quiet,' Mum shuddered. 'So painfully quiet.'

'Some people don't need to talk,' Beth said with a shrug.

'What's he doing in town, anyway?' said Mum, getting out of her chair to peer out the window at them.

I felt smug. 'It's perfectly obvious why Hannes is here.' He was here under the direct orders of his big sister, on behalf of the Leopold community. 'He is here to ask Dad to make you stop.'

Hannes was Juffrou du Plessis' younger brother. Although they shared the same high forehead and piercing eyes, in everything else they were complete opposites. Juffrou was a tormentor of the human spirit, Hannes was Leopold's hermit. He understood the land better than any other farmer. He rattled off the names of indigenous plants as if they were members of his family. He could treat almost any ailment with one of his foul-tasting bush remedies. In an emergency, the farmers called Hannes before they called the vet.

Marta passed us with a tray intended for the important business meeting.

'Marta!' said Mum, eyeing the full bottle of brandy, alongside the two glasses and large packet of biltong.

'Special request from Mister Tim,' replied Marta, avoiding Mum's disapproving eye.

There they stayed, Dad and Hannes, sinking into their deck chairs as the last of the day disappeared behind the house. We carried on with our usual Friday evening, eating fish and chips in front of *L.A. Law*, and then a video. Every now and then a low rumble of conversation or an eruption of laughter wafted in through the open window, but for the most part Hannes and Dad didn't say much. Later I heard Hannes' heavy footsteps through the house. I imagined him in his bakkie, slowly winding his way over the pass, and into the next valley, back to his sleeping farm.

Dad didn't make it out of bed until lunchtime, and that was only to stumble into the embrace of his favourite armchair.

'More Disprin, Doctor,' he croaked. 'And Meggie, close those shutters.'

'Why is it,' said Mum, delivering the tablets and a glass of water, 'that two men finishing off a bottle of brandy is seen as celebrating a cultural heritage in these parts, whereas if two women had to do that they would be publically flogged and driven out of town?'

'Because, Wife, you don't know how to drink brandy. If I were to sit you down with a bottle of brandy, you'd have started a revolution before you'd finished half of it.'

Mum punched his arm.

'I rest my case!'

'What did Hannes have to say?' Mum asked, feigning a casual tone.

'Hmm? Oh, the usual. Farm, baboons, rain.' Dad chuckled. 'Tokkie van Jaarsveld saw a leopard up in the foothills. Twice. Haven't had a leopard around here for ages. Someone needs to tell the spotted fellow to get the hell out of that valley.' Tokkie was the largest sheep farmer in the area. He hated leopards.

'I wasn't talking about farming chitchat,' Mum said.

Dad stiffened. He turned to Mum, the silence of the past week revealing itself in a flash of anger. Or perhaps it was doubt. 'You know very well what he came to say, Vivvy.'

Mum looked as though he had slapped her. 'I only meant –'

But he held his hand up and she stopped mid-sentence. 'Go phone your friend, Meg. Tomorrow we go to the mountains.'

CHAPTER ELEVEN

The dust cloud that had been travelling with us was momentarily so thick that it was impossible to tell where we were. As it settled, we found ourselves in a world of jagged rock and red soil and scrub bush. Clumps of gnarled and sawn-off boulder rocks littered the valley floor, stacked on top of each other, or balancing against each other at precarious angles, as though God had been building castles out of dominoes. We were in the belly of the mountains.

Ahead of us a footpath cut into the landscape, snaking its way diagonally up towards the saddle of the hill. Beyond the dip of the saddle, far away enough so that it looked a deep shade of browny-blue, was sheer rock face.

'This is it?' Xanthe asked.

'No,' replied Beth from the front seat. 'First we follow that footpath for about an hour, over the hill and down into another valley that looks exactly like this one, only flatter and hotter. *That* is it.'

Xanthe looked sideways at me. The dirt track up to the fossil farm had been worse than normal. Dad drove our old station wagon over the dongas* and potholes as though it were a rally car, which meant we spent a fair amount of the trip airborne.

Beth was not happy. Instead of hers and Dad's usual rendition of 'Ninety-nine bottles of beer on the wall', she had been silent the whole way here. Her sulk had started as Xanthe had emerged from the boarding house, wearing a pair of cut-off denim shorts and a T-shirt with a picture of a seemingly naked boy that said 'Manic Street Preachers'. Tattoed onto the arm of the boy were the words 'Generation Terrorists'.

'What's Manic Street Preachers?' Beth had asked.

'A band, obviously,' I'd replied, although I had no idea.

'Is it Christian?' Beth continued, which was fair enough as there was a large crucifix hanging around the neck of the boy.

'Not exactly,' replied Xanthe.

'Christian!' I'd laughed loudly and then felt stupid at the silence that followed. I hadn't fooled either Beth or Xanthe.

Dad opened Beth's door.

''What's that smell?' Xanthe asked.

'Dust,' replied Beth. 'And heat and boredom.' She turned to Dad. 'I'm staying here.'

Dad shook his head. 'Not a good idea, Bethie. We'll be gone hours.'

'I don't care. You can't make me.'

'True,' Dad agreed. 'I'm worried, that's all. The other day Koosie up at the Co Op told me he'd got the fright of his life. He was checking on a broken water pump in one of his boundary camps. As he climbed back into his bakkie, his leg like so,' Dad demonstrated, his leg hovering above the ground, 'a *tenth* of

* Gullies

104

a second away from putting his foot down, he stopped. And looked down.' Dad looked at each of us in turn. 'Under the accelerator was a cobra, thick as his arm, tightly coiled up.'

We three stared at him in mute horror.

'He reckons the bliksem* must have gotten itself curled around his front wheel, then managed to get up, through the carburettor and into the front cab.' He shook his head. 'Man, I hate snakes!'

Beth was out the car. Dad looked back at me and winked.

Xanthe fell into step behind him. Her long, skinny legs kept pace with Dad's wide stride. They made me think of Simon. Not only would Simon listen as Dad pointed out a rock formation that was in no way similar to other hundreds we'd seen that day, but he'd remember from the previous trip the names and shapes of Dad's beloved fossils. I tried to picture Simon in Europe. I tried to picture Europe. Did you feel a different person after looking at an ancient castle or travelling the tube?

Beth followed Xanthe at an infuriatingly slow pace. I brought up the rear, carrying the rucksack of sandwiches and juice. We had grown up walking these mountains on Dad's 'fun days out'. Each time we started up the path it felt like we were turning our backs on the rest of the world.

A distance opened up between Dad and Xanthe, and Beth and me. 'For God's sake, Beth, hurry up!' I ached to push past her, and stop Dad saying anything too weird. But Beth would have a fit if she were left at the back.

We caught up with them at the crest of the hill. The next valley was flat and shallow. Rocky outcrops dotted the floor,

* Scoundrel

home to dassies, wild cats and snakes. And fossils.

We passed the shell of an abandoned bakkie rotted slowly into the ground. There was a farmhouse in the furthest corner of the valley. It was more of a hovel, its walls crumbling and the thatch barely covering the roof in places. A sister and brother lived there, Hetta and Fillipus Jantjies, with their rheumatic, mangy dogs and their milky eyes. 'They're like hobbits!' Mum had breathed on one of her rare trips here. At least they wouldn't have read the article.

'Is this sea sand?' Xanthe bent down and picked up a handful of white sand. She looked up at Dad.

'Uh-huh,' replied Dad. 'You're standing on a very ancient seabed.'

Xanthe looked around at the rock-littered valley floor and surrounding mountains. 'No kidding,' she said.

'The shape of the mountains – you see the way it looks gouged out – that was caused by a glacier that pushed through these parts 420 million years ago,' Dad said.

'Wow,' said Xanthe, her head cocked to the side.

'When it melted, it deposited the millions of tonnes of rocks it had collected up north right here, and its water formed meltwater lakes. These icy lakes were home to some extraordinary organisms, many of which survive today as fossils.'

Xanthe stayed close to Dad as we descended into the valley, listening as he revealed the sacred mysteries of rocks. I used to think Simon feigned interest to show me up, but what was Xanthe doing?

I was bored, hot, and put out.

Beth flopped down on a rock in front of me and took a slug from the water bottle. 'Found one,' she called with a yawn.

Dad double-backed. 'That's a goodie,' he said, getting out his notebook. 'You've got a talent for this, Beth. Going to take after your old dad, huh?'

Beth snorted.

'What is that?' asked Xanthe, peering over Beth's find.

'A Spirophyton, most likely,' Dad replied. 'See the beautiful conical swirls. It was a small invertebrate animal that would have lived on the sea floor. That's why it's embedded in the rock.'

'How old do you think it is?' asked Xanthe.

Dad rubbed his chin. 'Anything up to 200 million years.' He took the stone from Beth and rubbed his finger over it. 'Each of these rock fragments is a story that is eons old. Each story is slightly different and it's all here. You simply have to know how to read it.'

Dad was such a nerd. A part of me longed to be as passionate about something, or someone, but nothing seemed interesting enough.

Xanthe took the fossil from him. 'That's amazing,' she said softly, running her fingers over the ridges and grooves the ancient sea slug made against the rock face.

Beth caught my eye and shook her head. 'Remember that one Simon found? That one *was* amazing.'

Xanthe raised an eyebrow as she turned the rock over.

'I'll tell you what,' Dad said. 'Fifty years ago you could find the most extraordinary things up here. This was the real Jurassic Park, not some Hollywood studio. Then holiday makers got

107

to hearing about them, and things started disappearing.' He shook his head. 'Now it's rare to find loose rock with fossil traces on them. It makes me mad.'

As we ate our lunch of cold sausages, cheese and soggy tomato sandwiches and tepid squash, Xanthe jumped up. She was holding a fragment of rock, small enough to fit into the palm of her hand. 'I found one! It was lying next to me, like it *wanted* me to find it!' She looked up at Dad, with shining eyes.

Dad leaned over to have a look. 'Not bad for a beginner! That's a lovely little crinoid shape.'

Xanthe held on to her treasure, turning it over and over in her hands. 'I found one, Madge! A crinoid one!'

I smiled at her, but didn't trust myself with words, on the off chance that I said: 'It's a frigging rock, Xanthe! Get some perspective.'

'My dad would laugh at me now, all hot and sweaty and fishing around in the dirt for fragments of rock,' said Xanthe later on.

I looked up. She never talked about her dad.

'His favourite saying is "He who dies with the most toys, wins",' she continued.

Dad laughed.

'What do you think, Tim?' Xanthe turned to him. It occurred to me that with Xanthe there had never been the 'Mr Bergman' stage. In Leopold anyone older than you was either 'oom'* or 'tannie' – even if you yourself were an adult.

Dad looked away, towards the hovering mountaintops. 'I don't know, but then I don't have that many toys. I think

* Uncle or adult man

we are all magnificently important and entirely insignificant. Each of us has our place and time, nothing we do can help us extend that. The San and the Khoi people who painted the rocks around here, who left behind their stories for us, they knew that. Their time may have passed, but their significance remains.'

In the thick afternoon sun a jackal buzzard screamed above us. Dad stretched. 'Enough mumbo-jumbo from me. Another half hour in purgatory, Beth, then we're off.' He turned in the direction of a clump of rocks nearby.

Xanthe watched him walk away. 'Your dad is cool, Madgie.'

As we bumped our way back along the track, tired and sun baked and dirty, I felt as irritable as though sand had been caught between the layers of my skin. Xanthe was supposed to think I was cool – not *Dad*! Each time I felt close to understanding Xanthe's world she changed the rules and left me as clueless as the day she arrived.

CHAPTER TWELVE

Xanthe was gone, back home for the ten-day September holidays, leaving me in the valley of death. Though I'd have not thought it possible, it was worse than before.

Dad had gone too, into his study, to his other life of paleontological hypotheses and publishing deadlines, his door firmly closed.

Marta had gone, to visit her sister and pick up Simon in Cape Town. Without Marta the house was slowly falling apart. The ironing grew into piles that Mum would stand and look at, and then leave. The kitchen stood empty and quiet. Without the smell of banana bread wafting through the house; without the sound of pots banging and the rhythmic drone of the gospel radio station; without a curry on the stove, it did not seem like our kitchen.

That left Mum and Beth and me. I wandered around the house, picking things up and putting them down again. I sat on the top step of the stoep, looking out over the garden until my bum ached so much on the hard stone that I couldn't bear it anymore. I was once again waiting, waiting away my life. In the empty days my mind kept pouncing on Simon's return. I had to talk myself away from the same panic I felt each time he was due back from school. But this time was different – I had Xanthe. I'd barely notice he was around.

Midway through the week I found Mum in the courtyard, kneeling over her pots of bulbs. For want of anything else to do, I sat down and watched her digging them up, shaking the soil off gently and then laying them down in a growing pile. She spent a ridiculous amount of time on them, when all they did was flower for a few weeks, then she'd pack them away again. She told us stories of the spring bulbs pushing through the hard winter earth in England, first snowdrops and then daffodils and bluebells, how they meant an end to the interminable cold. That world was as unreal to me as the Christmas cards of cheerful robins and snow-dusted windowpanes. Our wild flowers made a mockery of pots and flowerbeds. They burst through pavement cracks in rioting reds and oranges, squeezed out between walls and fence posts and rock face in violets and yellows and blues. They transformed whole valleys into a runaway blaze of colour. Mum's daffodils and irises seemed contrived in comparison, the opposite of what spring was about.

'Well that's it for this year,' Mum said without looking up. I was surprised; I didn't think she'd noticed me.

'What?'

'Spring. Do you know that you get more suicides in spring then any other time of year?'

'Why wait till spring?'

'Exactly.' She sat back and looked at me. 'Pass me that bag, won't you.' She pointed at a Checkers plastic packet lying a few feet in front of me.

111

I leaned over and chucked it in her direction but it landed in the space between us.

She gave me a withering look.

Making a big show of it, I got up and dropped it next to her, then sat down in a deck chair nearby. 'I feel pretty suicidal at the thought of many more springs in Leopold.'

Mum laughed. 'The worst of it is, you're going to look back on this as the best time of your life.'

'Kill me now.'

Beth appeared wearing one of Mum's oldest dresses – a floor-length 1970s evening gown. The hideous pattern was made up of large swirls of blue and green and mauve paisley.

'Oh, that dress!' Mum laughed, clapping her hands.

Beth had pinned her hair in a single braid around her head, Heidi-style. She stretched out her arms to show off the enormous blue chiffon bat wings and did a twirl.

'Going anywhere special?' asked Mum.

'Might be,' replied Beth as she sat down at the edge of a lounger chair. 'You never know.'

I snorted.

'What?' said Beth. 'You don't know what's going to happen ten minutes from now.'

'I have a pretty good guess.'

'You're wrong.'

'Beth, you look gorgeous. Far better than I looked in it,' Mum cut in.

Mum was right, Beth looked like a seventies pin-up. It made me even crosser.

'My mother gave that dress to me,' said Mum. As always the

words 'my mother' came out an octave lower, with a little shake of her head. 'She had it made for my first grown-up dinner party. God, what an awful night.' Mum sucked in her breath at the memory. 'She spent the evening steering me around the room, introducing me to all the suitable young men, saying: "Have you met my daughter Vivienne?" and then she would smile at them, but it was scary, she'd sort of bare her teeth.'

'Like this?' Beth mimicked the way Mum smiled at Hannes. Dad called it the 'Salisbury Rictus', after the day Mum presented him to my English grandmother.

'Yes!' laughed Mum. 'How did you know? It wasn't all bad though. That was the night I met Lawrence.'

'Lawrence! Of like Arabia?' said Beth, wrinkling up her nose with distaste. 'Who'd call their son Lawrence?'

'Oh, that was a long time before Dad,' said Mum. She flicked her hair. Unlike Dad's stories that grew more improbable and funnier with each telling, Mum's 'growing up' stories, about places and friends and family we'd never met, always felt like a betrayal.

'But look!' Mum stood up, soil raining from her lap. She walked over to Beth and picked up a sleeve. 'Moths!' The length of the sleeve was pockmarked with holes.

Mum was quiet for a long time, staring at the sleeve in her hand. Beth looked at me. I shrugged. Eventually Mum sighed, the weight of which pulled her whole chest downwards. 'It's just a dress,' she said softly to herself, and looking up at Beth and me repeated: 'It's just a dress.'

She let go of the sleeve and sat back into the chair next to me, all the time studying Beth.

'Do you want me to take it off?' asked Beth.

Mum smiled. 'No, no! It's lovely to see it again. I don't know why I keep it buried at the back of my wardrobe. I should wear it more often.'

'Oh dear God,' I said.

From behind the closed study door came the low rumble of Dad clearing his throat. Things weren't yet back to normal between my parents. Dad's continuing quiet made Mum skittish. She found reasons to avoid the shops, but Dad had been right about the talk. After two weeks there was nothing more to be said.

Outside a lorry clattered by on the cement road – *ka-donk*, *ka-donk*, *ka-donk*.

'My girls,' Mum smiled, looking at us. 'It's moments like these that a mother will never forget. Moments of quiet.' She said it with the tiniest of glances in my direction. She leaned back into the chair and closed her eyes.

Beth jumped up and, cupping her hands together at her chest, like Mimi Coertse, started singing 'Somewhere over the rainbow', in a falsetto. Mum laughed, still with her eyes closed and said, 'Let's have tea and cake out here.'

Beth broke off her song. 'There's no cake, Ma. There's nothing left to eat.'

Mum opened her eyes and sat up. 'There's always something to eat.' A few minutes later she returned with tea and a box of After Eight dinner mints.

Holding a mug of tea in her hand and with half a mint wafer in her mouth, Mum turned to me: 'Have you heard from Xanthe?'

'No.'

'Why don't you give her a call? Do you have her number?'

'No.'

'Was she going away?'

'I don't know!'

'She'll be with her Cape Town friends,' said Beth, licking chocolate off her fingers.

'Don't be cruel, Beth,' said Mum.

'Why is that cruel?' I snapped. 'I don't care.'

'She'll be back soon,' said Mum. Then, after a moment, in her careful voice, she said, 'She's very lucky to have you as a friend. She gets an awful lot out of this friendship.'

'What are you talking about?' I felt like a sea anenome when it's poked.

Mum pulled her mouth tight, then speaking slowly and delicately, said, 'I'm not sure that she gives as much as she takes.'

'Why do you always have to make everything so heavy?'

'And she's a troublemaker,' said Beth, pulling at the hem of the dress.

'Shut up!' I shouted at Beth.

'OK,' said Mum, holding up her hands. 'Enough.'

Having to listen to them was like having holes drilled through your eye sockets. I wanted to leave Beth in her ridiculous dress and Mum with her soil-encrusted knees, but I couldn't stand my room any longer, or the sitting room or the garden.

'Angel came by this morning,' said Mum. She smoothed out the green foil chocolate wrapper on the wooden arm of the chair.

'Angel?'

'Yup. Looking for Marta.'

'But –'

'I know. Her baby, her child, I mean, is sick. She needed money for the clinic.'

'What did you do?'

'I gave her some money and told her to come back next week.' Mum folded the foil in half and half again. 'But she won't.'

'Did you give her some condoms too and a pamphlet on sexual health?'

Mum looked up. 'Not so funny. She looked terrible, too thin.'

Of course she would be sick! In Mum's world Angel could never be healthy and happy and having a good life.

'Are you going to tell Marta?'

'I don't know. She's very caught up in Simon's return and what he'll do next.'

'It's not fair the way Marta's written Angel off,' I said.

Mum raised her eyebrows. 'The funny thing is that I always thought Angel sharper than Simon. Simon's quick and determined, but Angel – that little girl was something else.'

'Why would Marta do that then? It's not very Christian.'

'Perhaps she couldn't bear to watch her daughter end up with exactly the same life as her.'

'So if I do something you don't like, will you cut me off?'

Mum looked at me. 'What do you think? I'll make your life a misery, but I'll never let you go. That's what love is about,' she added quietly, looking down at her fingers. 'At some point we're all going to do something that hurts the people who love us. The more they love us, the more it hurts. It's a fact of life.

But love is bigger than actions.'

I knew she was talking about her own mother, far away in a town called Salisbury where it always rained, but even so I felt anger combust in every cell of my body. I dumped my mug on the stone and stood up. 'That's typical of you!' I said. 'That's exactly why we don't have any friends in this town, why people see us coming and cross the road. When you love someone, you don't do things that hurt them. You don't!'

I marched away. Safely on the other side of the kitchen swing door, my anger evaporated. I looked back out through the mesh. Mum was sitting perfectly still in the chair, looking down at the tiny square of green foil in her hands.

I sighed. 'It's not fair,' I said to the empty kitchen, to the space where Marta should have been.

CHAPTER THIRTEEN

Marta arrived the next morning as we were eating breakfast.

'Marta!' said Mum. Her cheeks filled with colour that had been missing since the article appeared.

'Good holiday, Marta?' asked Dad, looking up from his newspaper.

'Thank you, Mister Tim,' replied Marta. She was carrying a yellow plastic bag with the words 'Duty Free' in large red writing.

'Sister well?' continued Dad, returning to his article.

'As well as can be.' Marta did not think much of her sister's family-in-law. They were Seventh Day Adventists.

'It's been a long week, Marta,' he said, patting Mum's hand. 'Do I look thinner? I feel thinner.'

Marta tutted with pleasure.

'What's in the bag?' asked Beth. 'Did Simon bring you tonnes of presents?'

Marta looked down at the bag. 'Stuff and nonsense and Venetian glass.' She shook her head. 'Now what must I do with it? Imagine if Sister Bertha heard I had Venetian glass in my front room!'

Mum smiled. 'How is Simon?'

'He will be down to greet this afternoon.'

'Plenty of time for that,' said Dad. 'He probably needs to rest up.'

Marta sniffed. 'What has he been doing but resting this whole year? The child needs to make himself useful.'

'Send him to me,' said Dad, scanning the sports section, 'I'm in dire need of somebody useful.'

Simon sat on the wall of the stoep in the late afternoon sun, leaning back on his right arm. I froze, and then stepped back into the family room, into the dark shadow cast by the open door.

He twitched, a sensory movement, an intuition. His eyes flickered towards the doorway. I held my breath, but after a second he turned away.

'There is so much hot air circulating around this country at the moment,' came Dad's voice, 'I'm surprised we haven't taken off in the breeze.'

I examined this person who had replaced the grasshopper boy I knew, whom only nine months previously had sat on the same spot, mumbling and fidgety the day before he left for overseas. He wore long beige 'Out of Africa' shorts. Slipslops dangled from his toes. His brown ochre skin had paled away from the African sun. It would be a different colour on the chart now. Muscles moulded his arms where they protruded from his white T-shirt. I didn't remember muscles.

As he took a sip of beer from the Amstel bottle next to him, I noticed a collection of leather bracelets on his wrist.

119

And his hand, holding the green bottle, once too big, seemed to fit him perfectly.

'It's politics, Tim,' replied Mum. 'It's what happens in a general election.'

'Thank goodness for my wife, Simon, or how else would we navigate the modern world?'

I shook my head at my parents. They had entered into a careful truce, most likely for the benefit of Marta and Simon, but at least they were talking.

Simon smiled. His hair was cut very short. His face had changed shape, like silly putty drawn out wider and longer. He put down his beer and scratched his chin. It was stubbly now.

'Vivienne,' continued Dad, 'I'm perfectly aware of what happens in a general election, all I'm saying is that it's nonsense. No one is going to deliver on those election promises, not even Mr Mandela. They are turning a vision of the future into an election campaign.'

'Everything starts as a dream, Timothy,' replied Mum.

'People wouldn't vote for anything less,' said Simon.

His voice was still soft, but it had lost its apologetic tone. Any trace of Leopold had disappeared somewhere between his white English-speaking school and the rest of the world. It was a nomad's accent.

'We are impatient, we have waited too long,' he added.

We! I wanted to laugh. You can't do that, Simon, you can't spend five years benefitting from a white education and travel around Europe on a white-sponsored scholarship and call yourself a comrade. As I turned, he stopped talking and looked directly at me. I swallowed, my face burning. He'd known I

120

was there all along.

With no choice, I marched outside.

Mum looked up. 'Meg! Look who's here!'

'Do you want a little wine Meggie?' asked Dad, getting up to fetch a glass.

'Maybe not,' said Mum, 'it's a school night.'

'She's not going to drink the whole bottle,' laughed Dad and turned to me, 'are you?'

'I don't want any wine,' I snapped. My parents only offered us wine on special occasions. This was not a special occasion.

'Have you said hello to Simon?' said Mum

I closed my eyes and bit back the desire to scream. After a laboured breath, I opened them again and with a flicker of a glance at him, said, 'You're back.'

He smiled, leaned his head to one side. 'You've got so big!'

Oh my dear God. Was that all he could think of to say?

'You can't tell a girl she's "big", Simon!' said Mum in her most severe tone. 'A comment like that will have her eating nothing but lettuce leaves!'

'No it won't,' I said, pulling a face.

Mum laughed.

'You're gorgeous, Meg,' said Dad. 'You'll always be my princess,' he continued, laughing at his own joke, 'no matter how big you get.'

I couldn't stand it any longer. 'I'll see you at supper,' I said and fled.

Back in my room, I closed the door and leaned heavily against it. My breath came in gasps. My heart was pushing up at my shoulder blades and my stomach had plummeted, punching down on my sitting bones. Left behind in that space was both a deep hollowness and an intense pressure. Perhaps it was the beginnings of a heart attack, or some kind of seizure. I threw myself onto my bed but caught the wall with the back of my head, which sent a pain as sharp as a knife-edge into my skull, 'Aargh!' I shouted.

Beth burst through the door. 'Simon's here!'

I looked away, rubbing my head and blinking away the tears.

'Why are you crying?'

'I'm not! I hit my head against the wall.'

'Only mental people hit their heads against the wall.'

I rolled my eyes and continued rubbing my head.

But Beth wanted a rise. 'I'm going to tell Simon you've gone mental, and you're sitting in your room banging your head against the wall and crying.'

'OK, I'm mental. Go away, Beth, I beg you.'

Beth hesitated. 'Only if I get to sit next to Simon at supper.'

'Sure,' I muttered, 'No prob-le-mo.'

On the way to the dining room I found Marta in the kitchen.

'Why are you still here?' I asked. Marta was usually home by late afternoon.

'Have you washed your hands?' she asked in reply, a question she'd not asked me in ten years. I stared at her, wondering if perhaps everyone was going mental. Then I remembered – her boy, back from the moon, was sitting outside drinking a beer with my parents. I wasn't the only one feeling uncomfortable that night.

'Take this.' Marta placed the breadboard with a loaf and the butter into my hands.

'Marta's still here,' I said accusatorily at Mum as I sat down. Simon sat opposite me, next to Beth. Back in his old place.

Mum, half rising, called: 'Marta?'

'On my way, Miss Viv,' Marta appeared in the doorway in her street clothes, clutching her 'Duty Free' shopping bag.

The next second got stuck on itself, and the perspective in the room blurred so that Marta, standing in the doorway seemed shrunken, much smaller than normal, whereas Simon, looking across the room at his mother from his seat at the table, appeared much too tall. He looked like a man; as though he didn't belong to her. But the moment passed, and time speeded up again to make up for its glitch and Mum said, 'Why don't you join us for supper, Marta?' and for a moment Marta hesitated, then turned to Mum.

'Thank you, Miss Viv, but I am expected at the prayer meeting.'

'If you're sure,' said Mum.

Simon remembered himself, and jumped up, saying: 'Let me walk you home, Ma,' and reached out to take her bag.

'Gracious child, don't be silly!' Marta smacked Simon's hand away, although now she had to look up to scold her son. She turned, and raised her hand to the rest of us in greeting. As she disappeared back into the kitchen, she seemed to favour her right hip in a way she hadn't done before.

I watched Mum watching Marta. A shadow of guilt passed across her face.

Dad dished out mutton curry and rice. The table seemed shrunken tonight, making elbows and hands too close together. Under the table I could sense Simon's leg jigging up and down

123

though his face and upper body remained perfectly still.

'There's no air in this room,' I said, and got up to open the window. The evening outside was a riot of noise – the crickets and cicadas and birds were going wild in response to an electric static in the air. 'Storm's coming,' I said.

'What's that?' called Dad.

'Nothing,' I muttered and returned to my seat.

Mum demanded a blow-by-blow account of Simon's travels. Simon looked at both her and Dad as he spoke, but he was wasting his time – Dad hated Europe. I faced my plate of curry. I was determined to eat everything, despite being so big, but the tender meat scraped and cut into the back of my throat. I was sickened by the way Simon talked as casually about Covent Garden and the Houses of Parliament as I might a visit to the Co Op. And the grimy backpackers he stayed at in Earls Court – could it be the same one that Mum's old Australian boyfriend had stayed in twenty zillion years ago, the one with the green front door? Yes? Hilarious! Simon began to talk about the Eurostar, which was recently finished, and how odd it would be to know you were actually travelling under the sea.

Beth, who had maintained a dignified silence until that point, dropped her fork and squealed, 'Under the sea?'

'Imagine!' said Mum.

Simon glanced at me, but I was ready with a look that said, 'I'm fifteen years old, Simon. I don't care about a shitty little tunnel under the sea.' At least I hope it did.

'But that's insane!' Beth said, and spurred on by the laughter, continued, 'It's mental!' and flashed a look at me.

They moved on to Rome and the Vatican City and the

124

plundered treasures of the ancient world, before landing in Paris. Mum had a thing about Paris. She claimed that after Leopold, Paris was her next choice for a home.

Simon took a sip of beer and smiled. 'I had a moment, as I stared up at the Eiffel Tower. I had woken up that day with the thought, "Today I will see one of the most famous landmarks in the world!" and there it was, exactly the same as in the pictures and the movies,' he laughed, 'maybe a bit smaller.'

I looked up – that was the first interesting thing he had said.

'And I thought, why am I spending six months of my life travelling around a few countries, visiting places that I have been taught about, only to say "I've seen it!" Wouldn't it be better to spend six months exploring somewhere you knew nothing about? Wouldn't you learn so much more?'

Dad grunted.

But Mum wouldn't hear of it: 'You have to see Paris! You have to feel the *age* of Europe. You don't find that here.'

'Vivienne!' said Dad.

'I know this is the cradle of mankind and all that,' said Mum, 'but Europe is a different kind of old. Pass me some more wine,' she added, a sign she was losing confidence in her own argument.

As Dad passed the wine along the table, she said, 'You stayed in the Latin Quarter. How did you find your way there?'

'I had a good . . . guide,' Simon answered with a little laugh.

A clap of laughter from Dad and Mum exclaimed, 'Simon, you devil!'

'What?' demanded Beth.

'Never mind,' said Mum. But Dad leaned over and whispered

125

into her ear.

'Ooh la la!' shouted Beth and and made kissing noises.

'Simon, are you blushing?' asked Mum, in her maddening voice.

'Us coloureds don't blush, you know that!' he smiled.

My fork clattered to the floor. I bent to collect it, cursing my clumsy self. Simon had seemed to pick a new girlfriend each time he came home for the holidays. They'd hang about town looking bored. It annoyed me as I felt stupid walking past them. 'Why don't you take your girlfriend swimming?' I'd asked him one day.

'She can't.'

'So teach her.'

'Nah,' he replied, bored by the thought, bored by me.

'You must have done the Louvre?' Mum and Simon were now speaking a language that excluded everyone else at the table.

Simon nodded and smiled. 'All those pictures of white people in ancient clothes, like one big fancy dress. A big fancy dress party that not one single black person was invited to.'

'Obviously, ' I said, without thinking. 'It's Europe. What did you expect?'

Simon wiped his mouth with his napkin and looked at me. 'I suppose what I didn't expect was how insignificant, how expendable Africa was to the rest of the world.'

'Were there paintings of . . . *Chinese* people in the gallery?' I asked.

'Ja,' replied Simon.

'Yes, of course,' said Mum with a glance in my direction,

'All that wonderful Chinese art.'

How was I supposed to know that?

Dad looked at Simon. 'Africa wasn't expendable. It was propping up a wealthy Europe with crops and exotic exports and –'

'Slaves,' said Simon.

There was a pause in the conversation as Simon ate his food. The sharp definition of the muscles on his upper arm made me think that a cross-section of his body would be a perfect example to study in biology.

'It was an incredible nine months,' he said at last. 'The culture, hearing French being spoken by French people, seeing Italians riding scooters, ancient ruins in Rome, tasting proper coffee . . .'

'And ze French girls,' said Beth in a throaty voice.

'If you were having such a good time, why did you come home?' I said. In the silence I was aware of my parents looking at me. Inwardly I groaned as my petulant words bounced off the walls. It had felt like a perfectly reasonable question in my head. I felt Simon's eyes on me, willing me to look at him, but I would not give him that satisfaction.

'It was time,' said Simon, in a voice that seemed to be saying something else. He turned to Mum. 'Thank you for supper.'

'Thank you, but your mother makes the best mutton curry, she always has,' replied Mum, which called to mind Marta, making her slow walk up the hill towards the strobe-lit community hall and the blue linoleum floor and the hard plastic chairs and the feathery prayer book pages.

Dad cleared his throat. 'What are your plans now, my boy?'

'I'm waiting on those bursary responses,' said Simon.

'Have you decided on a university?' asked Mum.

'Wits,' he replied.

This was good news. Wits was as far away as he could go in South Africa.

'So we'll lose you again!' exclaimed Mum, but there was approval in her voice.

I'd had enough of this. At any moment Mum would start on about how a little bit of hard work afforded you such wonderful choice. 'I have homework to do,' I said.

'Actually, you've got the washing-up to do,' said Mum, gathering plates.

'I'll do it,' Simon said, standing up. He squeezed Beth's shoulder. 'You'll help me, Bethie, won't you?'

Beth and Simon disappeared into the kitchen, Beth jumping around him like a puppy. My parents followed them, leaving me alone.

I looked around the empty table. The favoured child had returned home, his initiation complete, bearing scars and stories from far-off lands. But Leopold was no place for a hero. Warriors on return get restless; with nothing to conquer, grow mischievous. Simon wouldn't last in Leopold; he couldn't stay. He had left behind his ability to return in some pavement café; he'd dropped it into a Roman ruin. With any luck he'd be gone again before Christmas.

CHAPTER FOURTEEN

I pulled at my T-shirt. Simon's return had brought the heat. He'd snatched away the last weeks of spring that were rightfully ours.

Xanthe was waiting for me outside the old gaol. Her skinny body seemed elongated against the flat-roofed, whitewashed building. She looked glum. Her eyebrows were scrunched together, her hands thrust deep into her pockets. As I reached her, she turned and started down Park Road. I knew this mood. The quickest way to get her out of it was to ignore her.

Park Road was my favourite in Leopold. It was the only part of town where you could be somewhere else. Bougainvilleas and jacarandas grew in abundance. Helicopter trees lined the road. It was four o'clock in the afternoon, and Bosmansberg's shadow was beginning to creep over the river, up the gardens towards the road. A trickle of gardeners and maids passed us walking in the opposite direction, making their way home. Apart from them, the road was deserted.

'My dad's on my case, Madge,' said Xanthe.

We passed a small brown-roofed house. The chicken-wire gate was open, a 'Beware of the dog sign' dangled off a nail. Dead leaves covered the path, the grass on either side was knee-high. Two of the front windowpanes were smashed through. The Portuguese family used to live there. The parents had run the local café for a while, but had moved to the coast two years ago. Beth and I used to stop and chat when we rode our BMX bicycles up and down the road. It was a long, flat road – a good road for bikes.

'I'm worried about the exams,' Xanthe said, looking at me sideways.

'Which one?'

'All of them. But science is the biggest problem.' She shook her head. 'My dad has this bizarre notion that I'm a sciences person, like him.'

I laughed.

'It's not funny. I have to get sixty-eight per cent in the exams to pass science this year. Sixty-eight per cent! Not a fucking hope.'

'You've got time,' I said.

'No, I haven't. There's too much to learn.'

For the first time Xanthe's careful nonchalance wobbled. She turned away.

'What would happen if you failed?' I said, my mind running ahead. She'd probably leave Leopold. If that happened I wouldn't be Madge anymore. I'd return to being Meg, the English girl with the empty desk beside her who spent all her time trying to be invisible. I shivered and looked up for the cloud blocking the sun, but the sky was a mocking blue.

'Failing's not an option,' replied Xanthe in a flat voice.

I felt helpless. I couldn't make her study, I couldn't write the exams for her.

'And to think the exam paper has already been set, and is sitting somewhere in the school, waiting.' Xanthe kicked a stone out of the road.

'In the printing room,' I said.

'What?'

'The door behind the big photocopier is a walk-in cupboard. All the exam papers are stored in there.'

'How do you know?'

I shrugged. 'Juffrou sent me there once. It's locked, of course.'

'Of course,' said Xanthe.

We walked on in silence. A curling poster tacked to the lamppost ahead advertised a Dinner Dance at the rugby club. It promised a swinging night with 'Little Jack and the Boom-Boom Band'.

Xanthe sighed. 'The last thing my dad said to me was, "I don't care how you do it, but don't come home without a decent set of results."' She swung around. 'They're not like your parents, Madge. They don't care whether or not I learn anything. It's all about appearances.'

If only Mum cared even a small amount about appearances our lives would be much happier. Xanthe was looking for sympathy but all I felt was envy.

We were in sight of the showgrounds. She quickened her pace. 'Come on, Madgie, they're waiting for us.'

I resorted to a triple to keep up. 'Who is they?'

'Miggie and them.'

I stopped. I had avoided thinking about this afternoon. When Xanthe told me of her plans, I'd simply blanked out the word 'dope'. It was a little word and easy to ignore. But now a voice in my head shouted the word so loudly that I looked around in case someone might hear. Xanthe was taking me to buy dagga, *illegal* dagga, from one of Leopold's dimmest characters. Miggie was Marta's nephew. 'Stunted body, stunted brains,' was Marta's well-voiced opinion of him, a 'textbook good-for-nothing-rubbish'.

'Miggie's a gangster, you know.'

Xanthe threw back her head and laughed. 'I can't imagine gangsters in Leopold.'

Two stone gateposts, as high as my head, marked the entrance to the showground. The slatted iron gates between them bore the words 'Leopold Skou' across them. The gates were always chained and padlocked, but everyone stepped through the hole on the right where the chicken wire had long ago come away from the post.

The Leopold Show was held in April, when the worst of the heat had passed. Lorries carrying livestock, bakkies piled with people and produce, and horse traps converged on the showground at first light. All day the smell of boerewors* and fried onion snaked through the air while squashbox music made the loudspeakers dance. Inside the marquees were stalls of preserves and pickles. Beth and I always went straight to the needlework. Amongst the towers of doilies was our favourite thing: the crocheted Sindy doll loo-roll covers in pink, green or purple with matching loo seat covers. We'd bought one for Mum once, but she didn't see the humour. Unlike her net curtains, a Sindy doll loo-roll cover was not ironic.

* Sausages

While the women helped themselves to tea and cakes, the men huddled in the beer tent, away from the doilies and the Dominee. We sat on the grandstands watching the gymkhana and drank Coke floats. The highlight of the day was always the tug-of-war, where the boys from the agricultural college took on the local rugby side. 'It's like a warped beauty pageant,' said Mum last year.

Today the grounds looked desolate. The grass grew in untidy clumps, the eucalyptus trees that lined the track seemed naked without their show-day bunting.

Xanthe followed the track around the back of the grandstand, and disappeared behind the stable block. I fell back and felt my stomach twist around itself. Why had I let her talk me into this? I didn't want to be here, I didn't want to smoke the drugs. I didn't want Xanthe to smoke them either.

I turned to look up at Bosmansberg. Was there something wrong with me? This was what teenagers did. This was exactly the sort of adventure I had been longing for. 'You want to be Madge – so move it!' I told myself.

I followed the sound of laughter around the far corner of the stable block. Against the fence, on a stack of old upturned peach crates, sat three boys. Closest to me was Miggie, with his skinny brown legs ending in oversized white basketball shoes, a yellow peaked cap perched on top of his head. Xanthe was opposite him, leaning back against the wall, smoking a cigarette.

I stepped forward. Xanthe turned and held out a box of cigarettes. I took one, and clutched it in my hand. Miggie raised his chin in greeting. Then, in delayed recognition, he raised his eyebrow, leaned forward and looked at his friends.

I followed his gaze. My heart stopped. A trickle of sweat ran clear of my armpit, down my side until it met the waistband of my shorts.

'One bankie or two?' I heard Miggie ask. I wanted to tell Xanthe that two bank bags full of dagga was absurd. But there was no room for words in my head. The internal voice had been replaced by hysterical laughter. Ahead of me sat Simon. He was trying to adopt a gangster attitude with a luminous-green vest T-shirt and a cigarette behind his ear. He looked ridiculous. Was this what you did with a first-class education and a year away? I felt like sneering. But after his initial surprise, his face spread into a mocking grin and I knew, sweet Jesus, I knew I was in a world of trouble.

'An entjie* for the road?' I heard Miggie ask. The deal must be done.

'No,' I said loudly. Xanthe turned at my voice and followed my gaze. Simon jumped off the crates. I looked away.

As he passed, Simon leaned towards me. '*Karraboosh*,' he said in his low voice. He tossed his soccer ball up in the air and dribbled it away.

Xanthe took my arm 'You know that boy?'

I looked after him. 'It's Simon.'

'Simon? "Simon-from-the-grave" Simon? He's fucking hot.'

'Don't be weird.'

'Where should we keep it?' Xanthe asked as we made our way out of the grounds. Xanthe had settled for one bank bag

* Cigarette

134

of illegal dagga.

Simon's face stuck in my head – his amused, mocking grin, his grown-up eyes. Would he tell my parents, or worse still, Marta? Or would this become his silent, smirking secret?

I shook my head to get rid of him. 'Not *we*. This has nothing to do with me.'

'I can't keep it! Are you mental?'

'It looks like it,' I snapped. 'Do you have any idea how much trouble I am in?'

'Why?'

'What if Simon tells my parents?'

'He won't tell. How can he?' She put her arm me and rested her head on my shoulder, the way Beth did when she wanted something. Unlike Beth, she made me feel awkard and stiff. 'Come on!' she said as if cajoling a dog into performing a trick. 'Stash it under a rock. Your garden is the size of a small farm.' She leaned over and stuffed the full *bankie* into my back pocket.

'I can't,' I said, handing the bank bag back to her. 'My parents will find it. Anyway, I'm not going to smoke it.'

'I'll teach you,' she replied. We had reached the top of Park Road. She placed the bankie in both of my hands, as though she were entrusting me with a precious gift. 'I'll stay over on the weekend,' she said. 'Margaret Bergman, it would make me proud.'

CHAPTER FIFTEEN

'Drugs Day' dawned, the early morning sun pouring colour into the pale sky and the cool and rested earth. It made me ache. It was the sort of beauty that immediately precedes the end of the world.

'Get a grip!' I muttered. This was supposed to be fun. Over the course of the week, my unease had grown into finger-chewing dread. What if Xanthe overdosed and had to be rushed to hospital? What if she died? I'd probably go to prison.

Since stashing the dagga under the rock next to the chicken coop, the subject wouldn't leave me alone. Each time my parents glanced at me I expected them to produce the discovered bankie. Drugs popped up everywhere – there was a cocaine haul off a container ship in Cape Town. As I hugged Dad at breakfast, he said 'Give me drugs, not hugs'. I looked at him, horrified, until I realised he was joking. Only Marta noticed something was wrong.

You've gone off your food,' she accused me, 'What's your problem?'

'No problem,' I muttered. 'Everything's hunky-dory.'

'Funny kind of hunky-dory,' Marta shot back, but left it at that.

Xanthe had decided we would go to the river. The last time I'd been there was when Simon had killed the cobra. He'd seen it first, even though he was behind Beth and me. The snake was blocking our path, only four metres away. Its black, scaly belly reared, its hood wide and evil. The rest of it was curled into an s-shape. 'Don't move!' Simon had shouted, 'and don't look it in the eye.' Not daring to breathe, I'd fixed my eyes on Bosmansberg and waited for Simon to save us. The cobra waved its neck. It rose up higher, enraged by our lack of attention. Simon made a wide circle and bashed it over the head with the spade he was carrying. Moments before he killed it, I couldn't help myself. I glanced into those black eyes. It was like looking into tiny pools of evil. Since then, I pictured the three acres that separated us from the river were crawling with snakes.

'Right then,' I said with a sigh now, thinking snake thoughts as we stepped over the low fence at the bottom of the garden.

The grass on either side of the path was thigh-high. I carried a bag with sunhats, water, towels and of course the dagga.

'Speak loudly,' I said to Xanthe, 'and stamp your feet, like this.' I showed her.

She watched me, a smile growing across her face. 'Is this a little game you like to play?'

'No, smartarse, its because of snakes. If you let them know you're coming, most of the time they'll get out of the way.'

Xanthe's smile vanished and she looked around. 'Where are they most likely to be?'

I laughed. 'Everywhere.' In a community where a fear of God was drummed into you, a fear of snakes was inborn. Everyone

137

was afraid of snakes: small children, superstitious grandpas who could tell you 'snake stories' from 1893, farmers strong enough to wrestle a bull – not even the Dominee was safe. Because a snake could kill you at any time, it could be anywhere: in your garden, under your roof, always just out of sight.

We passed the mulberry bushes that had grown into an impenetrable tangle. The grass became thicker and longer, then the blackjacks started, leaning over and grabbing at you. We reached the rickety style over the old fence that separated one mass of weeds from the other. That was the halfway mark – thereafter you couldn't see the house anymore.

Xanthe, ahead of me, had entered into the spirit of snake scaring. She belted out lyrics in a Queen falsetto. I crept closer and grabbed her shoulders. 'Xanthe!' I yelled.

'What? Where, where?' She spun around, eyes wild.

I laughed.

'That's not funny!' she shouted.

'Good reflexes,' I said, ducking out of the way as she lunged at me. 'Come on, we're nearly there.'

She delivered a venomous glare before turning back and marching on. We reached the river reeds. They were taller than us, in the absence of direct sunlight the ground was damp and mushy.

'*I want to break free!*' I sang. I leaned forward to see if she was smiling. But Xanthe did not like to be teased.

'Look, it's still here!' I said as we reached the riverbed. Five years ago Simon, Beth and I had spent the spring holidays digging and shifting stones, trying to deepen the middle of the riverbed where it widened into a natural pool. We had even hauled big rocks across from the far bank in order to create a path of stepping-stones to our freshwater paradise.

'What's still here?'

'The swimming pool!' I laughed. 'We made it with Simon.'

Xanthe looked up at the mention of his name. I threw off my T-shirt and shorts, and stepped across the stones, skipping over a lizard as I went.

The water in the pool rose past my knee. I gasped as my foot sank into the sandy bed. Despite the warmth of the day, the brown mountain water had not lost its wintry cold.

'Come on!' I said. Impelled by a territorial urge, I stretched out in the pool. The freezing water grabbed at my skin. High above a black eagle languidly rode a thermal. It dived as sharply as a tear, the white tips of its wings flashing as it disappeared from view.

Xanthe balanced on a stone, and peered down at me, a visitor at the zoo staring at a submerged hippo. I laughed self-consciously and sat up.

'Fuck!' she screamed, her legs convulsing in the air, her arms above her head. 'Snake!'

Out of the corner of my eye, my lizard darted away.

'See, it's a lizard.' I pointed.

'It was a fucking snake!' she said. 'I saw it!'

'No, Xanthe. It was a lizard.'

'Whatever. I'll leave you to your mud bath.' She stalked back across the stones, plonked herself down on the blanket, and pulled Dad's cricket hat firmly over her eyes.

I sighed, and scanned the sky for the eagle, but it had

disappeared behind Bosmansberg. One of the agricultural college's Jersey cows watched me from the far bank. She stood trance-like under a willow tree with unblinking eyes. How lovely to be a cow, how lucky to be untroubled by mothers and teachers and friends with dagga.

Back on the bank, I busied myself arranging my towel, then lay back and covered my face with my T-shirt. The sun seeped into my skin like a sedative. From the agricultural college came the rumble of a tractor, and the half-hearted lowing from the herd of cows.

I breathed in, until the air pushed back up my throat, and held it there and let my heartbeat drum throughout my body.

Xanthe was restless. She rummaged around in the bag. Then came the sound of paper crackling.

My toes curled in on themselves.

A *tchk-tchk-tchk* of her lighter. Then the crackle of burning paper and tobacco and a sweet, rich aroma. The smell was familiar, it belonged to the clumps of men on the Main Street hoping for a day's work on the farms. It belonged outside the off-licence.

Xanthe inhaled a couple more times.

'Your turn.' She prodded me.

I didn't reply.

'Hey!'

'No,' I said, underneath my T-shirt.

She lifted the shirt from my face. I squeezed my eyes against the aggressive light.

'Come on, Madge, get up.'

'I don't want to.'

'Don't be boring, I said I'd teach you.' She yanked at my arm.

I sat up. Her eyes were heavy and bloodshot. 'Now, watch me, OK? OK?'

'OK,' I mumbled.

'Are you watching?' she repeated as she relit the joint.

'Yes!'

'Good, because you must be sure.' She giggled. 'Inhale, like this,' her cheeks hollowed, 'swallow, and exhale.' A jet of smoke emerged from her pouty mouth. 'Easy, peasy, lemon squeezy!' She passed me the little white stick.

I took the joint and inhaled, watching the tiny embers light up at the end. As I dutifully swallowed, my chest exploded in pain, and I doubled over choking, coughing, and gasping for breath.

'No, Madgie, no!' Xanthe shook her head, so vigorously that it took a moment to stop.

I tried again – I had to get it right.

Retrieving the joint, she inhaled deeply, cupped my neck in her hand and pulled my head to hers. She opened her lips onto my mouth and blew in the smoke. It travelled down to my lungs. It swirled around my core. As I was about to pull away, the pressure of her lips changed and she pressed them into mine and it was not about the smoke anymore but about the lips and the pressure of her hand on my neck. Then the smoke inside forced its way out and I pulled away, spluttering out the foreign substance.

Xanthe lay down, arms stretched over her head. 'You'll get it soon enough.' Her voice was lazy and thick.

I stayed seated, staring straight ahead. The swishing branches of the willow trees on the opposite bank looked like a dancer's fingers gently trailing the surface of the water. 'That wasn't a kiss, why would she kiss you? Don't be weird, Meg,' they whispered as they brushed the water, dissolving the reflection of the sun.

My head was close to bursting. I lay down and closed my eyes. I rubbed my palms over the tufts of grass. It was cool and sharp and green in my hands. I realised I understood the colour green, I let it dissolve into me. As I filled up with greenness, I closed my eyes and felt the earth buzz beneath me. I could hear the earthworms busy underground. My eyes flew open. The force of gravity was weakening around me. I grabbed at clumps of grass. The reeds on the far bank had become a battery of spears, and were moving slowly upwards, as if to pierce the sky. The stepping-stone rocks hovered above the water, too heavy to float away, but unwilling to be bedded any longer. I covered my eyes to stop it happening.

But what if this was to happen to me? What if my brain shot out the top of my head? Keeping my eyes shut, I clutched the top of my head with both hands. Then I grasped back at the tuft of grass, to keep myself grounded. As I sat, one hand on my head and one clutching at the grass, Xanthe opened her eyes and started laughing.

'It's not funny,' I said through clenched teeth, in case they become loose.

'You're wrong,' she said through her giggles, 'It the funniest thing I've ever seen.' Xanthe chucked me my T-shirt and shorts. 'Come on, I'm starving!'

I looked at her under the too-big floppy cricket hat and from deep inside my belly laughter bubbled up. It felt as though it had been trapped there all my life. It had us bent over each other, clutching at our aching sides. It lasted back up the path, all the way home.

Mum found us in the kitchen, shovelling down leftover cottage pie. She shook her head. 'Teenagers have the strangest urges.'

That night, as Xanthe slept on the mattress next to my bed, I dreamt I was back at the beach we went to most summers. I chased Beth through the milkwood forest at the top of the cliff, ducking under the knotty branches, following the twisting sandy path. Then – pah! We stopped to take in the scene below. The beach was the shape that is made by your outstretched thumb and forefinger. Golden sand arched between long rocky outcrops on either side that reached out to sea. It was a small beach, and difficult to reach. It was the best beach in the world.

We were on the path, which was a narrow riverbed, running, sliding, sandy feet slipping over smooth rocks, all the way down to the sand.

The narrow beach made for terrific waves that crashed and pounded themselves up onto the shore. They picked you up and threw you about, dragging you down until your lungs were ready to burst and you didn't know whether you were facing up or down, then spouted you out, hair plastered across your face, gasping for breath. The thing about this beach was that you had to know how to swim it. The rocks and the shape of the tiny bay made for vicious side currents. Every few years somebody drowned there, either pulled out to sea, or dragged down and smashed against the rock edges. Two years before a father had gone in after his son, who had lost his footing. He saved his boy, but drowned in the process.

The side current didn't concern me. I ran down the beach. The water was delicious and cool, gently lapping at my feet, at my tummy. When I looked back I'd left Beth far behind and Mum was calling me back to the shore.

My throat was parched. Without thinking I gulped at the seawater, and drifted deeper into the ocean. But wasn't salt water toxic? I stuck two fingers down my throat but only swallowed more. When I tried to swim back to the shore, the outgoing current swept me away. Mum was screaming at me. 'Help me!' I shouted. I was swelling up with water. Mr Loubser, the biology teacher, appeared above me in the clouds. 'We are sixty per cent water!' he said, wagging his finger at me. I must be sixty per cent ocean by now; soon pieces of me would start dissolving until nothing remained. I looked back up at Mr Loubser but he had changed into Xanthe.

Xanthe was leaning over me, illuminated by the courtyard light behind her. She gripped my arm. Her lips were moving close to me in the gloom. 'You're making weird gasping noises,' she said.

I sat up and looked around my room, unable to shake my terror.

'Here!' She shook my arm and held out a glass of water. I shook my head and turned to face the wall, pretending to fall back to sleep.

CHAPTER SIXTEEN

Simon's photograph had disappeared from the fridge. 'I see him morning and night,' said Marta. 'A mother needs some peace.'

In the fortnight since he'd been back, Simon's junior school headmaster had called to say how proud the community was of him. He asked Simon back to his old school to talk about Europe. Father Basil made him stand up in church on Sunday and everyone clapped, even Sister Bertha, who was a sour-faced old crow. Marta relayed these stories with a tight mouth, careful not to look proud; rather that it was her duty to show my parents their investment had paid off.

Mum couldn't let that lie, though.

'But how is it for you, Marta, having a child back at home?' she asked.

I had brought my homework to the kitchen table. In the silence of my bedroom my mind kept jumping back to the river and the bankie sitting under the stone behind the chicken coop and the way Simon had leaned towards me and said *karraboosh*.

Marta humphed.

Mum took off her glasses and folded them on the table. 'Have you heard from Angel?'

I abandoned any pretence of studying.

'Why, Miss Viv?' replied Marta after a pause.

'Her daughter must be getting big,' Mum persisted. She leaned across the table with a querying look. Mum's nosiness was up against Marta's refusal to be drawn. The silent tussle continued until the hall clock struck a half-hour chime. Mum sat back in her chair.

I smiled.

But Mum was not finished. 'You should enjoy Simon's success, Marta. He's a credit to you.'

It seemed that Marta had not heard until she turned around. 'What is there of me in that child?' She pulled a yellow hankie from the pocket of her apron. 'I thought it was the right thing to send him away, and Mister Tim so kind with the school fees and goeters*.' She shook her head. 'My son has outgrown me. He is uncomfortable in his own home.' She dabbed at her eyes. 'I've lost my son as well as my daughter.'

'No, Marta!' Mum looked stricken. 'You're the reason Simon's achieved what he has. Our children have to leave us behind. But nothing replaces a home. Soon enough, if we let them, they come back.'

'Not me!' I said. 'When I leave Leopold I'm never coming back.'

Mum smiled. Marta adjusted her doek**, and stuffed her hankie back into her sleeve.

'Simon could give you a hand with your studying,' Mum said, ruining the pleasure I felt at making her laugh.

* Things
** Headscarf

146

'I'm perfectly capable of studying on my own, thank you very much.'

'He could help you get that elusive "A".'

'The only reason I don't get the "elusive A" is because you want it so badly,' I snapped.

'Maybe,' said Mum.

Mrs Franklin wanted to see me. Her office was situated in the original school building, the most attractive part of the school. It was separated from the secretaries' office by a wide, sunny foyer. A pane of glass, the width of the wall, afforded the secretaries a clear view of anyone who entered Mrs Franklin's office, but frustratingly for them, Mrs Franklin preferred them to keep their door shut.

The foyer was cut off from the rest of the school by thick glass double doors. Girls weren't allowed there unless summoned.

Three armchairs hovered on the edges of a neat rug in the middle of the foyer. The chairs were tightly sprung and designed so that the backs were higher than the tallest father. I stood near the chairs, ignoring the secretaries' curious glances. Perched above Mrs Franklin's door was an owl, carved out of local sandstone. Its wings were raised, ready to swoop, its claws curled around a piece of cedar wood that bore the inscription: *Vincit qui patitur* – he who perseveres, conquers. On the opposite wall was a dark wooden board engraved in gold lettering with the names of the previous head girls, dating back to 1933. For a moment I saw a new line at the bottom: '1995 – Margaret Bergman'. That would shut Mum up. Simon had only been a prefect. But head girls' fathers were elders in the church. Their mothers were tuck shop volunteers, not the local troublemaker.

The *clip-clip-clip* of Mrs Franklin's heels snapped me back to the present. 'A word,' she said without stopping. Her office was large and meticulously neat. In the sash windows wooden slatted blinds were drawn against the midday sun.

As she closed the door and turned, I realised why I was here. She knew about the dagga! Had Miggie told her? The thought made me so weak that I sank on to the edge of one of the two chairs in front of her desk. Did my parents know? Would I be expelled? I smoothed my palms over the skirt of my dress.

Mrs Franklin sat down. For a wild moment I thought about telling her everything – the drugs, the river, the growing uneasiness I could not name. It was the same rush I felt standing too close to the edge on one of Dad's mountain hikes.

'You look ready to confess, though as far as I know you've not done anything wrong.' She looked closely at me. 'But with a face as expressive as yours, I'm not sure you're cut out for the life of crime.'

I had no answer.

Eventually she said, 'This is merely a caution. You're a clever girl, Margaret. I have high hopes for you. I think you could be a bit of a star.' A little laugh. She sat back into her chair. 'Xanthe isn't interested in being a star, Margaret. Be prudent with your choice of friends.'

I found Xanthe lying under the oak tree next to the lower playing field.

She yawned by way of greeting. 'I've been thinking.' When

I didn't reply, she said: 'Don't you want to know what about?'

'Not really,' I replied. I was thinking of Mrs Franklin's words. The relief at not being found out had quickly turned into annoyance. Three months ago she had asked me to look after Xanthe, now she was warning me against her. If she was so sure Xanthe was a troublemaker, why had she offered her a place here? What did she mean by 'high hopes' for me? Why had I not heard about them before?

Xanthe sat up and leaned back on her hands. Since our conversation on Park Road, she seemed to have forgotten about the exams. I didn't want to ask whether she was studying for fear of what her answer would be. A squirrel shot past us and up the tree trunk. Xanthe laughed. 'Wouldn't it be great to be a squirrel? Racing up and down trees all day.'

'You'd be a crap squirrel,' I said, 'You don't eat nuts.'

'I'd be a hungry squirrel, not necessarily a crap one.' She looked sideways at me.

A short way off Elmarie was kneeling behind Esna, bending over her as she plaited her hair. I loved the feeling of someone playing with my hair. It made my scalp tingle and my vision blurry. It was the closest feeling to human purring.

'That's disgusting,' Xanthe shuddered, 'touching someone else's hair like that. It's like brushing their teeth.'

I lay back. The grass was dry and spiky.

After a moment Xanthe joined me. 'I've been thinking about Simon.'

'For God's sake, what is the matter with you all?' I banged my hand on the ground.

She rolled over onto her side and faced me, her head resting in her hand. 'You like him, don't you?'

'No!' I shouted, screwing up my face at the thought. 'He's . . . like a brother . . .'

'So then.' Her eyes were narrow slits.

'Xanthe,' I said, plucking at the yellowed blades of grass. 'You wouldn't –'

'What?'

'It wouldn't be right.'

'What wouldn't be right?' She looked amused.

'You know.' The thought of her and Simon together made me panic. It wasn't so much the scandal it would cause as the feeling that I was six years old again, watching Dad and Simon drive away.

'Are you a racist?'

I sighed. She was being deliberately dense. 'It would cause too much trouble.'

She looked at me with a small smile.

'Please,' I said.

'OK, OK,' she muttered and looked away.

Despite all the talk and fuss over Simon that would not go away, I had not seen him since the day at the show grounds. It was inevitable that at some point I would look around to find him watching me. All the same, the sight of him made me jump. We faced each other across a table of books.

Dad's study was my secret hideaway. I spent hours there when he wasn't around. It smelled of typewriter ink and old books. I liked the rhythmic click of the overhead fan. I liked the collection of fossils he kept in a glass display cabinet along the front wall, and the way each piece of rock was meticulously labelled on pieces of white card in his spidery scrawl. His books were stacked in horizontal piles across the bookshelves that lined the wall, as though he'd recently unpacked them, not had them that way for twenty-five years. Most of all I liked his chair. It was a swivel chair, covered in faded red leather. It was wide and deep and so old that it had moulded perfectly to the shape of his body. Sitting in it was like sitting on his lap.

That's where Simon found me, sitting in my bikini. Skin against skin. The bikini was new. It was turquoise with a white piping all along the edges. The top was nothing more than two blue triangles on a white cord. The same white piping ended in little bows at the top of each leg. Earlier, I'd paraded around the house feeling sophisticated, like a character from a Danielle Steel novel. Now I felt ridiculous.

Simon leaned against the doorframe, his hands resting inside his shorts pockets. His navy T-shirt said MATRIC '92 in US army-style lettering. I swivelled away, so that he could not see me blush.

'What are you doing?' he asked.

'I was trying to make the chair rotate at exactly the same speed as the overhead fan.' I said.

'Trickier than it looks?' he asked.

Instead of answering, I stabbed my pencil into my notebook until the nib broke off.

'Can I have a go?'

'No.' I looked down. All I could see was pale flesh. I lifted my legs so that my thighs didn't spread across the chair, I sucked in my belly. It made no difference. If I got up and left I'd have to walk past him and I was practically naked.

'I came to see your dad.'

'He's not here,' I said, paddling my foot until I could see him partially from behind the chair. 'You missed him.'

He stepped into the room and picked up a book from the table. He flipped through a few pages and then put it back down. The Simon that I knew was now pumped up and puffed out and possessed by a different person. Do I look different? I wanted to ask him, because I can't seem to find the old you.

He looked up, as if in reply. 'When I was in France we went to the Lascaux caves. The caves have some of the earliest examples of rock art in Europe. It was amazing. Their paintings are similar to ours, but these covered the walls and ceilings. In some places it felt as though you were walking through a herd of bison.'

He stepped closer and leaned against the table while still managing to appear upright. A movement without a movement. A hunter's trick.

'The funny thing was that we didn't actually go into the caves. We walked through an exact replica. The French place such importance on their history that only very specialised geologists or archeologists will ever see inside the real paintings.' He sank into the memory. 'I felt horribly homesick that day. I longed for the smell of heat and dust. For the taste of one of my ma's curries, for a game of soccer in the street.' He reached up and batted the overhead fan's cord so that it swung back and forth. 'I even missed you.'

This was the most Simon had said to me in five years. It felt strange but also effortless. At the same time all I could think about was that even if I went to all the places he'd seen, he'd have done something else by then. I'd never catch up. I'd always feel the way I felt now – a silly little girl.

'Sold any more drugs recently?' I said at last.

He moved over to Dad's fossil cabinet. 'Your friend is something else,' he said. Across the back of his T-shirt were the words THE BOYS ARE BACK IN TOWN! and underneath that the imprint of a pair of full female lips. He edged over the far right of the cabinet – he recognised immediately Dad's latest additions.

'What do you mean?' I demanded.

'Nothing.'

'Simon –'

He spun around. There was the boy I knew, that intense, inquisitive gaze, the way his neck came forward. In that moment of mutual recognition, he smiled his old lopsided 'knock-knock-who's-there' smile. I almost smiled back, I wanted to, but then I remembered Xanthe's comments under the tree, and a cold hand clamped around my heart.

I looked away. 'I've got work to do. We're not all straight-A students.'

He shrugged and left without a word.

CHAPTER SEVENTEEN

The next weekend was a mini-break. It was known in our family as 'Dad's Weekend'. He didn't get to dictate much in our house, being outnumbered and out-willed most of the time, but every year the camping weekend was his from beginning to end.

The preparation was as important for Dad as the weekend. It began with the tent. Dad laid it out on the grass and counted all the poles and pegs. Not for him the new lightweight pop-up tents – ours could have been used in the Second World War. Once the tent was in the boot of the car – a measure adopted after a disastrous year – he went to the garage to fill up the gas canisters; another lesson learnt. Next to the canisters went the crates labelled 'Camping', containing pots and a kettle, the braai grid, aluminium plates and bowls and cups, crockery, matches, tin foil, mosquito repellent, tarpaulins, sleeping bags, camping stretchers, aluminium folding chairs and four fishing rods, although it was only him that fished. On Thursday evening Mum produced the food, so that Dad could pack the car. 'Packing the car' had to happen on a Thursday evening because we left before dawn on Friday morning. There was no reason for the rush – our destination was a bug-infested riverbank. Dad insisted on the early departure so that we could get through the tunnel and have breakfast at the Wellington Wimpy. The full fry-up at the Wellington Wimpy made him very happy.

We sat in the same red booth each year. The restaurant was deserted but for two truck drivers sitting in the far corner. Two waitresses were part of the very loud conversation taking place behind the swing door to the kitchen. Beth slurped her strawberry milkshake while Dad, swimming in saturated fats, hummed happily. He was dressed for the occasion in his navy rugby shorts and 'Boland 10km run' T-shirt. He'd not actually run the race but Dad couldn't resist a freebie.

He sat up. 'The chops, Vivvie, did you remember the chops?'

'Yes,' Mum answered in a bored tone. Dad had been checking her packing at regular intervals since we set off.

A few minutes later: 'What about the matches?'

'No! We agreed last year that matches were on your list. Remember? Remember, girls?' She turned to us, her eyes wild.

'You two have this conversation every year,' said Beth. 'When are you going to grow up?'

Dad's chuckle rose out of his shoulders. Grey hairs had colonised his side burns. I realised I was happy to be spending a weekend with him and his stupid jokes.

Beth had been watching me all morning with a smug expression. No amount of my scowling or face-pulling shifted the little smile.

She held out until we were back in the car. 'Dad,' she said, as she flipped over a page of the *Archie* comic. 'What's dagga?'

I stared down at my lap. We were hours away from Leopold, and still I couldn't escape it! Where was the bankie? Behind the chicken coop, surely, under the big stone. Or had I left it in my room? 'Think, Meg!' I commanded myself, but any thought was drowned out by a hysterical voice that kept shouting, 'She's found the bankie! She knows! She's got it!'

'It's a plant, Bethie,' said Dad in a distracted voice. He was trying to overtake a long-haul lorry on a narrow, single carriageway. He manouevred the car into the middle of the road, but another truck was coming towards us.

Mum sucked in her breath but managed to stay quiet.

'People smoke it as a drug,' added Dad, back behind the truck.

Despite the grip around my heart, I felt like shaking him. How could he think she wouldn't know what dagga was?

'It's medically proven to fry your brain,' said Mum.

'That's right,' agreed Dad, moving the car back into the middle of the road. He pressed his foot flat on the accelerator. The car muttered and jumped forward.

Once we were safely in front of the truck, Mum turned around. 'Not to mention the fact that it's illegal.'

Dad looked back at us in the rearview mirror. 'Why do you ask?'

'Just curious,' said Beth lightly.

'Don't be,' snapped Mum.

I didn't give Beth the satisfaction of raising my head. I could picture the triumphant smirk on her face.

After an hour of bumping around on a gravel track, we arrived at the deserted river.

Dad jumped out and stretched his arms over his head. 'Who needs Sun City!'

While my parents argued over the position of the tent, I cornered Beth. 'Give it to me!' I gripped her arm, ready to twist it into a Chinese bangle.

Beth laughed.

'Come on, Bethie,' I dropped my voice, into something resembling a wobbly plea, 'Come on, now.'

'No!' she yanked her arm free. 'Why would I?'

'Because you're a lovely person.'

'Ha!'

'OK, so what do you want?' I began to negotiate. What did she most covet? 'My Kylie Minogue tape?'

She laughed, 'Nope.'

'My tortoiseshell sunglasses.'

She shook her head, that stupid little smile stuck on her face. Too late I noticed the bulge in her pocket. Her hand clamped over it. I wiped the sweat from my forehead. 'My A-Ha T-shirt!' I almost shouted.

She hesitated. I knew she loved it. I'd brought it along this weekend, though I hardly wore it anymore. Xanthe said they were crap. But from the disdain in her eyes I knew she'd never give up. I lunged at her, moments too late. She darted away and started across the campsite.

'Girls!' Mum's voice followed us but we kept running, past the loos and the outside washbasin, past the 'communal' braai area that was always exclusively ours, until we got to the long grass, where the thought of snakes stopped us both.

'You've been a bitch to me ever since Xanthe arrived.' She turned on me. 'I'm not giving it back.'

'But you like Xanthe,' I said. 'You were reading her magazine and everything.'

'Oh pu-lease!' Beth looked scornful.

I stepped towards her.

'Mum!' she yelled at the top of her voice, pulling the bankie out of her pocket and holding it high above her head. 'Mum!'

'Shut up!' I said, looking over my shoulder and backing away. 'But know this: I'll get it back. You're not going to get away with this, you little cow.'

Beth bled every last drop out of her secret. 'Meg's offered to do the washing-up tonight,' she said, looking me in the eye, and later, 'Meg doesn't want her marshmallows.' On Saturday afternoon, when she knew I had had enough, she offered to go fishing with Dad. The innocent delight on his face was pathetic.

I shook out her rucksack, I turned her sleeping bag inside-out. I looked everywhere I could think of, from the area behind the car seats to the stuffing of her pillow, but that stupid bankie was nowhere. I couldn't let my parents find it; that would be the end of my friendship with Xanthe, the end of my life. Tears spilled out. From the moment we'd set foot in the show grounds things had started going wrong. That bankie was radiating trouble. It made me terrified of my teachers and jumpy every time my parents spoke to me. Now I was swearing at Beth and she had me absolutely stuck and my whole life was spinning out of control. I lay back on my sleeping bag in the tent and cried until I fell asleep.

Beth and I slumped on the backseat, baked in sunshine. Our feet stuck out the open car windows, our eyes closed against the wind on our faces.

From the front came the continuous murmur of my parents talking. They loved to talk on car journeys, they'd chat for hours in a way they never did at home. Mum said that what convinced her that Dad was the man for her was that he was the only person she would happily travel the world with.

I turned and looked across at Beth. She'd fallen asleep; her lovely long dark lashes balanced shut against each other. She looked angelic; you couldn't believe that such an open, pretty face was capable of such –

I leaned forward cautiously. Her hand, the one that had been guarding her pocket all weekend, lay slack on the seat. I lunged over her. With my hand clamped around the bankie, I yanked it out and threw it out my open window.

'Bitch!' yelled Beth, waking with a start. We both turned around to see the small packet shrinking away from us.

'What's got into you two?' Mum demanded, a weekend's worth of annoyance showing on her face.

'Meg has . . .' Beth hesitated as I looked at her, 'Meg's torn my shorts pocket,' she said. I exhaled.

'Really, Meg, what's your problem?' Mum sighed.

That night, after I switched off my light, Beth came into my room. 'Why did you have the dagga?' she asked in the dark.

'It wasn't mine,' I said.

'Was it Xanthe's?'

'Leave it, Beth, please.' I sat up and switched on the light. She looked worried. I didn't like being responsible for the fear in her eyes, but this had nothing to do with her. I picked up

159

my sunglasses. 'Have them. I know you like them.'

Beth turned away, and left me feeling diminished.

A few days later Xanthe found me at my locker. 'What did you do with my bankie?' she said in a low whisper.

I snorted. 'Your bankie? The one that Beth found and was this close –' I held up my forefinger and thumb a few millimetres apart in front of Xanthe's face – 'to showing my parents?'

Xanthe's expression was the essence of patience. 'Where is it?'

'Somewhere between Worcester and here,' I said. 'I threw it out of the car window.'

Xanthe bent forward. 'Are you insane? After all that trouble we went to getting hold of it, you chucked it out the window? What's your fucking problem, Madge?' She stamped her foot.

Something had changed since that bankie. I wanted to go back to before the river, to before the day at the show grounds. I wanted my sister not to have found it. I leaned towards her and whispered: 'If you want more dagga, get it, keep it and smoke it yourself. Leave me out of it.'

CHAPTER EIGHTEEN

On Saturday afternoon, midway through the two weeks of exams, Mum found me eating a snackwich on the sofa. I wound strands of melted cheese around my finger and sucked them into my mouth as I watched my favourite movie, 'Listen to Me'. The movie made me ache. Jami Gertz was perfect. She was clever and brave and, most importantly, beautiful. What would it feel like to have Kirk Cameron resting his head on my shoulder while pretending to be asleep?

Mum stepped over my outstretched legs and switched off the TV.

'I was watching that.'

She stood in front of me, hands on her hips.

'What? I'm having a break.'

'Read a book.'

'Ridiculous woman,' I muttered.

'I beg your pardon?' Mum sat down on the arm of the chair. She had the air of having something to say.

I bit the inside of my cheek, preparing for a lecture about failing to live up to my potential.

'I ran into Mrs Franklin today.'

'And . . .' I stared at the dead TV screen.

'She said that you'd had a chat, that she was worried about Xanthe's influence.'

'That's rubbish! Xanthe's not *influencing* me. She's a friend, the first friend I've had in . . . forever.'

'I'm not the enemy, Meg! I was a teenager too. I know how it feels.'

'No, you don't.' I got up, purposefully leaving the plate on the sofa.

Beth was outside on the stoep, staring at a plate of apple and banana that had been allocated as her mid-afternoon snack. Mum devoted herself to coaching Beth through the exams. She made charts, marking up Beth's study time and break time. She even monitored her daily vitamin intake. By the time exams were finished, Mum knew Beth's syllabus by heart.

I was left to get on with it.

'Study break, huh,' I said.

Beth did not answer. She had been ignoring me since the afternoon I chucked the dagga out of the window. I missed her company, but then I realised it had been a long time since we'd really gotten on. It was a pity she let her jealousy of Xanthe get in the way. She was so used to being adored that she couldn't handle it that I had a friend. I tossed a Wilson's toffee into her lap and slouched back inside.

I'd hardly seen Xanthe in the past two weeks. Without her, 'Madge' was beginning to slip. I had even considered studying hard and getting that 'A', but I didn't want to show Xanthe up and I didn't want it to seem that I was in competition with Simon.

At night I had a recurring dream that I was kissing someone

– every night the person changed: Kirk Cameron, Shannen Doherty, Father Christmas – even Bles Bridges. Perhaps Mum was right – perhaps the dagga had fried my brain.

When I did see Xanthe she was distant and distracted, constantly disappearing at break and after school. I took it as a good sign; it meant that she was working. But everything depended on science, our last exam.

The mood in the classroom was jumpy on Friday morning. Isabel fired questions at Sonia, barely listening to the answer. Esna paged frantically through the textbook, as if that could make a difference. Xanthe, seated across the class for the exams, looked calm. That's good, I thought, that's a good sign.

Elmarie stopped at her desk. 'So, Santie, are you ready for the science exam?'

'We're writing science today?' Xanthe asked, making her face stricken.

Elmarie hurried back to her seat.

I laughed. Xanthe looked back and winked. She knew I was watching her when the question papers were handed out. She paged through the six-sided questionnaire, backwards and forwards, turned it upside down, and then shook it a few times. She looked back at me and mouthed the words, 'What the fuck!'

I giggled. But 'Please Xanthe,' I begged her silently, 'don't mess this up.'

Exam results trickled back over the next week. Esna and Elmarie checked the calculations on each script three times, as if an extra mark mattered. For the most part, I was stuck with an uninspiring 'B', which considering how little work I'd done, I was lucky to get.

Xanthe was fidgety as our science papers were handed back. 'Sixty-eight,' she said.

'Yup,' I said, looking over my sheet. Mum wasn't going to be happy, but it was a safely invisible mark. 'How about you?' I added too brightly.

'Sixty-eight,' she repeated, laughing.

'What?' I looked up.

Xanthe pointed to her exam sheet. 'How about that?'

'I don't believe it!' I said.

Xanthe looked at me sharply. 'Why?'

'I mean it's incredible. Well done!'

Xanthe leaned her head back and covered her eyes with her hands. 'Thank. Fuck.'

I frowned at the red numbers on my sheet. I couldn't believe it. I ought to be delighted for Xanthe, this was exactly what I had been hoping for. But Xanthe was supposed to be failing, I didn't see how she could end up with the same mark as me.

All that afternoon I returned to our conversation on Park Road. Why had I mentioned the exam papers behind the printing room door? Surely she wouldn't actually have stolen one? But how else could she have managed it?

The lawn in front of the school was bustling with girls and teachers and townsfolk and parents and farmers. It was the last day of term. The just-cut grass left the air sweet and damp, the beds of white roses were perfectly pruned. The morning sun bounced against the school's freshly washed sash windows. In Leopold everyone turned up for the end-of-year prize giving, even those without a daughter at the school. It was an event.

Dominee and Mevrou Dominee circulated with the attitude of dignitaries – smiling and nodding at members of their flock. The city parents had been arriving in their fancy cars since early morning, windows rolled up against the country roads, bringing the already busy main street to a standstill. They stood to one side, clustered together like iron filings. They fanned themselves and dabbed at their foreheads though by local standards the sun wasn't yet up.

I stole glances at the women in their white trouser suits and high heels. They patted their hair with red-tipped fingers, looking as though they had delicately stepped out of a magazine. One of them, whose long brown hair was arranged in big curls, was smoking. Every so often her friend leaned over and said something as she pretended to wipe the tip of her nose. They were laughing at us. I should be insulted, but instead I found myself standing taller, rearranging my hands at my sides to appear more elegant, clutching at a wild hope that perhaps I might stand out in this crowd of earthy farmers and dowdy wives.

'My dad calls them the "walkie-talkies",' said Xanthe, catching my gaze.

'The what?'

'The walkie-talkies. They're the sort of women who have walking groups. They meet up every morning. Gossip-gossip-gossip; walk-walk-walk. The better the gossip, the faster they walk.'

'Do they?' Sometimes I felt panicked at everything I didn't know.

We stood in the middle, my family and Xanthe, between the farmers and the city folk. Like a Venn diagram, we carried elements of both groups, but were a part of neither. Mum stood very tall. From her determined smile, I knew she was aware of the wide arc Juffrou du Plessis was making around us.

'Oh look,' said Dad. 'There's Hannes!'

'Great!' said Mum, in a forced voice.

Dad moved away from us and over to his friend. After a moment, he looked back at us and beckoned Mum over.

'Hi, Hannes! Lovely to see you!' called Mum without moving, her lips pulled back to the point that she resembled the police dog Kaptein.

Beth, forgetting her vow of silence, nudged me. 'She's doing it.'

'What?' Mum asked at our snorts. 'I'm being friendly.'

'No, you're being scary,' said Beth.

Dad returned. 'One of Hannes' labourers is unwell. I said you'd be able to help.'

'Surely the hospital –'

'Vivienne!' Dad's tone, close to a growl, made me glance up. A look passed between my parents.

'Of course,' said Mum after a moment. 'I'll go and have a word.'

Mum reappeared. 'Sounds like that labourer should really be in hospital. But I have a stock of meds in the clinic I'll send him.' She smiled shyly at Dad.

He beamed at her. 'Hey.' His eyes lit up. 'We should have

a party!'

Mum managed a barely audible 'Hmm.'

'A party?' laughed Beth. 'You!'

'Why not? It's been too long. We're hip, we're groovy, we're – what's the word – *kiff!*' he finished in triumph.

I stopped short. 'Don't ever use that word again.'

Dad was delighted. 'But I like it. We're kiff, aren't we, Vivvy, we're groovy!' He started walking towards the hall, in what was supposed to be a groovy manner. He looked like a spastic gangster.

'Timothy!' Mum laughed.

'Stop that!' I hissed. Elmarie and her parents were staring at us.

Beth clapped her hands and joined Dad in his ridiculous walk. Even Xanthe laughed. 'Tim, you are seriously kiff.'

He shot me a triumphant look and turned with his hand in the air, ready to high-five Xanthe, but she stopped. Her hand fell to her side.

In front of us was a woman, with her arms outstretched and a wide smile. Xanthe stepped forward and disappeared momentarily into the cloud of Red Door perfume. 'Darling!' said the lady. She stood on tiptoes and steadied herself by holding onto Xanthe's shoulders as she planted a kiss on each cheek.

'Mum. You're here,' said Xanthe, her tone matter of fact.

'Look at you, too thin! Always too thin! Don't they feed you here? Is the food terrible? Is it too hot to eat? It's bladdy-well nine o'clock in the morning and I'm close to fainting.'

Xanthe removed her mother's hands from her shoulders

and stepped back. The person smiling at us could not be more different to the mum I had made up for Xanthe. She was short and sporty. Her well-tanned arms were strong; the skin all the way up her forearms was slightly crinkled. She wore three chunky red wooden bangles on her right arm, a large red handbag to match, and a lot of gold on her fingers. Her blonde hair was cut in a perfect 'Princess Di' style. But as she lifted her white-rimmed sunglasses, I sucked in my breath. She had the same ice-blue eyes as Xanthe. As they looked at each other, they were looking into their own eyes.

'Mum, this is Madge, and her family.'

Xanthe's mum's gaze reluctantly left her daughter. A short-sighted frown flashed across her face before she replaced it with a delighted, 'At last! So pleased to meet you, I'm Shirley. Just call me Shirley, sweetie . . .' She kissed my forehead and shook hands with my parents.

'It's a pleasure, Shirley,' replied Mum. I looked at her and suppressed a groan. She was wearing a shapeless beige dress that ended below her knees, effectively amputating what were decent enough legs. Four strands of orange beads and large brown seedpods hung around heck. Her hair fell around her shoulders, partly obscuring her face that was free of any make-up. But what made me want to die of shame were her leather strappy sandals. She looked like a female Jesus of Nazareth.

Dad beamed and held out his hand.

Shirley was removing her hand from Dad's grip as Mrs Franklin appeared. She wore a green and white zigzag print dress, which had a neat green belt in the middle. Her green stiletto shoes matched the dress. Her hair was set so tightly it looked as though it might never move again.

'Mr and Mrs Bergman,' Mrs Franklin held out her hand, 'what a lovely morning. A great start to the holidays.'

'Absolutely,' agreed Dad, shaking her hand.

'You must be looking forward to a well-deserved break,' said Mum.

A tight smile from Mrs Franklin. She turned to Shirley. 'Mrs Muller.'

'Mrs Franklin. I was just admiring your roses. What's your secret?'

Mrs Franklin inclined her head in thanks. 'Perhaps it is the nurturing environment.' The grown-ups laughed a short, plastic laugh before Mrs Franklin moved to the next cluster of parents.

'She's very nice, isn't she,' commented Shirley. 'My old headmistress was more like the Bride of Frankenstein. We're very pleased with how Xanthe has settled into this school. Aren't we, darling?' Shirley squeezed Xanthe's arm.

We sat through the Dominee's forty-five-minute address. These were dark times; testing times for our nation. But this was not the time to cower because we were a chosen people. The Dominee held up his bible. *'I will give you every place where you set your foot, as I promised Moses.'* The Dominee's voice rose to fill the hall. *'As I was with Moses, so I will be with you; I will never leave you nor forsake you.'*

Murmurs of approval collected in the audience like a low humming sound.

'Be strong and courageous, because you will lead these people to inherit the land I swore to their ancestors to give them.'

Though I didn't look at her, I imagined Mum, white-knuckled and muttering under her breath. News reports these days seemed to be dominated by pictures and footage of thousands of people at election rallies. The authority in those speakers' voices was no less than the Dominee's.

'*Be strong and courageous,*' repeated the Dominee. '*Do not be afraid; do not be discouraged, for the Lord your God will be with you wherever you go.*'

My bum ached from sitting cross-legged on the floor. There was a point midway through prize giving each year when I imagined what it would be like to jump up and walk smartly to the stage, skip up the side stairs without a stumble, and shake Miss Franklin's hand as I accepted my well-deserved prize. Mum had been polite about my handful of 'B's, but instead of the expected 'could do better' lecture, she'd barely glanced at the results, which irritated me even more. I pictured her now, sitting next to Dad in the block of chairs reserved for parents, clapping and smiling, applauding somebody else's daughter.

Xanthe sat next to me with her head in her hands. Her science result was still bothering me. If I didn't ask her about it now, it was going to bother me all summer long. I jabbed her in the ribs.

'What?' she said after a pause and I realised she'd been asleep.

'You know the afternoon on Park Road . . .' I whispered.

'No,' she said.

'When I told you about the printing room door that didn't lock –'

Elmarie turned around. 'Sshhhh!'

'What about it?' whispered Xanthe.

170

'It's just. . .' Now that I had my opportunity, I froze. What was I doing? I was about to accuse her of stealing an exam paper and cheating. What if she hadn't and was so insulted that she never spoke to me again? What if she had? Did I honestly want to know?

Somebody poked my back. I turned around. Isabel pointed to Juffrou Kat who was glowering at me from the side of the hall.

'It's nothing,' I whispered quickly.

'Why don't you join us for lunch?' said Mum to Shirley, as we stood outside again, released for the holidays.

'Oh, that's nice of you . . .' said Shirley, 'But we should really be going.'

'You don't want to set off in the midday heat,' said Dad.

'The air-conditioning helps,' said Shirley with a little smile.

'Of course!' Dad made a funny face to cover up his embarrassment. 'But you cannot leave Leopold without trying the hotel's mutton curry. It's a tradition!'

'Oh!' said Shirley, fanning herself with the paper programme.

'Come on, Mother,' said Xanthe, 'It will make a good story for your bridge club.'

We sat in the cool interior of the hotel dining room. The Royal Hotel was where one marked an event in Leopold, and prize giving was one of their busiest days of the year. Every table was occupied. The heavy air-conditioning boxes, turned up to maximum, hummed in their efforts. A constant stream of serving staff emerged from the kitchen door with steaming

171

plates of tomato bredie*, frikkadel**, bobotie*** and of course, mutton curry, despite the outside heat. They snaked silently around the dining room in their starched white aprons over black uniforms, ducking out of the way of old friends greeting each other, pushing in chairs, picking up dropped knives off the floor. As our waitress moved around the table, adjusting our knives and forks, I saw Beth peering at the top of her bent head, at the starched white hat pinned onto her hair smoothed back with coconut oil. I caught her eye and smiled. We used to fold up Mum's napkins to look like those hats. We thought them very sophisticated.

To Dad's dismay, Shirley and Xanthe both ordered a Greek salad. Beth and I, as ever, chose burgers. Mum, after a moment's hesitation and a glance in the direction of Shirley, settled for the yellowtail line fish.

Shirley was a talker. She talked her way through her salad and a glass of wine, 'Oh, why not!' she'd replied to the offer, with a twinkle. She talked about her garden and the trouble she was having with the aphids. She told us about her recent trip overseas and how nice it was to get back home after all that travelling. She talked about tennis and her and her husband's love of golf.

'What line of work is your husband in?' asked Mum.

'Alan works for Shell. Been there for years. He's very happy there but he does have to travel a lot.'

'Sounds important,' said Mum. Shell was on her list of Large

---

* Stew
** Meatballs
*** Curried mincemeat

Bloodsucking Companies to Hate.

'*Pppf*,' said Shirley, waving the comment away, but a blush rose in her cheeks. She revealed her world in one story after another – bridge and book clubs and the rising cost of her weekly Pick 'n' Pay shop and the election next year. 'Let's not talk about that, we're having such a lovely day.' When she became animated, the red wooden bangles clunked against each other as her hands joined in.

Near the end of the meal, as Dad was sunk into his Malva pudding, Shirley took a spoonful of pecanut pie from Xanthe's plate, closed her eyes as she allowed herself a moment of bliss, then said: 'Alan and I are so grateful for the care you have shown Xanthe this term. We would love to have Margaret to stay these holidays, if it doesn't upset your existing plans.'

I sat up. I looked at Xanthe, who made a face. I looked back at Shirley, who winked at me. I looked at Mum and Dad, who were momentarily lost for words. I looked at Beth. She looked very glum. I looked back at Mum. 'Please, please, please!' I mouthed. She turned to Dad, who smiled and shrugged. At last she turned to Shirley.

'Why not,' she said, smiling.

I breathed out and gave her my most lovely smile. Shirley opened her diary and they agreed that I would spend a week with them after Christmas. In that moment my holiday was transformed from five weeks of an endless repetition of trips up the mountain, swimming and picnics on the dam, with a catalogue of chores for the sake of it, into what would most likely be the most exciting week of my life.

CHAPTER NINETEEN

Marta stood at the washing line, taking down the dry linen at the end of the day. She pulled down a pillowcase with one hand while returning the pegs into the waiting bag with the other. With a *flick-yank-pull* she folded it up into a perfect rectangle and deposited it on the pile of magnificent white that was already taller than the basket beside her.

She barely glanced at what she was doing. Her eyes flickered back and forth, her head tilted in response to a banging door. She swatted away flies, she shouted comments at Ethel next door. Eventually she turned to me, lying under the pecanut tree a few metres off. 'Make yourself useful, child.'

We faced each other across the breadth of a double sheet. 'Take the corners – not like so – like *so*. Pull tight.'

I pulled backwards.

'Tight!'

I yanked the corners, so that she had to take a step forward to steady herself.

She laughed. 'Now, drop the one side and pick it up with the other hand.'

I fumbled with the folded sheet.

'*Goeie hemel**,' she muttered as the folds twisted between us. 'Start again. Drop, pick up, fold and fold.'

Her small hands manipulated the folds of the expanse of crinkly white sheet with the expertise of an artist, nimble and confident against my thumby attempt.

'I'm going to Cape Town after Christmas,' I said.

'Uh-huh,' said Marta,

'To stay with Xanthe. For a week.'

'Even more reason to help out now,' she replied.

I laughed. 'Do you want me to bring you anything?'

'There's nothing I need in this life that I can't get here.'

'It's not about what you need.'

'Ha!' She dumped half of the sheets in my outstretched arms, picked up the basket containing the rest of the pile and marched off towards the house. 'That's what you young people think,' she said as she climbed the steps, 'You want to buy this, you want to go to travel the world, you want a big job with lots of money.' She dumped the basket on the stoep and turned around to face me. 'I hope that when you've finished running after all your wants, you'll turn your attention to what you *need* to do.'

'Like what?'

'Looking after your own, settling down to a sensible life and a job and responsibility.'

'There's plenty of time for all that,' I said with a laugh.

'So I hear. Has your report arrived?'

'Ja,' I said looking away.

'And?'

---

* Good Lord!

'Nothing like Simon's,' I said before I could stop myself.

Marta wiped her nose in a business-like fashion and stuffed her hankie back into her pocket. 'There's a lot more what goes into making a clever person than an "A" aggregate.'

'If you could have done anything, what would it have been?' I asked.

'Ha!' She smiled. 'I wanted to be a ballroom dancer. Professional.'

'A dancer?' I looked at her. There was not much of a dancer to be found underneath her yellow and green maid's uniform and brown lace-up shoes. I could not imagine Marta with her creaky knees and jammy hip being twirled around a ballroom.

'Oh, I could dance!' she said, so sharply that I blushed.

'I'm glad you didn't,' I said.

She launched a pitying look before disappearing inside.

I knew that Marta's life was hard, but I didn't want to know that she would rather have done something else. It was like hearing about Mum's Lawrence. My world was fragile enough. My very existence seemed nothing more than a random selection of multiple-choice answers. If there was no order in the way the pieces were put together, how could I ever hope to keep them in place?

Everyone was in the kitchen, including Simon, who had become Dad's official apprentice. He was sprawled out in one of the kitchen chairs, with his back to the door. The rooms in our house seemed to shrink in his presence. I couldn't imagine how he fitted in Marta's tiny two-roomed cottage.

'Excuse me, Simon,' I said. It was impossible not to touch

176

some part of him. 'Thank you,' I added, safely on the other side, loudly enough to make sure Mum heard.

Mum was engrossed in the newspaper. 'Look at this.' She held it up. The page was taken up by a photo of F.W. de Klerk and Mandela shaking hands and smiling. The headline read: PEACE LAUREATES – A TRIBUTE TO CONCILIATION AND PEACE.

'That's not something I thought we'd ever see.'

'The prize belongs to Mandela,' said Simon quietly.

'That's not quite true,' said Dad, 'FW let Mandela out and unbanned the ANC. Brave moves.'

I sat down next to Dad, only to find myself opposite Simon.

'He had no choice,' argued Mum, 'the country was grinding to a halt.'

'If nothing else, it sets a good example,' said Dad. He looked pointedly from Mum to me.

'What do you think?' said Simon, looking across at me.

'What?'

'Do you think they both deserve it?' His voice was quiet, yet crowded the room.

I looked around, expecting a reaction from Mum, but no one seemed to have heard the question. 'I don't know,' I shrugged.

'You must have some opinion.'

'Why?'

'Because it affects your future.'

'No it doesn't. I didn't make the rules, and I can't change them. Why should I care?'

Simon laughed. 'What do you care about?

I looked around the kitchen, thoroughly annoyed. Simon

didn't deserve an answer to such a stupid question and yet I had to say something. He was waiting. 'I care about lots of things, Simon, like being happy. Not some stupid politicians.'

Simon raised an eyebrow. 'Are you happy?'

'Delirious,' I snapped.

Simon shrugged away my answer and turned back to the newspaper. I stared at Simon, resentfully. This was my house, why was he here?

'The cake!' Mum jumped up, 'Sweet Jesus, the cake!'

'Plenty of time, Vivvy,' Dad responded in his mildest voice, 'it's only just December.' He turned to the back page of the paper.

Mum pulled down the egg-and-flour-encrusted recipe folder from the shelf above the stove. 'This year I've really done it,' she admonished herself. 'It will be a disaster.'

'Isn't the cake supposed to be made in October?' asked Beth.

Dad flipped down the side of the newspaper page and shook his head at her.

Beth continued: 'Why don't we have a chocolate cake this year? Or, or, an *ice-cream* Christmas cake!'

Mum shrieked. 'If your grandmother could hear you now!'

'But she can't,' Beth sang back at her under her breath, 'And she never will.'

'What was that?' Mum turned around, clutching a large packet of fruit mix. There was a smear of flour across her brow, like battlemarks.

'I love your fruitcake,' said Dad firmly. 'In fact this year I want two.'

'Two!' she shrieked again, 'You're out of your mind, Timothy.'

She only ever shrieked at Christmas.

I left the room. Mum forgot that stupid cake every year. From the moment she shrieked, 'My God, the cake!' a mania gripped her, demanding that we play out a pantomime only she understood. It began with an enormous Christmas tree from Hannes' farm. As she decorated it with her precious overseas decorations she'd say, 'Of course a *real* Christmas tree is a fir tree.' On Christmas morning as we'd tear into our stockings, which always contained oranges, for God's sake, in December, she'd shriek, 'Be careful, those are *real* stockings!' These bizarre rituals had seemed magical when we were little – no one else in my class had ever heard of a stocking. But the plastic sprigs of mistletoe and holly and 'ever-so-expensive' baubles from Harrods were out of place. Our Christmas Day lunch of turkey, gammon, roast potatoes and Brussels sprouts and bread sauce eaten in temperatures of forty degrees celsius, while the King's College Choir Cambridge belted out 'In the Bleak Midwinter' belonged in deepest, darkest Salisbury. Sometimes I imagined that it wasn't even us she was smiling at as she turned off the lights in anticipation of the flaming Christmas pudding.

There was no avoiding it. The yuletide machine had begun to grind. Dad woke me the next morning. He was standing at the end of my bed, jangling the car keys.

'I'm not a dog.' I sat up. He was wearing his long socks, veldskoens, too-short navy rugby shorts and a khaki short-sleeve shirt. It could mean only one thing. Today was the trip to Hannes' farm to cut down the Christmas tree.

'We've got to get over the pass before the farm traffic starts.'

'Take Beth,' I said and flumped back onto my pillows.

'Beth says it's your year to choose the tree.'

'Hooray!' I shouted, but Dad had left the room. The trip to Hannes' farm was what many years ago Dad had named 'the first day of Christmas' but I knew it was his way of escaping a day of Mum in her altered condition. It began with a hot and airless trip over the pass and into the next valley, windows closed against the dusty gravel spitting up around us. It involved sitting on Hannes' front stoep, which smelt of cattle dip, while he and Dad put the world to rights. This could require anything between one and four Castle lagers while Beth and I were left to sip flat Coke and try to outstare his two terrifying ridgeback dogs. Now and then the party line telephone would trill out a *short-short-short-long* or a *short-long-short-short* pattern. But it was never for Hannes. Eventually, Dad would slap the arm of his chair with a decisive, 'Ja-nee!' This was our cue that the worst part of the day had arrived, where we trudged up the mountainside to the pine forest. More often than not the tree was too big to fit in the car and stuck out the back of the open boot and we would arrive home scratched and scarred and covered in a thick paste of sweat and dust.

All of which was why, fifteen minutes later, I stropped my way into the garage. 'This is grossly unfair,' I said and kicked the door for effect. This is –' I stopped.

Sitting in the passenger seat, alongside Dad, was Simon. A lazy, patronising smile zig-zagged across his face as I passed his door.

I gathered the little dignity I had left and resolved not to say another word for the rest of the day.

180

After a few minutes, Simon pulled out an envelope.

'What's this?' asked Dad.

'Came in the post,' replied Simon.

'BP?' Dad leaned over to get a better look. 'Hey! The full scholarship?'

I watched Simon's shoulders shrug up and down in an awkward, throw away action. It was what he did after winning a race at sports day, or hearing that he'd been accepted at the Cape Town school.

'You did it!' Dad hooted in delight. I sank lower into the seat. Simon didn't say anything but I could tell he was smiling.

'That's my boy!' said Dad. In a reflex action of long ago, Dad reached over and ruffled Simon's head, although this time he had to reach upwards to do so, which made them both laugh. Dad whistled. 'To be eighteen years old all over again!'

We left the town behind. As we began climbing the pass I watched the ribbon of green that the river fed as it snaked its way up the valley. Here and there a koppie* pushed up through the earth, between the concentric circles of brown farmland. Higher up the valley the farmland gave way to scrub bush. Dad claimed that there were a hundred different shades of brown in the veld. But that was rubbish. Brown was brown.

A few kilometres after we passed the turn-off to the agricultural college, the tar stopped. The gravel made me feel sick. How would I possibly spend the whole day with Simon when I felt so angry with him that I could smack him? Last night I'd made a list all the things I cared about. I cared about my family, despite them being annoying. I cared about my

* Small hill

181

friends. Or my one friend. I cared about the four little graves in the corner of the churchyard. I cared about getting out of Leopold and never having to see Simon again.

'That's really good news, Simon,' Dad broke the silence. 'Now all you need to do is keep your head down, and stay out of trouble.'

When Simon didn't reply, Dad laughed. 'Not what a young man wants to hear.'

'This is our time,' Simon said softly.

'Quite right.' Dad sighed. 'I'm no revolutionary, as you know. I spend my time studying rocks after all.'

'You married Mum,' I said.

Dad laughed. 'The true revolutionary speaks!'

I pulled a face at his back and plunged back into my sulk.

We clattered onto the narrow farm road. Dad said, 'You and Simon can go get the tree while I chat to Hannes.'

'Terrific,' I mumbled as my insides bit into themselves.

Dad shot me a warning look in the rear-view mirror as he pulled up in front of the farm gate. There was a rule in our house that the youngest in the car got to do the gates. But the revolutionary spirit had taken hold. Instead of clambering out, I stared down at my stubby fingernails. After a few seconds of standoff Dad turned around and snapped, 'Meg!'

'I'll get it,' said Simon, opening his door.

I met Dad's glare with a glower. 'Snap out of it, my girl,' he growled as he swung the car into the drive.

As Dad unpacked a box of medicines Mum had sent, we made our way across a scrub-and-dust field behind the farmhouse until we reached the hill. The best trees were found halfway up. I let Simon walk ahead of me. Soon we were swallowed up by the trees. Forests made me nervous. There was too little light. The crunching pine needles underfoot seemed too loud against the eerie silence. I stopped. Simon didn't need me there to chop down the tree. I didn't see why I should trudge up the mountain only to stand there and watch him.

'Are you coming?' Simon called. He started back towards me, disappearing and reappearing between trees. He had taken his sweatshirt off and tied it around his waist.

What did he care about? Not his mother or sister. He thought only about himself.

'What's your problem?' I said.

'I beg your pardon?'

'I care about lots of things, for your information.'

'OK.' He turned away. His new arm muscles were glistening.

'What did your question even *mean*?'

'I thought perhaps you had an opinion, Meg. Let's get the tree.'

'I have opinions!' I shouted. 'What does it matter what I think about the politicians? What difference does it make?'

'A country is made up of individual opinions.'

'Rubbish! What difference does Mum make? None!'

'You're wrong.' He picked up the axe and stalked off.

I watched him, seething. I felt robbed of my position at home, of my closeness with Dad. 'What are you doing back here, Simon?' I shouted.

He didn't stop walking.

'Why do you keep hanging around Dad, hey?'

Still he ignored me.

'Need more money?'

I bit my lip. I had gone too far.

In a few strides Simon was standing in front of me, so close that I felt his spittle. I'd never seen him that angry before. He looked like he wanted to shake me. I felt intensely alive.

'I thought I'd screw your best friend. She's a dog on heat around me.'

At first his words didn't make sense. I stared at him. Then in a delayed realisation, I gasped and stepped backwards.

'This is the new South Africa, Meg. Us coloureds are allowed to answer back.'

I fled, running, slipping, tripping over needles and roots and tree stumps down the mountain. When I reached the bottom, blood prickling out of the scratches on my ankles and palms, I turned to find myself alone. I was so angry that he hadn't followed me that I screamed, 'You ruin everything in my life!'

I ran along the fence line as far as I could, until I doubled over from the pain in my chest. Simon's eyes burnt into my vision. He hated me. I shuddered. What did he mean 'dog on heat'? Did he really mean that – no, surely not! I sat down. Calm down, I told myself. He'd be off to university soon. Probably even before Xanthe got back and then everything would be fine. But as I forced my breath to slow, he sat down next to me.

I pressed my knuckles into my eyes to block him out. Hannes had once told me of a baboon he had shot. When the animal had seen Hannes' gun and realised he was trapped, he'd gouged out his eyes rather than face his death.

'Old Witbooi is still alive and kicking.' Simon broke the silence. 'He must be like 150 by now. And how's about that new mechanics store.' He whistled. '*Lar-ny** for little old Leopold.'

'It's not new,' I mumbled. 'It's been here at least a year.'

'Kind of new then.'

I opened my eyes. Darts of red and yellow criss-crossed my vision.

He picked up a stone and chipped away at the dry earth. 'How's school?'

Back to Xanthe. 'Considering I'm on holiday, fine.' I scooped up a handful of needles and jabbed their pointy tips into my leg. The leadenness in my heart threatened to leak out into my veins and stop my blood. I knew it was my cue to apologise, but after what he'd said about Xanthe, I couldn't.

'Stop trying to be friends, OK? You think you're God's gift to . . . everyone, with your fancy accent and your big overseas talk – well, I'm not taken in. Leave me alone.' I paused. 'And my friend too.'

Teetering at the top of the stepladder, I tried to lasso the string of Christmas lights around the top branches of the tree.

'This is the best one ever!' Mum enthused from beneath me. 'The best pine tree.'

I was still too shocked by the afternoon to answer. Simon had walked away from me without a word, and he'd been silent all the way home. Dad blamed me.

As I took a bauble from Mum's outstretched hand I looked down. I could tell by her tight mouth and the way her eyes

* Posh

185

darted backwards and forth that she was practising immense restraint not to say, 'Two hands!'

'Is everything alright, Meg?' she asked.

'I'm fine,' I muttered.

'Are you sure you want to go to Xanthe's? You don't have to,' Mum said a few minutes later.

'Of course I'm sure!' I shouted, wobbling in my violent reaction. I was now more sure than ever. The stepladder shook. Mum's eyes darted to the bauble in my hand.

I had to get away. I longed to be at Xanthe's almost as much as the prospect terrified me.

'They're different to us,' Mum said.

'What do you mean?'

'Their values.'

'What do you know about their values? You've only met Shirley once!'

'That's another thing.' She held out her hand to me, to help me down, but I ignored her.

The orange bauble was cupped in my hand, like a baby chick, the way Simon had taught me to do. 'Are you saying that I can't go?'

She smiled. 'You're fifteen years old, Meg, of course you can go. Only –' She sighed and looked around the room, as if her next sentence was waiting for her on the window sill, 'Know who you are. Don't be too impressed by otherness; it's nothing more than a façade.'

'Just because you ran away from the world, you think you're better than everyone else. But I *want* to be like them!' I shouted. The bauble flew out of my hand and smashed to the ground.

Even before the million splintered fragments of glistening orange and gold had settled I was clambering down. 'I'm sorry, Mummy,' I tried to reach her across the room. 'I'm so sorry.'

'It's only a bauble, Meg,' she said, and left the room.

CHAPTER TWENTY

Xanthe lived in a leafy suburb of Cape Town – in a double-storey Victorian house nestled into a tapestry of green. A thick cover of trees cascaded down the mountainside to the edge of their garden. It seemed incredible that this mountain, so green and flat and neat, was made of the same rock as the jagged, parched peaks back at home.

I had always longed to live in a double-storey house. Ours was squat and heavy – a tired, swollen-ankled matron. Xanthe's in comparison was a leggy model. A ground-floor veranda and upstairs balcony ran along the front and right-hand side. The long, thin poles that supported the veranda and the upstairs balcony looked elegant and sleek. Dove-grey wrought-iron broekie lace* decorated the underside of the upstairs balcony – jewelled fringes to this fine lady's gown.

I followed Xanthe up the garden path. A bamboo wind-chime hanging from the branch of an oak tree knocked lazily against itself.

'My mother has discovered *feng shui*,' said Xanthe, turning back to make a face. She led me up the steps of the veranda

* Ornate ironwork typically found on Victorian buildings

188

and in through the front door.

'Feng what?' I asked.

Pale floorboards ran the length of the wide front hall, across to the staircase. A suggestion of jasmine blossom floated in the air. Our house smelled of polish and thatch. To the left was a dining room; to the right, through a set of glass-paned doors, was a large sitting room across from which French doors opened onto the veranda, the garden and the mountain above.

'Feng shui,' said Xanthe. 'After her trip to Hong Kong last year she changed the whole house around, to keep the dragons out.'

'No, no!' Shirley had caught up with us, 'It's to allow the dragon free access through our house on its way down the mountain to the sea.'

'The dragon,' said Xanthe slowly, looking at Shirley.

'Why not?' With an expansive sweep of her arms, as though in an aerobics class, Shirley illustrated the dragon's passage down the mountain, in through the French doors, across the hall and out through the dining room. Shirley's hands hovered in the air as we examined the dragon's exit point – a rather small window.

'It's a bit of a squeeze for it to get out, but your father wouldn't hear of me putting in another set of doors.' She shrugged her shoulders. 'So I leave it open all the time.'

Xanthe shook her head. I turned away to stop myself from giggling. Inside the sitting room was a gleaming baby grand piano. On its closed lid was a vase of blue chrysanthemums and a cluster of silver-framed photographs.

'Do you play?' I asked Xanthe.

189

'I don't think it works. My mother bought it so that she had somewhere to put the photographs.'

'Xanthe!' Shirley laughed. I stepped closer. A few of the pictures were of Xanthe's parents together. Shirley held the same pose in each one – her arms around her husband's waist and a wide, radiant smile. His name was Alan – I remembered from the prize-giving lunch. He stood tall and stiff, one hand on his hip, staring intently at the camera – his brows drawn over the dark pools of his eyes. There was only one picture of him laughing: he was holding a fish a metre long. Even his eyes twinkled, as though the person taking the picture had said something very funny.

There were a lots of Xanthe: lounging on the back of a boat; sitting next to Alan on the steps in front of some ancient ruins – Rome, perhaps, or Greece. Simon would know, I thought and bristled at the thought of him. Another picture was of her standing in front of the Eiffel Tower, looking bored. I smiled. Only Xanthe could be bored in front of the Eiffel Tower. The rest of the pictures were of a podgy blonde child with a wide, impish smile. I leaned forward to peer at the little girl in a pink ballet tutu, standing on tippy-toes, ready to twirl away.

'Oh!' I said and looked up.

Xanthe laughed.

Shirley stepped beside me. 'My blonde baby,' she said, shaking her head. 'If you had that hair you wouldn't cover it in a mucky black dye, would you?'

'No, I wouldn't,' I said.

'Come and put your bag down, Meg. I thought about putting you in the guest room, but you can't very well have midnight feasts when you're all the way down the passage, can you?

'What?' Xanthe wrinkled up her nose.

'Midnight feasts, painting each other's toenails, swapping secrets. I remember it all!' said Shirley, leading the way upstairs.

Xanthe looked back at me and rolled her eyes.

At the entrance to Xanthe's room I stopped. She had my curtains! Not my disgusting purple ones, but the curtains I'd imagined would change my life. Metres of the beautiful fabric billowed gently in the breeze, from the top of the tall sash window, gathering in an indulgent pile on the carpet.

'Wow!' I breathed. A quilt was folded over the end of her cast-iron bedstead. It was made of striped fabric in the same green and buttercup yellow as the curtains. Along the far wall was another window. This one had a deep seat. I could spend days there, reading and dreaming.

'I love these curtains!' I said. 'It's Biggie Best fabric, isn't it?' I said, running my hand over the quilt.

'If you say so. Stop stroking my bed.'

I laughed. In a room like this I would always be happy.

Shirley arrived carrying a set of towels. 'We are going to have so much fun!'

'Go, Mother!'

The sudden silence left behind by the banished Shirley made a week seem a long time. I remembered Xanthe lying on my bed the first time she came to lunch. It felt like such a long time ago, and yet I still couldn't think of anything to say. 'How was Christmas?' I asked.

'Fine,' Xanthe shrugged. 'Usual.'

I thought back to the excruciating weeks of waiting, to the

191

irrational fear I had felt that something would prevent the trip from happening. And what of that day at Hannes' farm, of Simon's words? I had thought at home that I'd ask her what he meant, but standing now in Xanthe's room I knew it was another thing I couldn't ask her about. I busied myself with my bag.

Xanthe picked up my copy of *Emma*. I had packed it imagining the two of us lying by the pool, reading our setwork books. She reached across to a small writing desk and chucked a large yellow book on it in my direction.

I picked it up. 'Why would you buy the study guide?'

'Why would you read the book?'

'You read Chekhov.'

'Chekhov is short. Chekhov says what he means and is done. This –' she fanned through my book – 'is like spending 450 pages inside my mother's head.'

I found things that I loved in every corner of Shirley's house. I loved the floral wallpaper in the downstairs loo, and the way the little soaps had been arranged in a patterned dish. I loved the deep green-covered loungers around the side of the pool. Shirley's tea, served in botanical print porcelain mugs, tasted different to the tea at home. We ate homemade toasted granola sitting on bar stools at the breakfast island in the kitchen. Beth would die, I thought; she believed breakfast islands to be the height of sophistication. The floral fabric on the peg bag hanging up on the back of the kitchen door matched the oven gloves and the apron Shirley wore to do the washing-up. They were a set. It made my scalp tingle.

On Friday morning, the day after I arrived, Shirley stood at the bottom of the stairs, handbag over her right shoulder. Her orange-red lipstick – 'Hawaiian coral', I decided – matched her fresh nails. As we descended, Xanthe in her Doc Martin boots and skinny jersey dress, I in my jeans and polo shirt, she said: 'Meg looks so pretty and neat, don't you think, Xanthe?'

'Doesn't she,' replied Xanthe.

Outside, Shirley stopped to lock the security gate. 'I don't know where Wellington is today. I'm at my wits' end with that man.'

'Didn't his father die?' asked Xanthe.

'That was a month ago. He took two weeks to bury his father. But if it's not one thing, it's the other. Two months ago he had to go to an uncle's funeral, before that an aunt. Three funerals in three months. How much family can one man have?'

As we snaked through the garden, Shirley pointed to the yellow rose bushes. 'See my Germiston Golds, Meg. They never let me down. And look at my water feature in the corner! The birds go mad for it.' The interior of her car gleamed. Instead of map books curling out from the seat pockets and sweet wrappers stuffed into the ashtrays, there was a tube of Wet Wipes.

Shirley returned to the problem of Wellington. 'Don't get me wrong, I feel for him. I lent him money to pay for his father's funeral, don't tell your father, Xanthe, he'd kill me if he knew. And I've never found out what happened to that Mont Blanc pen of your father's. I don't like to think.' She sighed. 'Does your mother have the same domestic issues up there in the Karoo?' she asked, facing me as she reversed down the drive. I

193

smiled, wondering whether I should explain that we didn't live in the Karoo, that Leopold was part of the greater Cederberg Mountain region, and only three hours away, as opposed to the Karoo that was five hours away and where there was hardly a *koppie*, let alone a mountain.

Shirley didn't like silences. The subject did not matter; she skipped happily from cousin Nicole in England who had forgotten to phone her mother on her birthday, to Mary from bridge who was having a new kitchen put in. Shirley did not approve of this; there was nothing wrong with the old one. But then Judy had had new curtains in her sitting room and Mary had always been competitive.

Xanthe ignored her. She fiddled with the radio stations, jumping between Radio Good Hope and Radio Five, so it was left to me to 'yes' and 'no' and laugh at the appropriate moments.

We turned onto the freeway, following an arc along the edge of the suburbs that nestled at the bottom of the mountain. As we passed a sign for Newlands Forest and Rhodes Memorial, Shirley interrupted herself and said: 'Don't you think it would be lovely to climb the mountain, darling?'

'No,' replied Xanthe.

'We can walk up Skeleton Gorge. Make a day of it.'

'Madge is sick of the mountains. It's all she knows.'

Shirley smiled at Xanthe and patted her thigh. 'You're a very thoughtful girl,' she said as she slowed the car down to stop for a red light.

Nelson Mandela was smiling at us from a poster, surrounded by happy children of all races. Next to the ANC's slogan, were the words: 'A better life for all.' In Leopold the ANC's posters were confined to the Camp.

'Lock your doors!' Shirley shouted, leaning over Xanthe to push down the knob. She swivelled around to make sure I obeyed. Ahead of us, making their way through the three lanes of cars, were two boys of Beth's age. One was selling boxes of grapes, the other bunches of roses. 'I don't drive into town anymore if I can help it. It's full of hooligans,' said Shirley in a low voice, not taking her eyes off the boys.

As she pulled away, a mini-bus taxi cut in front of her. The car jerked as she braked. 'Look at that! "Bad Boy",' she said, reading the name on the back of the van. 'Bad Boy indeed!' At the next set of traffic lights Shirley pulled up in the lane next to 'Bad Boy'. She hooted, leaned forward and shook her fist at the driver. 'Where's your blooming licence?' she shouted at him, through her shut window. The driver, dreadlocks piled high in his rasta hat, laughed and turned his music up until the van was rocking to the *doof-doof-doof* of the base.

'Outrageous,' Shirley tutted. 'They're out of control.'

Eventually, after starting along a one-way street and a traffic-stopping three-point turn, Shirley pulled up opposite Greenmarket Square. 'I'll see you here at three o'clock. Be careful of your bags. There are so many skollies around these days.'

Xanthe planted a kiss on Shirley's forehead and slammed the door behind her.

'Thank you very much,' I said, trying to keep up.

We stood on the pavement facing the market, watching Shirley drive away. 'That woman is the perfect example of someone who has never learnt to think,' said Xanthe.

I laughed. 'Mothers who think are no use to anyone.'

Xanthe shook her head. 'She sits alone in that house all day, worrying about her garden and how to fill her sandwiches at her next bridge day. You don't see it, Madge, but your mum is cool.'

The last few storeholders were setting up, filling the air with the clanking of metal poles. Seagulls swirled and squawked in the morning sun. Across the road a group of traders leaned against a trestle table drinking from styrofoam cups. They were watching a man offloading T-shirts from his van. The man's belly spilled out between his top and shorts and was mismatched with his bendy legs. He reminded me of the pictures we used to draw of Father Christmas – a circle for his belly and two sticks for his legs. Suddenly he dropped a large pile of shirts and rushed into the road, waving his arms and shouting at a bakkie that was about to reverse into his van. '*Jislaaik boetie!** Look with your eyes! You crash into my van, you write off my life!'

The coffee drinkers laughed.

To their left a tall, very dark man with a collection of carved giraffes and hippos was in an animated conversation with a passer-by on the other side of the road. His rapid soft-syllabled speech made me think he must have travelled a long way with those animals.

I followed Xanthe into the market. We passed a table of Kenyan baskets. Bright sarongs looped around the top of the stall. The green, red, yellow and turquoise fabric flapped, <u>festival-like,</u> as though everyone was making a special effort

* Jeepers, my brother!

for me. How exotic to be a storeholder and be surrounded by so many people every day! The parched, dust-covered Leopold was a faded dream. Here anything could happen.

Xanthe pulled my wrist. 'The first thing we need to do is replace that horrible shirt.'

I looked down at the white polo shirt I'd asked for especially for Christmas.

Xanthe stopped in front of a spread of psychedelic tie-dyed T-shirts. She held up one and handed it to me. Concentric circles of green, pink, blue and yellow radiated outwards.

I took a breath. 'That's very bright.'

'It's perfect. Put it on behind that mirror.'

I stood in front of the mirror, staring at the loud top. Xanthe grabbed the polo shirt I had tossed to the side. She beckoned over a street child that was hanging around and gave it to him.

'Xanthe! It's brand new. My mum will –'

Xanthe and the boy looked at me.

'Forget it,' I muttered.

Xanthe clapped her hands in satisfaction at the T-shirt, her mouth spread unconsciously into a smile.

'Peace, sister,' said the longhaired stallholder, as I paid for the top.

'Peace,' I agreed, which made Xanthe laugh.

Past the drums and the counterfeit CDs and the shorts made from recycled maize bags, I stopped at a stall selling rings. Some of them were plain silver bands; others were decorated with black and white ying-yangs. One tray was full of skulls and cross bones. Right in the front was a collection of rings with semi-precious stones – moonstones, quartz and cats' eye.

Some of the stones were fatter than your finger, others small enough for a child to wear. A row of turquoise stones set into silver rings caught my eye. Beth loved rings. In a rush of guilt at her at her being stuck at home while I was here, I chose one for her. As I paid for the ring, I pointed to a tray of the smallest rings I'd ever seen. 'Those are tiny!'

'Toe rings,' replied the bare-chested stallholder. He had a large tattooed lizard crawling up his arm. Its tail wound around the bulge of his bicep.

I laughed, 'What, like a ring for your toe?'

'That's right.' He looked at me as if I was backward.

'Oh.' I hurried away.

The market was filling up. We jostled and squeezed between knots of shoppers leaning over tables. As we stood to one side to let a family pass, I looked towards a small clearing where children were performing acrobatics. My heart plummeted. Standing amongst the crowd was Simon. 'Oh no!' I said.

'What?'

I strained to see him, but he had moved. I saw his head again, coming towards us. He disappeared and was suddenly in front of me. 'Thank God!' The boy looked nothing like him. 'I thought I saw Simon for a moment.'

'But he's not here,' said Xanthe.

'What do you mean?'

'Jeez, I don't mean anything. I thought he was in Leopold.'

'Xanthe!' called a gravelly voice. 'Hey, Xanthe, wait up!'

We turned about, in search of its owner.

'Here, man!' A tall girl with straggly blonde hair emerged from behind the 'Crazy About Cape Town' T-shirts. She had on the same Doc Martins as Xanthe, black leggings and an oversized lumberjack shirt.

'Howzit, Xanth,' she grinned. 'Thought you'd fallen off the planet.'

'Karen! Don't ask.' Xanthe shook her head.

'Did your parents really send you to that school?' asked Karen, pulling a pack of Peter Stuyvesant cigarettes from her bag and offering one to Xanthe. I waited for her to offer one to me, trying to think up a clever way of saying no, but she put them back in her bag.

Xanthe and Karen lit up.

'It is the arse-end of the world,' said Xanthe, blowing out a stream of smoke. The cloud hung about her.

I laughed, not knowing what else to do.

Karen looked at me in surprise.

'I'm Meg,' I said.

'Hi,' she said, 'Nice top.'

Xanthe flashed me a smile of triumph.

'Fuck man,' Karen continued, returning to Xanthe, 'What a bummer.'

Xanthe nodded. 'It's everything you've heard, only ten times worse.'

By now I thought my smile would split my face in two. And yet for all my manic grinning, I seemed to be invisible to them.

'Why don't you come to the Heidelberg tonight? They hardly ever check for IDs anymore,' said Karen.

Xanthe's face brightened at the suggestion. Then she remembered me and sighed. 'I'd better not.'

I looked away. In the silence that followed, I imagined them exchanging a glance.

'Pity,' said Karen, not sounding particularly concerned, 'Give me a call when you're, uh, free. Bye . . .'

'Meg,' I said again.

As she disappeared into the stalls, I turned and picked up the closest thing to me, while I tried to blink away my tears.

'Let's go,' said Xanthe behind me but I didn't answer. I was sick of my life. Every time I believed that I wasn't that pathetic girl stuck in apparently the arse-end of the world, reality marched up and spat in my face. Karen couldn't even remember my name for five minutes. I didn't belong here, even if Xanthe had invited me.

Then I remembered that it had been Shirley who'd invited me to stay, out of an obligation to my parents. Xanthe was probably counting the days until I left.

A fat man wearing a Springboks rugby shirt jostled past me, pushing me against the edge of table. I wanted to be back at home, on the stoep, staring out over the empty garden.

'Madge, hey, what are you doing? Why do you want that?'

I blinked and focused on what I'd picked up. It was an ostrich egg. Hand-painted angular Bushmen with fat round bottoms and stilt-like legs clutched oversized bows. Glinting gold arrows flew all around them. 'What? No!' I let go of it in surprise and stepped back.

We watched it fall and disintegrate into tiny pieces around my feet. Xanthe started laughing and pulled my arm. I turned to the stall owner, but he had his back to us, talking to a tourist dressed from hat to socks in khaki. Xanthe pulled my arm again and we ran, weaving and pushing along the narrow paths between the stalls, squeezing through the crowd around the second-hand books, the bright animal mobiles, the wide-rimmed leather hats. I laughed in gasps as we ran, not daring to look back until we reached the edge of the market. I followed Xanthe across the cobbled road to the stone steps in front of a church, where we flopped down. Each time we looked at each other, we started laughing until my tummy ached. I leaned back on the step behind me.

'Why don't you want to go that place?' I asked, my eyes against the sun on my face.

'Karen's full of shit. They always check for ID at the Heidelberg,' she replied.

'You have a fake ID?' I asked, although I knew the answer. 'You should go, I don't mind.' I opened my eyes. 'I'm sorry about earlier, I was –'

Xanthe stood up. 'Come on, let's go.'

'I thought you were going to –'

'I saw a dress I like,' said Xanthe, talking over me. 'Come *on*, Madge, there's so much more to do.'

I lay awake that night. Police sirens and cars passing on the road below were a constant reminder that I was surrounded by city life yet I felt as alone as I did in my bed at home.

Xanthe turned over in her sleep.

Visions of the day flashed back at me. I loved the market and the freedom of being dropped off for the day. Then, when I met Karen it had all gone wrong. I had failed a test, Karen's test. Friendship with Xanthe felt exhausting. It hadn't felt that way with Simon, but then I supposed Simon hadn't been a real friend.

CHAPTER TWENTY-ONE

There was no sign of breakfast when we arrived downstairs the next morning. It was New Year's Eve. Newspapers covered every kitchen surface. Shirley was in her cotton nightgown. Next to her was Lizzie, Shirley's maid. They were studying the papers.

'What have those men achieved, Lizzie? That's what I don't understand,' Shirley said.

Lizzie clicked her tongue. 'They are mad for blood.'

'Who is mad for blood?' asked Xanthe, leaning over Shirley's shoulders. 'Oh my God!' She went pale, looking up at me quickly, and then back at the paper. 'That's the Heidelberg! What happened?' Lizzie shuffled out of the way to make room for Xanthe.

'Three men burst in there early this morning and opened fire on the full bar. On their way out they shot the man from the Portuguese café who was standing on the street. They had no reason other than to kill.'

'Fuck!' said Xanthe.

Shirley smacked her hand.

'Were lots of people hurt?' asked Xanthe.

'It says three women were shot. Young girls,' said Shirley.

Xanthe mouthed the word 'Karen!' at me. I sucked in my breath and stared at the pictures. If it hadn't been for me, Xanthe might have gone. If it hadn't been for the ID-checking, I might have gone. The horror of the pictures seemed more like a movie scene than a bar twenty minutes down the road. Suddenly Mum's St James massacre victims came horrifically into focus. They became people, whereas before they had simply been part of Mum's general diatribe.

'Have you spoken to Judy today?' Xanthe asked Shirley, with studied casualness. She picked up a carton of orange juice.

'I called her first thing,' Shirley replied.

'Karen OK?' asked Xanthe, looking at me.

'Fine,' said Shirley, looking up at the question. 'Do you want to invite her around for a swim?'

'Nah,' said Xanthe, and left the room with the carton of orange juice.

Mum was beside herself. The papers hadn't been delivered in Leopold that morning, so she had nothing more than the national radio reports about the massacre to go by. She made me read her every article.

'And what does *The Argus* say?' came her voice down the phone line.

I sighed. '"Heidelberg Pub Massacre. Four die, six injured as gunmen blast popular Observatory tavern." There's a picture of an ambulance guy picking up the body of a woman, and one of some men helping another, and one of a guy sitting with his head in his hands.' I looked longingly through the door towards the kitchen, where Shirley, in her distress, had cooked a full English breakfast. Mine was untouched as Mum gabbled on. 'And they say APLA have claimed responsibility for it?' she asked for the second time.

'Yes, Mum, whoever they are.'

'For goodness' sake, Meg! They're the armed wing of the PAC.'

'OK,' I said. I wound the phone cord around my finger.

'The Pan African Congress,' she elaborated slowly.

'Yup,' I replied. The coils had become twisted. There was an ugly hiccup to the pattern halfway along the cord that hadn't been there before I had started fiddling. I panicked. I was in Xanthe's dad's study. The room gleamed like a hospital theatre. From our one meeting he seemed the sort of man who cared about ugly hiccups in the phone cord.

'What happens now?' said Mum. I assumed she was musing, but when she said nothing more, I realised she was waiting for an answer.

'Life goes on, I guess,' I mumbled eventually.

'For the lucky ones.'

I rolled my eyes.

'Are you having a lovely time?'

'Yes.' The phone cord was fixed.

'And you're being polite, cleaning up after yourself?'

'Mo-ther!'

I heard Beth shouting in the background.

'Hang on, Beth,' Mum said. 'What have you been up to, Meg?'

'Stuff.' I was bored.

A deeply dissatisfied silence issued forth from Mum. I gave in. 'Greenmarket Square market, the beach, a bit of shopping.'

'That sounds lovely! Any plans for tonight?' Mum's attempt at sounding casual and gossipy did not work.

'Drugs,' I replied, 'lots of them. And unprotected sex.'

'Honestly, Meg –'

'We're going to the beach for supper. And maybe some fireworks.'

'Thank you. We're not really –'

'We've had pizza – twice!' Beth's voice shouted into the phone, 'And Coke, every day, and Mum and Dad let me watch *Dirty Dancing* –'

'Wow,' I said, and yawned for effect.

'I'm not finished! And Mum's bought me a pile of new clothes!'

In the background Mum laughed and said, 'That's a gross exaggeration!'

'And,' Beth paused for effect, 'Simon and I went canoeing all day on the dam.'

'Hooray!' I said. I didn't care how Simon chose to spend his time. At the same time, I was relieved to know he wasn't here.

'Yip. We had so much fun he wanted to do it again today, but he had to catch the early bus.'

'Where was he going?'

Beth sighed in exasperation. 'The bus only goes to Cape Town.'

Later that morning I sat on the porch, and nursed a cup of tea. Why would Simon be coming to Cape Town? It must be to visit his aunt and cousins, or perhaps his larny school friends. Shirley and Wellington were busy in the flowerbeds. Wellington rested on his haunches, muddy gumboots over his blue overalls in the middle of the bed while Shirley was primly positioned on the edge of the grass, on her floral print gardener's mat, wearing gardening gloves and a sun visor. As she bent forward two diagonal stripes of her pants appeared across her shorts in a 'v'. Every now and then she'd say something to Wellington, who'd grunt in reply. I closed my eyes, and leaned my head back against the wall, lulled by the late morning sun and the distant hum of a lawnmower.

'Eh! Those two!'

I opened my eyes. Lizzie stood next to me.

Her soft body cushioned out from her baby-pink maid's outfit. She held a tin of Brasso and polishing cloth and at my glance made a half-hearted attempt at the front door knocker but soon enough she was leaning against the front door frame, soaking up the sun behind me.

'Uh-uh. Tennis, bridge or the garden.' She counted off the options on her fingers. '"Why do I employ a gardener, Lizzie?" says Mister Alan when he phones.' She laughed. 'All day in the garden, bent over those flowers. And all the time talking to Wellington.'

'What does she talk about?'

Lizzie chuckled. 'A river flows. Some days it's fast, other days slow. Some days deep, sometimes shallow. But it's always water.'

Shirley straightened. 'No, Wellington! *Haai*, my friend! We need to clear there,' she pointed to her left, 'and there.' Her hand swept around the far edge of the bed.

Obediently, Wellington got up and repositioned himself with his garden fork. Lizzie looked at me and shook her head. 'You looking for Miss Xanthe?' she asked suddenly, remembering why I was there.

'No. She's inside I think,' I mumbled. Since making a telephone call earlier, Xanthe had been in a mood.

'Where is your family?' asked Lizzie.

'Leopold,' I said.

She looked unimpressed.

'Near Piketburg,' I tried.

She shook her head, a slight frown on her face. After a few minutes, she said, 'Is it near PE?'

'No,' I replied, 'It's in the middle.'

'What do you think, Wellington?' Shirley's voice wafted back across the morning air. 'By the time we're done here, we'll have a garden fit for your new president, hey.' Shirley laughed. 'For Madiba.'

Wellington grunted.

Lizzie shook her head almost imperceptibly. 'He's a Zulu, Madam,' she scolded Shirley softly. 'Madiba is not the Zulus' president.'

Shirley sat back on her heels and stretched.

Lizzie was back polishing the knocker. 'Madam!' she called, a pre-emptive strike, 'Miss Judy called. I say you call right back.'

Shirley turned and smiled: 'Thank you, Lizzie,' and returned to her shrubs.

Every table in the restaurant was occupied by the time we sat down. The atmosphere crackled. People talked and laughed loudly, as though in competition with their next-door neighbours. We sat near the front of the restaurant, overlooking the palm tree-lined beach below. 'When my mum says "on the beach", she means a restaurant overlooking the beach,' Xanthe had explained earlier as she shook the bottle of Vixen nailpolish. 'Shirley doesn't do tomato sandwiches.'

I watched the clusters of families with blankets and cooler bags spread on the beach below us.

The waiters wore white vest tops, long blue aprons and jeans. They called each other 'babe' and 'sweetie'. The girl hovering next to Alan had long blonde hair scooped up into a high ponytail. She belonged on *Baywatch*.

'Champagne, I think,' said Alan, after a glance at the wine list.

'Ooh, yes,' said Shirley, 'I do like my bubbles.' She giggled in my direction. She was wearing a sparkly gold blouse that showed off her deeply tanned cleavage. Her cheeks were flushed.

I giggled too.

'Here we go,' said Xanthe.

She had drawn thick black eye liner across each lid. She looked incredible. I stole glances at myself in the mirror across the restaurant. Xanthe had made me wear a green dress she had found at Greenmarket Square. Shirley had done my eyes. 'Oh my God!' she'd said. 'Look at that! Just like Bridget Bardot!'

Alan looked around the table. Shirley was much more twittery around him. When he spoke his words were clipped and quick. 'Enjoying Cape Town, Meg?' he said as he passed the menu back to the waitress without looking at her.

'Yes, thank you very much,' I said quickly.

'Loosen up, Dad, you're scaring her,' said Xanthe.

'I'm fine,' I squeaked.

'How can you tell your father to loosen up?' Alan demanded, forgetting about me.

'You're killing the vibe,' said Xanthe.

Alan laughed. Shirley and I joined in after a fraction of a pause.

Our waitress returned with the bottle of champagne. 'Two glasses?' she asked Alan.

'Four,' said Xanthe.

'Oh, I don't know.' Shirley glanced in my direction.

'It's New Year, Shirl,' said Alan, 'we don't want to kill the vibe.'

The champagne was dry and bubbly. The champagne Mum and Dad occasionally drank at home was much sweeter. This filled my nostrils and made me want to sneeze.

'How did you do in the exams?' Alan returned to me.

'Alan, please,' Shirley tutted.

'Is it you we have to thank for helping Xanthe make such an improvement in science?' he said with a dismissive pat on Shirley's arm.

'Oh no, I had nothing to do with it,' I said quickly.

Alan sat back in his chair. 'Did you actually work for these exams?' he asked Xanthe.

Xanthe smiled.

'I always knew you were a sciences person.'

'Blah, blah, blah,' said Xanthe, grinning. Her eyes flickered up at Alan's and for a moment I saw the chubby blonde girl in the photographs again.

Alan looked across at his wife. 'Not like Shirl. Shirl's more

209

of an arts person.'

'Nothing wrong with the arts,' said Shirley.

After supper we drove around the coast to the next bay. Large boulder rocks that lined the shore divided the bay into four small beaches.

'We'll see you here, in Fourth Beach car park, not a minute after one o'clock. Fourth Beach, not Second or Third. Do you understand?' said Shirley.

'I'm quite sure the whole beach understands you,' said Alan and Shirley giggled.

'I've got to get my bag out the boot,' said Xanthe and when Shirley swivelled around, she added, 'Jerseys and stuff.'

'Clever girl. There's always a chilly wind in Cape Town.'

As Alan reversed the car, he shook his head and laughed.

'What?' said Shirley. 'It's perfectly true.'

The beach was dotted with groups of people come to see in the New Year. Some had lit small bonfires and sat around it. Others sat inside circles of glowing candles in brown paper bags. Several hi-fis competed with each other. A man with blonde dreadlocks and wearing multi-coloured clown trousers sat on an upturned crate strumming 'Bye-bye Miss American Pie' on his guitar.

'Hey, Bruce,' Xanthe called out as we passed. He looked up and nodded and in reply. Halfway down the beach Xanthe plonked down and unpacked the bag. The 'stuff' was a six-pack of beers. 'My dad won't miss them,' she said. She pulled out some sachets of clear liquid, bit them open and squirted the contents into each of our open cans. 'Flavour,' she grinned. The wolfish look was back.

The 'flavoured' beer tasted disgusting – bad enough to spit out. But Xanthe sipped it without making a face, so I did my best to copy her. A boy, not more than Beth's age, ran in front of us, carrying a bottle half full with bright green liquid. Two other boys ran after him. They tackled him to the ground and the bottle went flying. For a few seconds the three of them looked at the bottle and the green liquid that was seeping into the sand before starting to push and shout at each other.

'Kids, huh,' said Xanthe.

I managed to get through the first can of beer and started on the second, which tasted less toxic than the first. The stars wiggled out of their fixed positions. Shouts, singing, laughing and stereos melted into one happy background buzz.

Xanthe looked at her watch. 'I'm going down the beach to see if I can find some friends. They're always here at New Year,' she said.

'Shall I come?' I started to get up.

'No, no, you stay here with the bag and stuff. I won't be long.'

'OK.' I sat back down. The sand felt warm. I took off my shoes and squiggled my toes around in the sand. I could feel each grain of sand separately. I tried to estimate how many grains of sand would be in contact with each foot. I smiled and waved at passers-by. After what seemed like a long time but also none at all, the thought that I needed to find Xanthe popped up with a pinging sound, like a cash register. It was such a surprise to hear the noise that I sat up. I put everything into the bag and stood up. The sand felt very uneven. I dug my toes into the sand to steady myself. A few paces down the beach, after having weaved through and around and over groups of people, I stopped and looked back, in case she might have returned.

An arm hooked around my waist, a mouth clamped down on mine. The lips were hard and rough and chapped.

'I beg your pardon!' I said, taking a step back, trying to focus on the person in front of me. He was tall, with crinkly eyes and messy, shoulder-length brown hair.

He started laughing. 'Sorry, love. Wrong girl.' He had an English accent. 'Happy New Year, anyway,' he said and kissed me again before disappearing into the blur of people.

Someone had built up a bonfire in the middle of the sand and crowds of people sat around it, their faces luminescent in the orange light. Bruce the guitar player sat to the side, playing 'Sing us a song, you're the piano man'. He looked up as I passed, and winked at me. I walked on, hoping to bump into that strange boy again.

I found her, on the other side of the beach, where the boulders form a barricade at the edge of the sand. More precisely, I found her shoes. 'Xanthe!' I shouted, but the words were caught in my throat. I started running over the resisting sand.

At the shoes I stopped and started turning in a circle, in a panic so thick I could hardly see. Where the hell was she? *Water-water-sand-sand-sand-rocks* – a movement in the rocks made me stop. I blinked but could see nothing. The boulders ahead leaned over each other to form a hideaway of sorts, a cave. I walked towards the cave, with dreading feet. There again was the flash of movement and a leg – pale, almost luminescent. Had she passed out? How was I going to get her all the way up those steps to the car park?

And then I stopped. A hand appeared on the pale leg – long, dark fingers against the skin.

'Xanthe!' I screamed, running, my heart thumping in my ears, throwing myself over the endless sand, diving over the last distance, until I was in front of her. In front of them.

'Happy New Year, Madge,' she said. She sat up and tried to yank her dress back down over her tummy as I stared. I could not think. I could not breathe.

'What's the time?' asked Xanthe. In a quick movement she lifted her bum to pull her knickers back up.

I turned away and caught myself staring at Simon's crotch as he pulled up his trousers. A spasm caught me and I jerked my head back to Xanthe. She had seen that. She had been watching.

'Come on, then.' She crawled back out a few paces, stood up and pulled her blue dress down. She picked up her shoes and without a word or even a backwards glance at Simon, started walking back down the beach.

A few steps later I looked back, to make sure it was actually him. He was sitting on the sand, arms slung around his knees. He was looking at me, not at Xanthe, as if he had been waiting for me to look back. I heard his words again, *She's like a dog on heat*. I turned away, humiliated.

When I looked back again, Simon was staring out to sea.

CHAPTER TWENTY-TWO

Sleep was no refuge. I dreamt that I had drowned. I couldn't breathe. Something heavy, sticky and salty was wound across my neck and mouth. After a moment of panic I realised that it was my hair. I threw it off but couldn't stop shaking. I shut my eyes, forcing my breath to deepen until I felt my heart drop back out of my ears. The window above my stretcher bed was open. The breeze was so cold that I knew it must be very early, long before dawn. I was shivering and sick. I staggered into the lit bathroom and shut the door. My pink fingers clutched the white basin. I looked into the mirror, into this new version of me. Shirley's heavy mascara formed black rings around my bloodshot eyes. I looked ghoulish. I closed my eyes, but that brought back the image of Simon's crotch. I shuddered and opened them again quickly.

Simon had a birthmark, the colour of wine dregs, behind his right ear. It created the illusion of his right ear being bigger than the left. He used to say that he would know when he found his father as he would have a matching birthmark. The impossibility of this did not bother him.

I touched it once, when I was ten and he was fourteen. We

were behind the chicken coop. I wanted to know whether the dark patch felt any different to the rest of him. As I reached out and brushed it with the tips of my fingers, he turned and nudged me backwards, until my head knocked against the white-washed brick wall. Then he pressed his lips against mine and prised open my mouth with his tongue and stuck it inside. That moment marked the end of our friendship. A nail driven into dry wood, splitting it apart. I shoved him backwards and spat, until my mouth was dry. My spit lay between us – dark stains on the dry sand. By the time I looked up he was gone. After that day he'd stayed away from our house. From me.

I switched off the bathroom light. I knelt over the loo and stuck my fingers down my throat but nothing came out.

When I woke again Xanthe's bed was empty. I stood under the shower with my eyes closed and let the water chip away at my skull and shoulders. Back in her bedroom I sat down at her dressing table. I opened her drawer looking for something to get rid of the black smudges around my eyes. I rummaged through an untidy collection of ear buds, sticks of mascara, lipsticks and moisturising cream until I found some make-up remover. As I was about to close the drawer, I spotted a small cardboard box right at the back. I opened it, expecting a necklace, or a ring, but caught my breath. It was the fossil she had found that day in the mountains. How typical of Xanthe to steal it – after listening and nodding as Dad made his speech about not taking anything away. She took anything she wanted. I traced the spiral shape with my fingers, remembering that day, the heat and dust. I felt homesick and ashamed. Dad had trusted her.

215

I put the box back exactly where I found it. I wrapped the fossil in a pair of knickers and buried it at the bottom of my bag. I would take it back to where it belonged.

Xanthe was downstairs, lying on the sofa in the TV room. She pulled in her legs to make space for me, but I chose an armchair close to the door. I felt woozy, like my balance was gone. Seeing her, stretched out like a lazy cat had brought on the sensation of someone kicking at my brain with steel-capped boots.

I sat back into the chair, out of her grasp. 'How did Simon know you were at the beach? Did you plan it?'

She shrugged and picked up a *Homes & Garden* magazine.

'And by the way, how could you leave me, *drunk* and all alone? Anything could have happened to me.'

Xanthe dumped the magazine on the table and left the room. I followed her. I knew I was making her angry, but I didn't care.

'You owe me an explanation,' I said in the kitchen.

She opened the fridge door and then stopped. 'Why?'

'Because this is not how friends treat each other!'

'Your problem, Madge, is that you're living in an Enid Blyton book. Ginger beer?' She attempted an ironic smile as she held out a cold SodaStream bottle of water to me. When I didn't respond she shrugged and inserted the bottle into the machine. As I started speaking again she pulled down the lever and pressed the button. The *touf-touf-touf* drowned out everything I tried to say.

Eventually I gave up and shook her arm.

She shook me off, her hand on the button again.

'Xanthe!'

'What?' She stamped her foot.

216

'That's going to explode if you keep pressing it.'

She flung back the lever. As the bottle slid down the tube a whoosh of fizzy water spilled over her T-shirt and onto the floor.

'Fuck!' She banged the empty bottle on the counter and turned on me. 'You and your crazy little town, you don't get it. You're all so fucking weird – you, your family, and fucking Simon!' As she said his name she screwed up her eyes.

I wasn't surprised at her calling me or my family weird. That much was a given. What shocked me, tore at me, was the pain on her face as she said Simon's name.

Xanthe chucked her wet T-shirt in the direction of the back door. She turned to the sink to find a cloth. 'He helped me study for the science exam.'

'So? Why didn't you tell me?'

'Because you're so fucking weird about him –'

'I am not!'

She knelt down to mop up the water on the floor. 'Ja, right. Anyway, once I got to know him, I realised he's . . . unlike anyone I've ever met.'

I watched the knobbly line of her spine and ripple of ribs along her pale curved back, as pronounced as an exoskeleton. No one had ever said that about me.

Shirley bustled into the kitchen. 'Ha-lo-o! You won't believe the chaos out there. The whole world was trying to get to Woolies this morning. Traffic was a bladdy standstill. And it's so *hot*!' Shirley dumped her shopping bags on the breakfast island and wiped her brow. 'Huh!' She looked around. 'Tea is what I need.' She flicked the switch on the kettle and turned to Xanthe. 'Why are you semi-dressed? It's almost noon! Really

217

and truly!' She laughed.

I looked at Xanthe. She took a while to respond to Shirley. Without her tough outer layer, she seemed tiny. Simon had done it again. Not satisfied with merely beating me at school and at home, he'd taken Xanthe too.

That evening I stood in the kitchen, spooning Shirley's curried egg mixture into hard-boiled, halved egg whites. Judy and Stuart were coming for supper. 'Nothing fancy,' I had heard Shirley say into the phone after lunch. 'Whatever I find in the fridge.' She had been in the kitchen all afternoon.

'Thank you, sweetie,' Shirley bustled past me, 'I'm lost without Lizzie. But she always goes to church on New Year's Day – one of those eight-hour jobbies.'

It suited me. I'd stayed by the side of the pool all day, avoiding Xanthe and her parents. Everything was turning out horribly wrong. I was furious with Simon. I could not forget the twist of Xanthe's mouth as she said his name. I would never forgive him. I was furious with Xanthe, yet without her I wouldn't be in Cape Town. I would be at home, wishing away my life. More than anything, I was furious with myself.

An hour later Stuart and Judy arrived. Shirley was worried about the table we had set outside. Was it warm enough, was there enough light? She fussed and muttered and bustled about, until the moment she heard the front gate click. In an instant she whipped off her apron and turned around to greet her friends, as serene and composed as Mother Teresa. After a chorus of 'Happy New Year!' and 'Another one gone!' Judy presented an exquisite lemon meringue pie. The weightless tufts of whipped egg-white were cooked to the palest hint of beige. 'Oh, it's nothing.' She waved it away. Judy's smile transformed her face. The crow's feet that fanned out from the far corners of her eyes concertinaed up like a squash-box; her eyes twinkled, her mouth spread surprisingly wide. It made you want to smile back. But it faded quickly. The natural set of her face was pinched and anxious. Mum claimed that by the age of fifty you had the face you deserved. But Judy had probably never seen that look on her face. It seemed unfair for her to unconsciously give away so much about herself.

Judy kissed Xanthe on the cheek. 'Xanthe my darling! What a lovely surprise! I thought you'd be out jolling. I wish I could have made Karen come. She said she bumped into you at Greenmarket Square! She's at a party tonight, another party, at Grant McCullam's house. Tomorrow she's off to Plett*. I swear she treats me like a hotel. Do you know Grant McCullam?'

Xanthe shook her head, admirably disinterested.

'She runs rings around you,' Stuart's gruff voice cut in. Stuart looked like Alan – large, thick-set gingerbread men cut from the same mould – only Stuart had turned out more sloppy: he sagged around the tummy and neck.

'She does not!' laughed Judy uneasily.

'You have no idea who she hangs out with these days,' said Stuart, talking over his wife.

'I do too!' protested Judy. 'Tonight she's at the McCullams' house. You went to school with Pete McCullam, Stu. You've known that family forever.'

* Plettenberg Bay, a popular seaside town

219

'Piet *Skiet* McCullam!' laughed Alan from the far side of the Weber braai where he was tending a thick slab of fillet steak. 'Shot the maid, when he was a boy,' he said, I assumed for my benefit.

'It was a mistake!' Judy cried.

'He was cleaning his hunting rifle,' said Shirley, straightening a knife as she cast a last eye over the supper table, 'and it was only her toe.'

'Never could bowl a cricket ball either,' said Alan.

'He's done very well for himself, thank you very much,' said Judy. 'Big house in Constantia, pool, tennis court. All his kids in private school. Went to Italy on holiday last year –' she took a sip of wine – 'even took the kids.'

'After April there'll be no more overseas trips for anyone,' said Stuart.

Alan grunted.

Shirley dispatched Xanthe and me to the kitchen to fetch the salads, curried eggs and potato bake. As we returned I stopped in the light that splashed over the edge of the porch. The night was warm. The memory of a sea breeze hung through the air. Lights shone out from hiding places tucked away inside the beds that lined the perimeter of the property, illuminating the deep greens and purples of the dark garden. Alan was at the head of the table, his large frame stooped as he carved the meat. Stuart sat opposite him. Shirley and Judy were each settled to the right of their husbands. The flickering light from two fat church candles in the middle of the table shimmered in the tall wine glasses and bounced off their animated faces. As if on cue, the conversation erupted into a shout of raucous

220

laughter. Mum and Dad had never had an evening like this; they had no shared friends who knew them inside out. I wondered how different they would be, how different our life would be, if they did.

By the time I sat down the conversation had taken a more serious turn.

'It's too close now,' Judy said. 'Six months ago they burst in on a church full of people and randomly opened fire, and now its a tavern of young folk. And not only whites – there were coloureds and blacks there too. Those were innocent people minding their own business, thank you very much. What right do they have? That's not "freedom fighting", as they like to call it. I don't care what you say, they're bladdy terrorists.'

We waited as Judy wiped her eyes. Stuart leaned over and rubbed her back. After a moment she sat up with a resolute sniff and continued, 'Karen doesn't even know where the Heidelberg is, thank God, it's not her kind of a place, but where will it be next time? How do you protect your family from these people? What kind of a life is it when you don't feel safe going to church anymore?'

'It's a big bloody mess,' said Alan, standing up to pass the platter of thinly sliced steak to Shirley. 'If Mandela thinks he has the skills to sort it out after splitting open rocks on Robben Island for twenty-seven years, I say good luck to him.'

'Please, Alan, no politics tonight.'

But Shirley was drowned out by Stuart. 'I don't agree. We don't stand an arsehole's chance with a black government.' His glass landed heavily on the table.

Shirley looked nervously at Alan.

'I'm a businessman, Stu, I don't care who is in charge of the country – black, white – whatever. I care about my assets and I care about being allowed to get on with what it is that I want to do.'

'And you care about your family,' said Shirley.

'You're my biggest asset!' said Alan, winking at her.

'Don't be so rude!' shrieked Shirley.

Stuart shook his head. 'It's not that simple. Everything we have built up, everything our parents worked for – will be lost overnight. And it doesn't stop there. One day they're in charge of the country, the next thing your daughter will be marrying one of them.

'Stuart!' said Shirley.

'Why not? Isn't it every woman's fantasy?'

I spluttered on a mouthful of Coke, sending painful bubbles up the back of my nose.

'Stuart, please!' Judy glanced in my direction, 'That's not nice talk!'

'What do you think, Xanthe?' Stuart bulldozed on.

I looked at Xanthe. Yes, I thought, what do you think? And what do you think your parents and their friends would say if they knew what you were up to last night?

'I don't see why not. Half the Afrikaner nation is mixed blood as it is.'

Alan chuckled and winked at Xanthe.

But Stuart didn't appreciate Xanthe's answer. 'I, for one, will not be allowing Karen to run off with the first Sipho* she comes across.'

* A Xhosa boys' name

222

Xanthe's smile was unreadable.

'Have some more wine, Stu.' Alan stretched across the table with a full bottle. Shirley turned her back on Stuart and made frantic 'time-out' signals at Alan. I was unutterably grateful Mum was not here. It made me shudder to think what she'd make of Stuart. It was too easy in Leopold to label Afrikaans and racist together. But here were English-speaking people, as well educated and well travelled as Mum, saying things that surely belonged to 'the enemy'.

'There is a list of properties that the new "cabinet"' – Stuart's fingers formed quotation marks –'have chosen for themselves.'

Alan laughed uproariously. 'Stuart, you don't seriously believe –'

'It's true,' Judy cut in. 'Bishops Court, Constantia: whatever takes their fancy. Soon they'll be slaughtering sheep and brewing beer under our noses.'

Alan sat back in his chair, enjoying himself. Shirley glanced in our direction and mouthed: 'Plates!' with a jerk of her head towards the kitchen. Xanthe settled deeper into her chair.

'Have you started stockpiling tins yet, Judith?' Alan asked, leaning forward with an earnest face.

'Too right.' Judy looked like a ruffled hen. 'And light bulbs.'

'Light bulbs!' said Alan. 'But when the revolution comes there'll be no electricity anyway.'

Judy looked to Stuart. He leaned forward, tapping his finger on the table. 'When the revolution comes, we're out of here.'

Shirley sat back in protest. Alan smiled and toyed with the saltshaker.

Silence rested on the table. There were no cicadas or crickets

223

or frogs. There wasn't even a moon; it was blocked out by the wide strokes of high-level clouds. A burglar alarm went off nearby, piercing the darkness. 'Bladdy cat again,' Shirley muttered.

'You've got to know when to think of yourself. And your family,' Stuart said eventually. 'You've got to know when to jump.'

Judy nodded in agreement.

'Oh, for pity's sake!' said Shirley. 'I am not Australian or Canadian! This is my home – I could never leave. You can for-*get* it.' She smacked the edge of the table.

'Thirty years ago you were having such a good time in Europe you didn't want to come home!' Alan, softened by the wine, rubbed her arm.

Shirley sniffed. 'Thirty years ago the rand was as valuable as the pound. Now, we would be poor wherever we went. And what about my garden, my roses? I'm too old to start again.'

'Speaking of starting again, did you hear about the van Niekerks? Unbelievable. That man couldn't hold onto his money even if it was glued to his body . . .' Alan's voice rumbled on and the conversation changed course. The candles were swimming in their wax, rivulets spilling over the top and down the sides.

As the talk around the table drifted to people and places I knew nothing of, the words became sounds and rhythm and space between sounds, like flat palms on a drum.

I breathed out. In the last few days I had seen and heard so many shocking things that I didn't know what to think. '*Not waving, but drowning,*' said Mum's 'quoting voice' in my head. But what did I feel? I felt like a page divided up into tiny squares and triangles. I was orange and purple and white. I was a light shade of pink and a murky, dirty brown. I was a raw and painful red. I was a silly, spotty, pointless green. I was an infinite blue. As long as I could keep the violent red from soaking through into the ethereal blue, everything would be fine.

CHAPTER TWENTY-THREE

I was happy to be home at first. My contentment lasted all the way out the car and in through the front door. But as it swung shut behind me, the shuttered house rubbed itself back into my skin and I yielded to gloom. I couldn't be outside. The light was too bright, the grass underfoot felt serrated. Eating made my jaw ache. My bones didn't fit into their sockets. Mum's eyes followed me, the line of her mouth small and tight. The only bearable place was on my bed, with my body perfectly still so that I could focus my mind into a place of silence. I had climbed inside the heart of misery and, despite Mum's threats, I had no intention of 'snapping out of it'.

Two days passed as I lay under the disgusting curtains. The careful calm I had maintained throughout the visit to Xanthe was ruined. The spotty green leaked into the pointless pink. The orange and purple muddied the bright white. Soon I was a stagnant brown I could neither shift nor make sense of.

I picked up my setwork book, but it did nothing for my mood. *Emma* deserved a fat slap, the silly bitch. She had everything, yet she spent her time fannying about, interfering with the likes of poor Harriet, who didn't have much going for her.

But instead of getting her just deserts, Emma landed the hero, whereas her much-wronged friend ended up with a farmer. I knew this because I'd skipped to the end.

On the evening of the second day I watched the gathering shadows harden into dark. Night soaked through the open curtains and settled in the room. The saccharine theme tune of *Beverly Hills 90210* drifted through the house. It must be nine o'clock.

A gecko appeared on the windowpane. Its tiny intestines made a dark silhouette against its translucent underbelly, like a specimen on a microscope slide. I watched the little sucker feet propelling it upwards and shuddered. Geckos' feet gave me the creeps. One of my greatest fears was waking up in the middle of the night with one crawling over my face.

Then I noticed the moth knocking against the top of the window, *flutter-flutter-bang, flutter-flutter-bang*, consumed in its own stupidity, unaware of the danger creeping closer. I wasn't sure whose side I was on. Did the moth, obsessed only with getting through the impenetrable sheet of glass, deserve to get away? Geckos killed moths – that was the nature of things. Who was I to alter that? All the same, I felt an overwhelming impulse to tap on the glass, to intervene on behalf of the moth. I couldn't watch, knowing what was about to happen.

When I returned from the bathroom, the gecko and moth had been replaced by Mum and Dad.

I retreated to the corner of my bed. Neither of them spoke. The hunch of Dad's shoulders gave away that he was there under duress.

I raised my eyebrows. 'Can I help you?'

227

Dad shot me a warning look.

'What is the matter with you?' Mum's annoyance swirled around my room.

'Nothing,' I said, looking up at the ceiling. Kirk Cameron's nose was askew.

'Because from where I'm standing you look like a very spoilt child.'

'Thanks for sharing,' I said, not quite loud enough for Mum to hear.

'Look at me when I'm speaking to you!' snapped Mum.

I hoisted myself up, and fixed my eyes on Dad.

'I don't quite know what you're playing at, young lady, but you are sorely trying my patience,' continued Mum, warming to the sound of her voice.

Xanthe might have thought Mum cool, but she didn't have to put up with this. 'Am I trying your patience?' I asked Dad.

He sighed and shook his head. I had gone too far; I was on my own.

'You see, Timothy!' Mum turned to Dad. 'That's what I'm talking about.' She jabbed her finger at me.

'That? I asked.

'Your attitude! Your complete self-involvement. You cannot live your life with such disregard for anyone other than yourself. Every day people are being killed in this country in terrible violence, people who have been fighting all their lives to attain the freedom that you take for granted.'

'How will my attitude change that?'

'You're an intelligent person, Meg. You can't simply stand by and watch events unfold – that's how apartheid lasted for forty years! All you care about is your own needs –'

'I'm a teenager! That's what I'm supposed to do.'

'I'm not finished!'

'You're never finished!'

'How dare you speak to me like that! You are fifteen years old, Margaret, and as long as you are under my roof, you will respect my rules. For the love of God, I don't know what's got in to you! You have a tantrum every time I try to educate people about a disease that will kill them, because it makes you feel a little uneasy. You're so caught up in your little adolescent friendship with Xanthe that you can't be bothered to extend a cordial greeting to Simon.'

'I have heard enough about Simon!' I screamed back.

Dad turned and left.

'And what about you?' I launched back at Mum. 'You'd love me a whole lot more if I got that "A", if I were more like Simon! Even Beth has to perform for you even though it half kills her.'

'Rubbish! But I'll tell you something while we're on the subject. Simon's not letting his circumstances hold him back; he's determined to make something of himself. You – on the other hand – mooch around, bored about this, whining about that, letting your life slip between your fingers.'

'And Marta?'

'What about Marta?'

'Do you think she's thanking you and Dad for taking her son, like a laboratory experiment, giving him a first-class education, setting him up in his brilliant new life? Because now she has no one.'

Mum stepped backwards, as though I'd smacked her. 'You

229

have no idea what you're talking about.'

'I was there, Mother. We both heard what she said, that Simon has outgrown her. That's your fault!'

'Simon is more his mother's son than ever.' Mum's voice was quiet. 'This is my final warning. If I don't see a dramatic improvement in your behaviour, there will be no more trips to see Xanthe in Cape Town.'

'Fine with me!' I shouted.

She looked at me, startled, but I concentrated on picking at a loose thread on my pillow. It had been a childish response, but would that be such a bad thing? Had I been more miserable before I met Xanthe than I was now? Though I tried to dismiss it, the question hovered at the corners of my mind.

I heard Mum breathe out. 'Meg,' she paused. Her voice sounded unsure.

Go away! I shouted in my head.

'You will tell me if there's anything wrong? Something you want to talk –'

'I don't to *talk*, I want to be left alone!'

The walls around me felt heavy and old, as though the strain of holding up the roof was becoming too much to bear. From the sitting room came the sound of rock music, squealing and laughing as a bunch of American teenagers had the time of their lives.

Late that night a wind stormed through the valley, a freakish thing for that time of year. I awoke on its approach, as it tore down through the pine and cedar forests, gathering ferocity and speed over the empty fields on the valley floor. The moments before it struck were silent and breathless, as though all the air had been sucked out of town into the approaching fury.

It hit like a Chinese dragon, mutating its form, growing larger and smaller, curling back in on itself, tunnelling down the main street. It twisted up and down lampposts, and sent shop signs spinning. Its fingers tore down every side street, and around the back of dustbins, each new surge and gust its ferocious breath. It howled and raged and tossed things around, driven wild by some jealousy. I lay in bed, in the submissive darkness, identifying each clash and rattle: the steel watering can in the courtyard, the loose shutter outside the sitting room, the window in the bathroom. The plastic chairs skidded about the stoep, colliding with the table and bouncing against the walls.

I snuggled deeper under my duvet. Above me the eaves creaked their disapproval. The wind whipped around the house, mustering pace and ferocity, until it felt strong enough to snatch us out of the ground. After two days of feeling nothing, the wind seemed to jump-start my heart. I understood its anguish and rage. 'Take me away,' I begged the wind. 'Take me with you.'

A clap, as loud as a bullet. My heart raced against the top of my skull. An image of the Heidelberg victims flashed through my mind. Another bang followed, and again. I sat up. It was the swing-door outside the kitchen banging shut on itself, but even so I fumbled for my bedside light switch.

'The electricity is down.'

I jumped. I hadn't spoken. The darkness was absolute. The wind whispered and hissed. Ghosts didn't scare me – in a town like Leopold the number of dead far outweighed the living. And a ghost wouldn't discuss electricity. It was Beth.

231

I lifted my head.

'The electricity is often down,' I said, 'you know that.'

The wind dropped, its silence more eerie than its rage. I could hear Beth breathing across the room. 'Come here,' I said. A shuffle and a creak and Beth's body shifted in beside me. We lay silent for a moment, getting used to each other. We listened to the wind reorganising itself.

Beth sniffed. 'Everything's changing.'

'Like what?'

'Everything. Soon you're going to leave and I'll be the only one at home with *them*.' She jerked her head backwards on the pillow in the direction of Mum and Dad's room. 'It was horrible without you.' She shook herself, as though she was expelling a demon.

'I still have two years at school,' I said, feeling grown up.

'More, if you fail,' she said.

'Thanks.' I knocked her elbow gently.

The wind chased itself around the house, growing wilder with each circuit.

'What about the radical time you had with Simon?' I asked drily.

Beth sighed. 'He thinks I'm a child.'

I smiled into the black. 'Don't worry about Simon, he'll be gone soon.' Lying next to Beth felt like finding a long-lost treasure. Yet she had been here all along.

'I don't want him to go. I want him to stay and you two to be friends, like before.'

'I don't think it can be like before, Beth.' Again I saw Simon staring out to sea.

232

Across the courtyard the kitchen swing-door clapped again.

'So, was your week amazing?' Beth yawned loudly.

I reached my arm behind my head. 'It was different.'

'It must be better than Leopold.'

My little sister was changing. Until a week ago, Leopold was the best place on earth. 'You can't lie in the middle of the Cape Town Main Street on a Sunday afternoon.'

Beth giggled. 'Or listen to other people's conversations on the party line.' She yawned and then said sleepily, 'I'm glad you're back.'

Next to me Beth felt like the most comforting thing in the world. I wanted some of her completeness, her sureness of herself. I remembered the ring I'd bought her in Greenmarket Square. 'Remind me in the morning, I have something for you.'

There was a low murmur from my parents' next-door room. Then came a heavy *tha-donk* and, 'You bugger!' as Dad tripped over something in the darkness. A few moments later I heard a *clacker-clacker-clacker* of the wooden curtain rings as Dad drew one aside.

'It's gone,' we heard him say through the wall, and his words reached the furthest corners of the night.

It was true. The storm had rolled itself up and disappeared; silence settled on the battered night. The howling wind was no match for our squat, square house. The metre-thick walls felt for the first time like a bastion against the outside world.

CHAPTER TWENTY-FOUR

The shriek, of a kind we had not been expecting for another eleven months, reached us from the depths of the house. Beth and I were in the courtyard, lolling in deckchairs in the dappled afternoon sun. I looked at her. Her head popped up, her eyes swivelled from side to side, like a mongoose. Dad appeared at the door of his study, notebook in hand.

'What's happened?' I asked him.

He glanced back inside. 'Your mother's on the phone,' he said. He blinked in the sunlight. One could almost imagine he was developing a nervous tic.

That morning, at breakfast, he'd paused in the kitchen doorway.

'You're up!'

'Yup.'

'And eating.'

I nodded as I licked Marmite off my hand.

'And you're not going to cry, or shout or throw anything,' he said, still in the doorway.

I laughed. 'I promise.'

'Cause to celebrate!' He'd clapped his hands.

But once again he could smell trouble. We all could.

Mum appeared now, in a state of wild excitement. 'Bibi is here!' She held out her arms, like Father Basil proclaiming the good news on Easter Sunday. 'Not here, obviously, but in Cape Town. She's coming to see us tomorrow!'

'Bibi?' asked Beth.

Mum laughed. 'You know, my crazy friend from uni.'

'Don't be funny, Ma, you don't have friends,' said Beth.

'Is that necessary, Beth?' Mum frowned at her, then turned to Dad. 'Isn't it exciting!' She clapped her hands.

On hearing that name, my fragile equilibrium shattered. That woman, who was responsible for planting all the AIDS education ideas in Mum's head, who had the most stupid name in the whole world, was coming to stay in my house. That interfering no-gooder, perpetrator of untold misery. Imagine if Juffrou du Plessis got wind of this! It was like housing a terrorist.

'Bibi is the one who wrote the article,' I said to Beth.

'Which article?'

I stared at her. One day she was going to have to leave her parallel universe, where everyone loved each other and nothing bad happened.

'THE article,' I said, rolling my eyes.

'Why is she here?' asked Dad, stepping down into the courtyard. He placed a restraining hand on the top of my head.

'She is on her way to Natal, to cover the pre-election violence around Richmond.'

'Poor her,' said Dad.

We giggled.

'Why?' asked Mum.

235

'Why?' laughed Dad, but seeing the look on Mum's face, stopped. 'Tough assignment.'

'If anyone can do it, she can. She has a big job at the BBC. It's taken her all over the world,' said Mum.

I bit the inside of my cheek. Who cared about the BBC?

'And now she gets to see Leopold!' said Dad.

Beth stood up and clapped her hands. 'She must do the tour!'

'She must buy the veldskoens!' I added, seeing Mum's face pale.

'She must drink the tea,' Dad concluded, nodding gravely.

Mum was not amused. Dad coughed and leaned forward to kiss her. 'Only teasing, Vivvy. That's very good news.' He rubbed his hands together. 'Now, if you'll excuse me, there's work to be done.'

'Where are you going?'

'To the town hall! I must inform the mayor at once.'

Marta, caught up in Mum's excitement, spent the day preparing for Bibi's arrival as though it were a state visit. She vacuumed and scrubbed and dusted. We were enlisted to polish the silver. I found it offensive to be made to polish silver in honour of a trouble-making community wrecker, but I was not brave enough to bring it up with Marta.

As we sat at the kitchen table, under Marta's watchful eye, a foreign sound reached us from the sitting room. It was the sound of women laughing.

'It's Bibi daahling,' Beth mimicked, in an accent that was more *Dynasty* than the Queen.

We dissolved into giggles.

Marta clicked her tongue.

'So glaaaad to see you, Bibi,' Beth continued, undeterred. In our new alliance we were unstoppable.

'It's char-ming, simply charming,' I said through splutters of giggles. Beth banged her head on the table by mistake, which had us screaming with laughter.

We didn't immediately notice the two figures watching. The woman next to Mum was tall and seemed to be constructed out of angles: a big triangular nose, a straight back from which her long thin arms jutted out, hinging awkwardly at the elbows. Her dark curly hair escaped in tufts from an indigo scarf that was tied around her head much in the same way Marta tied her doek. She was so pale that the hair on her arms was startlingly dark against her skin. She wore a khaki sleeveless top and trousers, as though she had arrived back from a day in the bush, and Jesus of Nazareth sandals like Mum's.

We examined each other across the kitchen. Mum looked different next to Bibi. I thought of the memory matching games we used to play when we were small. It was the first time I saw Mum correctly matched up.

'Beth, Meg, and Marta our housekeeper,' Mum introduced us. I turned in time to catch Marta's raised eyebrow at her new title.

'We meet at last!' said Bibi, revealing a mouth of big teeth, 'Look at you, beavering away!' She opened her mouth and delivered a loud braying sound. 'Is the boy, Simon, around? I've heard so much about him over the years.'

Mum looked embarrassed. 'He's not a boy, Bibi, he's nineteen!'

'God, I feel old!' laughed Bibi. She looked around. 'But what

237

a wonderful old kitchen, it's the real thing!' she exclaimed, as though we were mannequins in a museum display.

'It's not true Cape Dutch, but it was the first homestead to be built in the town. Now through here,' Mum pushed open the swing door to the courtyard, 'you can see the original stonework . . .'

With a backwards smile, and a right-angled wave, Bibi followed Mum out through the swing door into the courtyard.

Beth kicked me under the table. 'She doesn't shave under her arms!' She pulled a face.

'And her toes have tufts of dark hair growing on them,' I said.

'Why wouldn't she shave?' asked Beth. Beth was desperate to start shaving, but Mum was adamant that nice girls only started shaving at the age of fourteen, if at all.

'It's because it always rains in England. They need to keep warm.'

The donkey laugh and chitter-chatter continued throughout the afternoon. It made it easy enough to avoid them, but towards evening they cornered Beth and me in front of the TV.

'Bibi's brought you presents, from London!' By the tone of Mum's voice, it was required of us to sit up and be excited. Beth sat up. She had no willpower.

'That's nice,' I said, not taking my eyes off the TV.

'Not much – a few things my colleagues tell me are popular with young girls at the moment,' said Bibi. She produced a Body Shop bag, with the usual lip-gloss and body cream, and some stripy fingerless gloves. 'I know, wrong time of year!' she laughed.

There were some luminous plastic bracelets – 'Fun!' said

Mum, and a teddy bear from Harrods – 'I'd forgotten you were so big, Beth,' said Bibi. At the bottom of the bag was a bottle of Vixen nail polish.

'That's for you, Meg. All the girls your age are wearing it. It's brand new this year!'

'Oh wow!' said Mum with a laugh. She took the bottle and examined the colour, then handed it to me.

'It's not brand new,' I said, putting it down. 'It's been around for at least six months. I already have some,' I lied.

Beth pinched my thigh.

'But thanks anyway.' I delivered my sweetest smile.

Marta had laid the supper table outside. But after a pre-supper glass of wine, Bibi started rubbing her ankles and wound her cardigan around her head to ward off the mosquitoes. As she reached for the insect repellent for the fourth time, Mum stood up and ushered Beth and I to move everything inside.

'Don't move on my account. I'll be fine,' said Bibi.

'We almost always eat inside,' said Mum. 'I don't know what Marta was thinking.'

Ten minutes later Dad appeared, looking confused at the change of plan. He placed a roasting tin groaning with meat in the middle of the table and hovered next to Bibi as he ran through the contents of the tin. '*Ribbetjies*,' he pointed out the lamp rib chops, 'mutton chops, and some Malmesbury boerewors. It's a secret recipe.' He winked at Bibi.

She laughed loudly and said, 'Yum! I do love red meat!'

Dad beamed.

'Unfortunately, I'm trying to limit myself to white meat only.

239

So dreadfully dull!' She produced a packet of what looked like birdseed and sprinkled it on her salad.

Dad handed me the meat, with a look that made me snort with laughter, but a glance from Mum killed it.

'How do you like our country, Bibi?' asked Dad.

'Wonderful. So beautiful. A little bit warmer than I'd imagined,' she said with a laugh, 'But at least it's not humid.'

'Natal is chronically humid at this time of year,' I said.

'Thanks for the warning,' she smiled.

'And it's a malaria area of course,' I added, hoping I was right.

'It's beginning to sound like *Heart of Darkness*,' she laughed.

I stared at her.

'The book,' she said, glancing from me to Mum, who smiled in a strained way at me.

'I think Bibi can deal with a few mosquitoes and a little heat after all the places she's visited,' she told me.

Bibi laughed. She turned to Dad. 'Tim, it's so exciting what Viv has achieved with her AIDS awareness programmes. Now that we have secured funding, we can approach it in a much more organised fashion.' She stopped for a sip of wine.

My fork jabbed into the roof of my mouth. I blinked away the stabbing pain. I looked at Mum, but she would not meet my eye. I looked at Dad. Bibi was waiting for an answer.

'Yes, indeed,' he said. He didn't look happy, but neither did he look surprised. My fork landed back on my plate. My hands were trembling. I sat back in my chair. Mum had promised not to cause anymore trouble. I'd believed her. All the time she'd been planning more organised, *funded* trouble! And she had the cheek to rant at the politicians about transparency. Did

240

no one tell the truth anymore?

'Such an exciting time in your country,' Bibi's voice droned on. Would she never shut up?

I looked up and realised she was talking to me. 'What?'

'I said it must be very exciting to be your age at this moment in your country.'

'Why?'

She laughed, baring her oversized teeth. 'To be a part of the historic changes that are taking place! Isn't that exciting?'

'I don't know.' I shrugged my shoulders. 'You're the expert.'

In a mad confidence I held her gaze until she looked away.

'There's only so much you can learn from books and reports,' she said to Mum.

'I've always thought so,' I replied, 'but you wouldn't know it. Read any British newspaper article and you'd think we're a bunch of stupid racists, us white South Africans.'

Bibi sat back.

'Margaret! Enough!' growled Dad.

'That's what it said! What gives you the right, Bibi, to write an article about a community you know nothing of, that you've never even been to?'

'Margaret!' Dad's fist landed on the table.

I was not finished. 'You English think you're so much better than us, with your grand statements. You don't understand what you're writing about. You have no regard for the impact of your throw-away lines.'

'They do not!' said Mum.

'"They"?' I laughed, swinging around to her. 'You've been here for seventeen years and you still can't speak the bloody

241

language. You talk about England as home. You'd like to save us, but you stand outside of us. You're no different to her!' I jerked my thumb towards Bibi, then got up and left the table.

As I reached the door, Mum stood up. 'I will not tolerate you speaking to my friend like that. Come back and apologise.' Her fury sliced open every word.

I turned around.

'Viv, it's fine,' Bibi murmured.

'It's not fine,' said Mum, not taking her eyes off me. She put her hand on the table to stop it shaking.

As I took in a deep breath, a new voice, one that had been sitting at the pit of my stomach for a very long time, answered. 'No,' I said quietly.

I held Mum's gaze a moment longer, in which she appeared to shrink, and wither, like the speeded-up 'Life of the bean plant' films at school.

Bibi stayed one day instead of two in the end: she blamed her bosses in England, she blamed the tensions in Natal. Everyone was relieved to see her go. Mum was so angry with me that she could not speak to me. She couldn't be in the same room. Mum's anger bubbled and boiled for three days. I felt nothing. She was a liar and a hypocrite.

Marta didn't see it that way. 'Respect.' She poked my shoulder as I sat outside on the stoep. 'What you lack is respect.'

'But Marta –'

'No buts.' Another stab at my shoulder. 'No ifs, no buts, no nothing. Finished *en klaar**.'

* Properly finished

CHAPTER TWENTY-FIVE

It was only when I was halfway across the quad, clutching my brown 'Paddington Bear' suitcase that bumped against my knees, that I realised everyone was looking at me. Worse still, they were laughing and pointing.

'What?' I demanded, turning around as I scanned the sea of girls. Each time I tried to focus on one of them, their eyes and nose and mouth disappeared. They were featureless apart from a pencilled-in underlined capital T like the characters in my children's bible. At last I spotted Esna and Elmarie, at the front of a growing crowd. At least their faces didn't disappear, but they were shaking their heads in disapproval.

'My dad says it not right to walk around naked,' Esna said, wagging a finger at me, before they dissolved into giggles.

'Where's Xanthe?' I asked.

'Who?'

'Xanthe!'

They conferred in whispers behind their hands. Elmarie shook her heads. 'We don't know a Santie, there's no Santie here.'

No Xanthe! What had they done with her? Then I caught

sight of my reflection in the glass door opposite. I was seven again. And I was naked, except for my white ankle socks and Clarks T-bar shoes. Where was my uniform? I'd been dressed a moment ago.

'I'm sure my clothes are here somewhere!' I said, sounding like Mum in a crisis. I bent down and flicked open the suitcase. The children had formed a ring around me. Frantically I pulled out one thing after another: my turquoise bikini; an eggshell-encrusted Easter card I'd made for my parents, one where you pulled back the top half of the card flap to reveal a yellow chick; my First Love doll, who had never recovered from a severe haircut; and a diary from when I was thirteen. Then came Simon – I pulled him out by his ear and flung him to the side, where he landed face down on the doll. I had run out of options; there was nothing left. The crowd was closing in. There were faces above me, to the side, stamping feet getting closer. They chanted, 'Meg has lost her panties! Meg has lost her panties!' I crouched forward, head tucked into my knees to block out their faces, my arms locked around my legs. Behind them was the sound of Mrs Franklin's stilettos stalking across the quad; the echo of the spiky heels bounced against the four walls. Everything went quiet. She stood over me, blocking out the sun. When I dared look up she had become the evil old hag in *Snow White*, with her hideous crooked, warty nose and toothless grin. She stretched out her witch's hand and extended a gnarled talon. She was going for my eyes.

Uuurghwah! I pushed my way back through the layers of semi-consciousness, and sat upright in bed, breathing in shallow gasps. As I caught the lingering smell of roast chicken from supper, I talked myself back from the dreadful dream. I was awake, school hadn't yet started. I wasn't a seven-year-old anymore. I was me.

The dream was trapped inside the walls and low ceiling. To avoid my parents' bedroom, I crossed the moonlit courtyard and slid back into the inky-black kitchen. I padded past the hulking shadows of the dining-room chairs, like highwaymen crouched over in trench coats, past the squat crouching leopards of the sitting room furniture and at last into the family room. Moonlight streamed in through the glass pane above the doors that led out on to the stoep. I opened the door and stepped out into the hot night. I sat down on the bench and spread my toes against the cool stone. I dug my spine into the wooden slats. Slowly the dream lost its focus and released its pinch on my mind. With a deep yawn I closed my eyes and rested my head back on the smooth-rough surface of the wall behind me.

'You scared me.' Mum stood in the doorway, wearing one of Dad's old T-shirts and some awful homemade shorts. 'You look like a former occupier of the house. For a moment I wasn't sure.'

'Sorry to disappoint you,' I mumbled.

'Shift over, you're in my spot.'

I looked up.

'I'm quite nocturnal. I've spent many nights musing here.'

I moved to the other side of the bench. The moon cut a neat crescent high above the pecanut tree, a spotlight its inky branches. The garden was alive with scurries and rustles in the undergrowth, the sporadic *kaark* of a sleeping chicken and the creeking of crickets. We sat side by side, neither of us willing

245

to break the silence for fear of what had to come.

Twice Mum started to say something. Eventually, tucking her hair behind her ear, she said: 'I feel like I'm losing you.' She wiped her eye and laughed. 'I don't know how to let you go gracefully. I'm not yet ready.'

Hearing her tired, small voice punctured my anger. 'I'm sorry about the Bibi . . . thing. I was rude.'

'Yes, you were.'

'But the thing is –'

'I know.'

I felt her body sigh, as if letting go of a burden. Then she started laughing, a little trickle at first, but soon it turned into a rumble and as it gathered pace, it drew me in. 'Oh my God!' She wiped her eyes. 'That was quite a performance.' She pulled me towards her. 'I can't think where you get it from.'

When Mum spoke again, it was with the tone she saved for grown-ups. It made me want to listen. 'My first years in Leopold were such a disaster. I rushed in, desperate to become part of the town. I knew it would be hard. What I didn't expect was that the Boer War would still be a current topic of conversation.'

Her hands were very still in her lap. I covered them with one of my own and it swivelled around and grasped mine, still bigger than mine even though I was fully grown.

'I spent years trying to fit into this town. But I'm different to them, Meg. It's like spending sixteen years trying to be someone else. I'm no good at that. It's a difficult way to live, feeling that you are not allowed to be whom you are. It can do funny things to your head.' She squeezed my hand. 'This AIDS work has made me feel valuable again. I know I will make a difference and it's made me feel excited about being who I am. You and Beth will be off and away soon. I need to find myself again before that happens, or I might lose myself forever.'

I had a question for her, before she got up and kissed me and went back to bed. 'Mum,' I started, 'do you think . . .'

I sighed. What should I say – that I suspected that Xanthe wasn't actually a very nice person, nothing like Jami Gertz or Queen Isabella of Spain; that she took drugs and had sex at the age of fifteen and didn't seem to care about anyone but herself? I had a million reasons, each of them enough in themselves, not to speak to Xanthe again, but I couldn't remember them anymore. Perhaps my expectations had been too high. The thought of returning to my life before Xanthe was miserable, and surely far worse than any of the bad things she had done, or could ever do.

Mum was waiting, but I couldn't find a way to begin.

'It's OK to have . . . colourful friends,' she said, carefully. 'They can be very good for people like you and I; they shake us up. But it's not OK when you find yourself swallowed up in them, when you lose sight of who you are.'

It was the answer I'd hoped for, it was the absolution I needed. But after my initial relief I felt I'd tricked her into it because I knew that taking drugs and having underage sex in a public place didn't fit into the same category as 'colourful friends'. And I knew that I would never tell her about any of it.

'Sometimes it's hard to know what the right thing to do is,' I said.

'Sometimes it is. And there will be some choices you will

make that you will never know if it was the right one.'

'So how do you ever make a decision?'

'You do what feels right in your heart.' She pulled me very close to her, so that I could feel her heart beating against her ribcage. My breathing slowed to match hers and it felt as though the whole world breathed with us, in and out, in perfect time.

Later, in the kitchen, while Mum boiled the kettle and warmed the tea pot, because 'no matter what time of night it is, tea tastes better in a warm pot', I reached up above her and pulled down the cake tin with the remains of the Christmas cake.

'I hate Christmas,' she said, peering into the tin.

'I know,' I said. 'Because it's not a proper Christmas, because it's not cold, because it's not English.'

'Quite the opposite. I've always hated Christmas, even as a child. It was my terrible secret. I thought it was evil to hate Baby Jesus' birthday. But watching the way my mother wound herself up until she was teetering on the point of collapse, I never saw the point of it.'

I stared at her. 'So, what's with your annual hysteria?'

'I do it for you and Beth, to try and make it different for you. Each year I think I might finally have outgrown the familiar dread it brings. But mostly, I do it for my mother. An act of penance I suppose, to do one thing that would have made her proud after a lifetime of disappointment. And I bugger it up every year!' She laughed.

I looked down at the dense fruitcake, and suddenly understood why it had never tasted right. 'Let's chuck it away!' I looked up. 'Go on, throw it in the bin!'

'Oh, I don't know.' Mum shook her head. She ran her hand through her hair.

'Go on!' I said. 'It's a bunch of ingredients.'

She looked at the cake for another moment. 'I can't throw it away.'

'Mother!'

'Only because your dad likes it so much,' she said with a small give-away smile.

CHAPTER TWENTY-SIX

On the last Saturday of the holidays, I bumped into Juffrou du Plessis in the Spar. She was at the check-out counter, in the entrance of the shop. I saw her first, and for a moment thought of ducking behind the pile of *Die Burger* newspapers and the stack of braai wood, but there was no escape. The ratio of grey to brown in her bun had tipped over the holiday in favour of grey. Beads of sweat glistened across her hairline in the breathless morning. Her navy-blue and white polka-dot dress clung to her legs. Before I knew it, I was carrying her shopping bags to her car.

She paused to catch her breath next to her white Toyota Corolla. 'Something is different about you – what can it be? Taller? Maybe.' She studied me with an intensity that made me look at my feet. My green slip-slops were covered in red dust.

She was still frowning at me when I raised my eyes.

'Your face is slimmer,' she decided disapprovingly. 'It's hard for us,' she continued as she watched me lift her shopping bags into her boot, 'seeing you girls turn into women, and leave without a backwards glance.'

'Who said I was leaving?' My flash of confidence fizzled and popped under her look.

'This town is no place for a bright thing like you. Every year we lose the best of our young people to the world. For those who stay behind, it's not a life of many choices.' She looked up at Bosmansberg behind us. It was impossible to imagine Leopold without Juffrou, but would she have left, had she been given the choice?

'We prepare you as best we can. Education isn't about grammar and tenses. It's about knowing right from wrong. Understanding the bond with your family and your community is the most important lesson of all. That's your backbone.'

I couldn't listen to these words from the woman who'd gone out of her way to emphasise my family's apartness for as long as I'd known her. 'Juffrou, you don't see my family as a part of the community. We're the trouble-making Englishers, remember?'

Juffrou looked wounded. '*Wragtie* child! For someone with a good brain, you can be very dense.'

She looked hesitant then, caught by a private thought, but dismissed it with a shake of her keys. 'Let us not get ahead of ourselves – we still have two more years together!' She banged the boot shut, her familiar glower back in place. But before she reversed into the street, she turned back and winked.

I walked home, puzzling Juffrou's words. Perhaps Mum relied on Juffrou's disapproval as much as Juffrou relied on Mum's revolutionary streak. In a strange way they complimented each other.

I set up camp next to the pecan tree. I had my Coke, Nik-Naks and chocolate digestives, my Walkman and, if all else failed, the irksome *Emma* to keep me company. I had pulled out our old red, green, yellow and blue-striped beach umbrella from the garage and planted it diagonally in the grass. It was my shield against the heat.

But not Simon. From the moment his eyes had met mine on the beach in Cape Town, my familiar jealousy and resentment had started to transform into a violent desire to fight him. But that was absurd. Instead I had stayed out of his way.

Now, a day before he was due to leave for university, he was suddenly beside me. I had forgotten Simon's ability to move in silence, as if his footsteps left no imprint on the ground.

'My mother finally told me who my father is. Was.'

I shifted away. A black mussel shell had dropped out of the folds of the fabric when I'd set up the umbrella. I clutched it, pressing it into my skin.

Simon pulled out a cigarette. He lit it, holding it between his thumb and first finger, like the skollies who hung about outside the off-licence. I reached out and took it out of his mouth, stubbed it out on the grass and broke it in half.

He laughed and pulled out a handful of Wilson's cola-flavoured toffees and offered them to me.

I pushed his hand away. 'You know I only eat the black ones!'

He shrugged, took one and put the rest away. 'I thought that you might have changed your mind at some point in the last five years.'

How dare he discuss toffees! Why was he here? Hadn't he caused enough trouble for one holiday? I turned until I had my back to him. The mussel shell was cutting me open. I opened my hand and watched it fall to the grass.

Simon glanced down. We were back at the beach. I was looking at him, sitting alone on the sand, staring out to sea.

'How could you, Simon?' I blurted out.

'What?'

'After everything else you've been given, how could you steal the one friend I've ever had? How could you be so cruel?'

Simon glared back at me, at first with disbelief and then anger. 'What have I been given? I have had to prove myself worthy of everything I have, whereas you were born with it.'

I bit the inside of my cheek and stared at the ground. That was beside the point. 'I don't want to talk about this.'

'OK.' He shrugged his shoulders.

But the anger returned, more violent than before. 'Who do you think you are, sauntering back after your fancy overseas trip, with your big fucking attitude?'

'I thought you didn't want to talk about it.'

'Perhaps you're too sophisticated for this silly old town anymore. But for your information it's not OK to have sex with someone on the beach.'

'Why not?'

'Why not?' I shouted. I knew there must be a perfectly good reason, but I was too angry to think of it.

Simon spoke again, his voice cold and mocking. 'What's upsetting you, Meg? The fact that I was having sex on a beach, or that I was having sex with Xanthe?'

I smacked him in the face. He pulled back, his eyes wide but he said nothing. He didn't even lift his hand up to the red mark that spread across his right cheek. I sat back, struggling to push my breath back beyond my throat into my chest. I was

253

shocked at how much my hand stung, but also at the satisfaction it gave me. I was shocked that as soon as I'd hit him, my anger evaporated and I had to wonder why I'd done it.

'Xanthe's not like you, Meg.'

'I know, OK? I get it!' My cheeks were burning.

He frowned at me. 'That's a good thing.'

'How can it be a good thing when she's the one with the amazing life?'

He picked up the shell and traced its curved perimeter. 'She's not that cool. It's all for show.'

I watched his finger. The curve of the shell reminded me of an ear. Maybe Simon was right. What actually lay behind those impenetrable, ice-blue eyes?

Beyond the striped canvas, high above, a fish eagle's cry pierced the silence, heralding in the early evening. 'What about your dad, then?' I prompted, after a pause. 'Your mother . . .' I searched the sky.

'Father Basil has been preaching about forgiveness and transparency in the new South Africa, so Ma thought it time I knew.'

I raised my eyebrows. Those were dangerous words in a town like this.

'She was right. He was a good-for-nothing *rubbish*.' His laugh was hollow and painful to hear. 'I never thought that knowing would be worse than not knowing.'

'It can't be that bad,' I mumbled, pulling at a tuft of grass.

'It is,' he insisted, 'because when you don't know you can be anybody. But when you know –' He sighed. 'For the first time in my life I am ashamed of who I am.'

254

I realised that for as long as I could remember, I had resented Simon for infiltrating my family, as if he didn't deserve to be part of it. I had been wrong. What he didn't deserve was to feel ashamed of his family. Nobody deserved that, least of all him.

'Your background means nothing, Simon. Look at Mandela.'

'What about Mandela?'

'Look where he came from. Now he has a Nobel Peace Prize and is set to be president.'

'Meg, he was pretty much royalty. His father was the chief of his tribe.'

'Oh. Not a great example, then.' I stole a glance at him. 'Parents are heavily overrated.'

Simon smiled.

'And at least your mum doesn't suffer from delusions of sainthood.'

'She's doing something important, Meg. She's going out of her way to try and save the lives of people whom nobody else sees as important enough to bother with.'

'I guess,' I shrugged. I hadn't thought of that before.

The milking bell rang across the river. Simon and I had made up and suddenly I didn't want him to go quite yet.

'How did it feel coming back?' I asked.

He looked at the shell. 'It feels like I'm a loose fossil trying to fit back into my original rock bed. Time and weathering and, exposure,' he paused for a breath, 'have changed my shape. I don't fit.'

I didn't like that comparison. It reminded me of the little box at the back of Xanthe's drawer. 'Or maybe it's like waking up to find you've turned into a butterfly. But essentially you're still a worm.'

Simon laughed but it died quickly. 'I don't like the way my ma looks at me. It's like she's seeing a stranger. And sometimes she talks to me like she's speaking to . . .'

'To?'

'A white person,' he muttered.

'Simon . . .' I wanted to reach out and place my hand on the cheek I'd hit, but my arm didn't feel long enough.

He looked up. 'She didn't need to tell me about my dad. I think she did it in case I start forgetting who I am.'

'No!' Marta wouldn't be that cruel. But without Simon Marta was alone – a small woman shrinking with age.

'Why won't she talk to Angel?'

Simon shook his head.

'Why not?' I insisted, ready to argue Angel's case, but the look on his face stopped me.

He sighed. 'It's not my battle, Meg. That one at least is not mine.'

'Do you think that going away to school and overseas has changed you? Do you think your essence has changed?'

He was quiet for so long that I wondered whether I'd spoken my question out loud. Then he turned to me, his brown ochre neck tilted to the side, with a smile that made me smile back.

'No,' he said.

Simon had escaped Leopold and travelled overseas, but he was still alone. Perhaps lonely was not the same as being alone.

'Remember when I went to school in Cape Town and I wrote you those letters? You never replied.'

I looked at my stubby fingernails, feeling ashamed. I had

been so jealous of Simon for leaving, for being singled out, that I had not replied out of spite. 'I still have them,' I said. 'They're very funny.'

'Will you write to me this time? Tell me everything that's not happening in Leopold?'

Something inside me jumped at the idea. He'd tell me about life at university, about things I needed to know. But I was also afraid. I thought back to my dream at the beach, of being pulled further out to sea, away from the receding shore. 'Oh, Simon, you're going to be too busy with your new life to reply.'

'For every letter you write, I'll write back. OK?'

'OK,' I said, meaning it.

In the late ripeness of January, too early in the summer to even dream of the cooler days of March and April, Simon reached across the diagonal pole of the beach umbrella. He turned my chin so that I could see him – his straight nose, his jaw, wider than before, and his eyes. I knew his eyes well, I recognised the intensity, the quickness, but there was a new darkness I felt I understood.

His lips touched mine for a moment, although it didn't feel like that. It felt like talking and laughing and dreaming in the same moment, carried on a current that pulsed between us. I was sure he felt it too.

'I have to go and pack,' he said.

I looked down to hide the glowing red that spread up my neck. The imprint of his lips fizzed. The current throbbed around my body, stuck inside. A gecko's severed tail writhing about uselessly.

He held out a yellow piece of paper folded into a square.

'This is my address.'

'OK,' I said, avoiding his eye.

'Bye,' he said.

I looked up. 'Karraboosh.'

He laughed, raised a hand in a single wave, and walked away.

CHAPTER TWENTY-SEVEN

Early on Monday morning Dad made his daily walk around the house, closing all the shutters. It was not something you could sleep through, but this morning I was awake long before his face peered in through my window.

'It's going to be hot as hell today,' he said with a glint in his eye, a deranged sailor forecasting stormy seas. 'The barometer's doing the Loop De Loop!' He bolted the shutters and my room plunged into slatted green darkness.

I reached for the yellow piece of paper next to my bed. *Ernest Oppenheimer Halls of Residence, 8 Trematon Place, Parktown.* In two years I would be giving my address to Beth. If only it were today!

What would I say to Xanthe? I couldn't ignore her. I didn't want to. *'Hi Xanthe, I'd like to be your friend, but from now on it will be different.'* I could imagine the look on her face. It sounded worse than something out of *Beverly Hills 90210*. *'And by the way, I don't mind about the beach thing anymore.'* I shuddered as the throbbing sensation I'd felt under the pecanut tree returned. As I was about to leave me room I hesitated, then grabbed the folded paper and stowed it in my pocket.

A talisman.

At breakfast the Raisin Bran scraped down my throat. In the end I gave up and stared at my mug of tea.

'A new year!' said Dad, appearing in his rugby shorts and "I'm too sexy for this shirt!" T-shirt. Both he and Mum were unnecessarily cheerful. They didn't even try and hide their relief at the start of another term.

'The year of the "A",' said Mum.

'The year of leaving Meg alone,' I said.

'How would I fill my time?' said Dad, reaching across the table to pick up newspaper.

'Get a job?'

Dad laughed. He yawned and stretched his arms over his head, revealing under his sexy T-shirt a hairy belly.

He tapped the folded newspaper on my head in farewell and disappeared in the direction of his study with a mug of coffee and the newspaper under his arm.

'Come *on*!' Beth hopped about in the doorway of the kitchen, her satchel already on her back.

'Don't wait for me,' I muttered.

She disappeared, back up the hill to school, to the newly white-washed building, to the mass of girls, the shiny-floored corridors, and the notice boards that would be cleared of last year's artwork and lab reports and sports fixtures. Ready to start again.

Eventually Marta shooed me out of the door. 'Get!' She flicked her dust cloth. 'Leave me in peace.'

The break-of-day freshness was already burnt off. As I reached the Main Street I caught tannie Ester's eye, clutching her basket like Mrs Tiddlywinks, on her way to open the library.

'Lekker dag!'* she called before disappearing into her air-conditioned sanctuary. Across the road hotel staff hurried through their outdoor jobs. Two of them beat a pair of runner rugs that hung looped over the outside beams of the front verandah. They pounded away with long-handled brooms, causing dust clouds to rise up above them and hover for a moment before settling back into the rugs.

A little way along Witbooi and Mr Pretorius from the bank leaned over the churchyard wall, peering into the graveyard. I crossed the road to have a look.

'That bladdy dog,' Witbooi rasped. 'Give me a gun and I'll shoot him *fokken* dead.'

'Come now,' chided Mr Pretorius. Kaptein, the police dog, had found a nest of starlings in the night. I turned away.

Marta, with her instinct for trouble, had caught up with me. 'Go to school before I smack your bottom!'

I laughed and turned up the path next to the graves. As I left them behind I heard Witbooi say: 'Mr Pretorius, you must write a letter of complaint. That dog is a menace. Mauling a nest of birds to death is against the new constitution.'

'Write to Mr Mandela,' said Marta, 'Tell him we've got Dr Basson's dog here in Leopold.'

At the top of the churchyard I paused for a moment in front of the four little graves in the corner. I hadn't visited them in a long time. If I too forgot about them, their faint imprints on the world would be scuffed out forever, as if they had never lived.

The first day of school traffic rumbled by – cars and

_____
* Have a nice day

dust-sprayed bakkies, even one or two lorries. As I reached the bottom field one of the groundsmen was busy on a tractor, painting white lines back onto the field. I stopped. What a satisfying job, to create a perfectly straight white line against a green field, to look back at the other end and see such unbroken precision.

The school bell rang. Latecomers swelled around me before being sucked into the buildings ahead.

Juffrou's classroom was a clamour of laughing and hugging and six weeks of gossip. Elmarie sat on one of the front desks, whispering something to Isabel. As I squeezed past her, she stopped and glanced at me.

'What?' I said.

Instead of replying, she turned over her shoulder and looked towards my and Xanthe's desks. They were both empty. Xanthe had not yet arrived.

'So?' I said, looking at Elmarie. Her skin was better this term. From far away you wouldn't see the spots.

But she hadn't been looking at my desk – her gaze was on the next row along, on the back two desks, which up until now had been empty.

There was a new girl sitting there, a city girl you could see by the smirk on her face. On the far side of her sat Xanthe.

I looked back at Elmarie. She was waiting for an explanation. Of all the scenarios I'd rehearsed while waiting for morning, this was not one of them. I pushed past her to my desk. The wooden seat shrieked as I sat down sat down in a rush. I blinked. This is fine – *this-is-fine-this-is-fine-this-is-fine-this-is-fine-this-is-fine*.

Girls wandered back to their desks, happy to be with their

friends, oblivious to my private misery. What a big-fat-bloody-fucking fool you are, Margaret Bergman! And yet at the same time I was expecting Xanthe to slip in to the desk beside me, muttering: 'Madgie, where the fuck have you been?' The din of voices died down. I could make out the sound of the new girl's voice.

'Oh my God,' she said. 'Look at them all!'

There was a pause, and a short laugh from Xanthe.

'Did you go away for New Year?' said the new girl.

'No,' replied Xanthe, in Alan's *'Enough now, Shirl!'* voice. 'I was at home.'

'Cool,' said the girl. 'What did you get up to?'

I held my breath. This was the moment when Xanthe would laugh, call my name and everything would return to normal.

'Not much,' said Xanthe.

With that Madge slipped away silently, without so much as a backwards glance.

All of it came to nothing. In the end I was still only Meg, the English girl, with the empty seat beside her. I clamped my hand around the folded paper in my pocket.

I felt Xanthe looking across at me. I didn't need to see her face to know it would be scornful, as if to say, *'I did warn you, you knew I wasn't good at this.'* It was true. Maybe she had been like this all along. Maybe I'd constructed the Xanthe I'd wanted out of somebody quite different.

Juffrou du Plessis huffed into the classroom, carrying a pile of textbooks. She let the books drop to the floor next to her desk with an almighty thud that brought the class to silence.

She caught her breath, then turned to Isabel. 'What's keeping

263

you, child?' she said with exaggerated patience.

'Juffrou?' asked Isabel.

'Hand out the books!' said Juffrou and left the room.

Dad believed in stories. He said each one of us was born with a story, that it was ours to live. Simon's story was a hero's one, but it demanded a great deal of him in return. I thought of Mum, a British–South African Joan of Arc. My story wasn't going that well. Sitting alone, the desk beside me once again empty, I realised that the difference between Simon and I was that he was trying to be the best at what he was, not somebody else. It seemed laughably simple.

I knew something that the girl who'd sat here, alone, six months ago didn't. I'd rather be alone than uncomfortable trying to be somebody else. 'Xanthe is cool,' I told that girl, 'but she isn't that brave.' And her parents, and Stuart and Judy, for all their beautiful homes and lifelong friendships, weren't brave either.

'Meg!' Elmarie rattled my pencil case.

'What?'

'My dad says he's going to phone your mum.'

Not today, please God. 'Why?' I asked.

Esna swung around. Isabel stopped to listen, balancing the pile the books on the edge of my desk.

'He's going to ask your mum to come do a clinic on the farm, to teach the volk about her disease,' said Elmarie.

'Why?' asked Isabel.

'He says the last thing he needs in this life is for them to start dropping like goddam flies,' said Elmarie.

Esna gripped Elmarie's arm, her eyes wide at the impending apocalypse. Isabel started to say something, but Juffrou walked back in and she hurried away.

'So,' continued Elmarie, shaking off Esna's hand, 'Maybe when your mum comes to our farm, you can come too. To visit.'

I looked at her, registering slowly. 'Maybe.'

Juffrou stood at the front of the class. She mopped her forehead with a hankie and tucked it back into her dress. She looked about the room, examining each of us in turn. Her eyes rested on the empty desk next to me, then shifted across to the new girl and Xanthe beside her. Juffrou's eyes narrowed. I knew that her glare was a protective one, but I still felt shame prickle my skin.

When the bell rang, I was the first one out of the classroom. Instead of turning left for science, I kept walking, out of the building, down the hill. I caught my breath on the Main Street, my tears smeared hot and sticky on my face.

Mum stepped out of the old coloured entrance to the post office. She turned towards me carrying a large box. It would be from overseas, from Bibi. I waited for the anger, but found nothing. Instead I heard Simon's voice, *'She's helping people whom no one else sees as important enough to bother with.'*

I smiled.

She stood in front of me, her eyes taking me in. 'When I was fifteen Bibi and I went to Paris for the weekend without telling our parents.'

'What?'

'I was in so much trouble,' said Mum, laughing, '*worlds* of trouble when I returned.'

'Paris! Was it worth it?'

Mum's lips twitched, but she didn't say anymore.

I looked up at Bosmansberg, so close that it could be leaning in to hear the story too. Mum followed my gaze. The prospect of going anywhere, let alone Paris, seemed so ridiculous that we started laughing.

'Walk with me,' said Mum, shifting her box onto her far hip and threading her arm through mine.

We started up the Main Street – past the library and the off-licence and the Volkskas bank. Soon we would be at the top of the road. There we would turn right and make for home.

Acknowledgements

I owe an enormous debt of gratitude for unwavering support and inspiration from Aty Georgopoulos, Alison Nagle, Gerda Pearce, Rochelle Gosling, Sarah Morris Keating, Elspeth Morrison, and Charlotte Edwardes. Thanks also to Maggie Hamand of the Complete Creative Writing Course, and Shaun Levin for many years of creative nurturing; and to Dr Sally Cline, who taught me, among many other things, the correct use of the word 'so'.

Huge thanks to Claire Wilson, for seeing the potential of an imperfect draft, and to Emily Thomas, Georgia Murray and the Hot Key team.

To my wonderful family and friends – each of you are a thread in a tapestry I treasure very deeply.

And of course, Johnny, who dared me to dream.

Rosie Rowell

Rosie Rowell was born and grew up in Cape Town, South Africa. These days she lives in West Sussex with her husband and three children. LEOPOLD BLUE is her first novel.